I0692028

A Dead Pig
in the Sunshine

by

Penny Burwell Ewing

The Haunted Salon Series

A Dead Pig in the Sunshine

Cover Art by *Angela Anderson*

The Wild Rose Press, Inc.
PO Box 708
Adams Basin, NY 14410-0708
Visit us at www.thewildrosepress.com

Publishing History
First Fantasy Rose Edition, 2017
Print ISBN 978-1-5092-1680-2
Digital ISBN 978-1-5092-1681-9

The Haunted Salon Series
Published in the United States of America

Staring down at the mangled, half-eaten body lying face up behind an old headstone gave me the sense of an outer body experience. The Snow White costume had been ripped and torn away by the scavenging forest creatures. The cracked headstone with splatters of blood, the bloated corpse with part of the mouth ripped away, and the white teeth exposed in a taunting smile with Mini Pearl clasped in the victim's hand. The wind whistled through the tall grass and trees spreading the stench of death. God, how I hated that smell.

Twice I swept the flashlight beam across the grisly scene, imprinting the ugliness into my memory to be recounted I'm sure hundreds of times in the days ahead. Bradford's hand was strong, firm, protective, but still I shivered.

"Can you identify the gun?"

"It's mine." My breathless voice faltered as my gaze roamed over the pink gun with pearl grips. "Not another like it in the States. Custom made. I had Mini Pearl engraved on the barrel. I thought I'd never see it again."

My mind flashed back to the day I'd discovered my .32 caliber snub-nosed revolver stolen from my car. I'd arrived out at Pineridge Plantation to conduct tours of the antebellum mansion for the annual fall Whiskey Creek Pecan Festival. Increased activity from the re-enactors arriving could be heard, so I followed the sounds around past the back terrace and into the rose garden. During my absence, my wallet had been emptied and Mini Pearl taken.

And used in the commission of a crime. Just as I'd feared.

Penny Burwell Ewing's
The Haunted Salon Series

DIXIELAND DEAD
UTTERLY DEADLY SOUTHERN PECAN PIE
A DEAD PIG IN THE SUNSHINE
BEIN' DEAD AIN'T NO EXCUSE

Dedication

For my aunt, Dorothy Jean Salter,
who inspired the character of Billie Jo
and her vivacious love of life and family.

Cast of Characters

Jolene Claiborne—Planning her sister's wedding is hell enough, but coupled with a new mystery from the netherworld has the oldest Tucker sister wishing heaven would give her a break.

Deena Sinclair—Her wedding plans threaten to go up in smoke.

Billie Jo Hazard—Midlife hands the youngest Tucker sister a big surprise.

Annie Mae Tucker—Now that her newly published cookbook has been launched, it's time for sun and fun on the warm beaches of Florida.

Harland Tucker—The Tucker patriarch wants to sell the peanut farm and retire to sunny Florida where the only problem will be his golf game score.

Detective Samuel Bradford—The pragmatic police detective never gave much thought to the afterlife until a citizen of the invisible world invaded his aura and refused to leave.

Vanessa van Allen—Her Dark Enchantment Vampire Series is worth millions. There's even talk of a movie deal. There's only one problem—someone's out to take a bite of the Queen of Vampires.

Maylene Lovett—This book critic is referred to as "The Terminator" because her reviews can make or break a writer.

Peaches Noble—This Romance Writers Southeastern Division Leader is sick and tired of playing second fiddle to her best friend. If only she could stab her friend in the back and get away with it.

Purvis Dupree—He's hot to land a big name author for his small Atlanta publishing company.

Cash Hitchcock—Vanessa's Atlanta literary agent knows how to suck the blood out of any deal.

Careen Halsey—Sometimes dreams do come true. Unfortunately, some dreams can turn into a nightmare.

Michael Halsey—Careen's older brother is double-dealing from the bottom of the deck.

Betty van Allen—Vanessa's mother keeps secrets close to home.

Sophia—The van Allen's maid is loyal to the bone.

Sheriff Cleaster Snellgrove—What's this good ole boy really up to?

Scarlett Cantrell—Heaven's PI is on the job again. Her newest assignment has her rounding up a wayward ghost with no sense of direction.

Chapter One
Halloween Hoedown

The trouble began on Halloween. I awoke that morning with a keen sense that my world was, once again, about to change. The initial signs pointed to an all-out frontal attack from the Great Beyond. A black, hazy film skirted across the October sky, reminding me of the old classic Hitchcock film, *The Birds*. Static electricity buzzed through the walls of my redbrick home, causing Tango, my orange tabby, to prowl about the house screeching like a banshee. His fur standing on end like an angry pufferfish gave me cause for concern. And then, the undead started arriving shortly after my first cup of coffee with threats of retribution over unfinished business among the living.

With the creep factor off the charts, I didn't linger long over breakfast and hurried off to a full appointment book at my beauty shop, Dixieland Salon—where the day spiraled downhill from there. Strange incidents plagued the shop, and I suspected the undead shadowed me and had taken up residence in the facial room. By the end of the day, one frazzled hairdresser had packed her implements and stormed out, and there were several threats of lawsuits from disgruntled clients with fried hair.

By evening my patience had taken a hike when I ran out of trick-or-treat candy and a couple of loveable demons in the neighborhood toilet-papered my front yard and smashed my jack-o'-lanterns all over the front porch steps.

Halloween. A rent in the veil between the living and the dead, and once my favorite holiday. Not anymore. That sentiment had died a quick death when the dead made a startling appearance during my mid-life crisis. People might call me a psychic, a seer, a medium, or whatever the most popular term at present would be. I prefer "ghost coordinator." The term makes me sound hip, cool, even slightly normal. Which I'm not.

Daddy says I was born this way and not the result of some tragic event in my life. Since my childhood had been chaotic at best, I tended to believe him. For a time, Mama scoffed at the idea that her eldest daughter could communicate with departed souls, but after several visitations from friends and acquaintances that had met with violent, premature deaths, she began to explore the possibility that perhaps she'd been wrong in calling me crazy.

The first time had been when Scarlett Cantrell, a local television celebrity, had been murdered in my beauty salon with a facial mask, of all things. Sound crazy? Well, the crazy part happened later when her ghost showed up threatening to take up permanent residence in Dixieland Salon if I didn't help solve her untimely demise. Owning a haunted beauty shop in the Deep South wasn't a prize to be desired, so I tracked down the killer and before long, Scarlett zoomed off to that fabled golden city in the sky.

The second time had come in the midst of the fall Pecan Festival. While conducting tours out at Pineridge

Plantation, I stumbled upon a ghost with a terrible secret that kept him bound to the blood-soaked land. Before I could high-tail it out of there, I had an ancient key that would unlock a century-and-a-half old mystery involving lost Confederate gold and murder. Of course, to make my life a living hell, Theodore Herrington keeled over dead during the pecan pie contest, and the finger of suspicion pointed directly at Daddy. I solved that case, too. Well, with Scarlett's help, of course. She describes herself as an overworked heavenly private eye who hires her services out to the dearly departed.

It sounds like a child's tale, but believe me, I'm not making this stuff up. But thankfully everything had finally calmed down, and at the moment I find myself ghost-free. Of course, with it being Halloween, and the evening still young, I'm keeping my fingers crossed that I'll make it through the night without all hell breaking loose on my quiet, sleeping hometown. Little did I know, Halloween was to herald in one of the biggest mysteries I would ever encounter.

Later that evening I was finishing up the last touches of my Halloween costume for Mama's cookbook launch party when the doorbell rang. I glanced over at the digital clock on the bedside table, noting that my date had arrived several minutes early. Settling the mask over my eyes and the cowboy hat on my head, I hurried to the front door to discover a tall, dark-haired Native American standing on my front porch. He whistled, flashed me a wicked smile, and pointed at his white Lexus SUV. "Ke-mo sah-bee, your horse awaits."

Laughing, I locked the door behind me and took Preston's hand. "Then let's saddle up, Tonto, and hurry along before we miss all the fun."

"Didn't you tell me that this party is being given by that famous author who writes those erotic vampire books?" Preston asked me once we'd settled into his car.

I adjusted the toy gun and holster strapped to my hips before fastening the seat belt. "Yeah, Vanessa van Allen and Mama are close buddies. She mentored Mama through the process of writing her cookbook. Since it was just released, Vanessa had the idea of combining a Halloween party with a book launch. The caterer used only recipes taken from *Mama Tucker's Ole Fashioned Southern Good Eats*."

"Hey, catchy name," he said. "How do I get my hands on one? No, make that two. I'd like to give one to my mother for Christmas. She collects cookbooks, you know. She's got all of Trisha Yearwood's. Maybe your momma will become a famous Southern chef, too."

I considered my newest beau and a warm, fuzzy feeling washed over me at his enthusiastic prediction of Mama's future. Preston Neally was a nice guy. Not handsome, but presentable. Younger than me by several years, and a successful doctor to boot. We'd met through an online dating service, and he'd been a welcome surprise after I'd endured several disastrous first dates with my other daily matches. At least he still had his natural teeth! You wouldn't believe how many toothless guys I've met this past year. I'm tempted to swear off dating completely. I can't face another blind date no matter how "cute" he promises to be.

Bradford's rugged face resurfaced in my memory before I could stifle it. The previous warm, fuzzy feeling vanished under the onslaught of piercing blue eyes that seemed to mock me and cause my insides to clench with despair. Whiskey Creek Police Detective, Samuel Bradford, my former boyfriend. He dumped me over a ghost, and I'm still fantasizing that he'll see the error of his way and beg me to take him back. At the moment, my fantasy's failed to materialize. He's moved on with another woman more to his liking.

A heavy sigh escaped my lips Preston reached out, lacing his fingers with mine. "Worried about tonight? I wouldn't fret overmuch. I'm sure your mother's cookbook will be well received."

My face relaxed into what I hoped was an engaging smile. "You're right, Preston. Everything will go off without a hitch. What could possibly go wrong on a night such as this? Although anything can happen with that weird group of writers Mama's hanging around with. Wait till you meet them and you'll see what I mean."

He brought my hand to his lips and dropped a gentle kiss on my gloved knuckles.

"Everything will be perfect, you'll see. Most authors are normal people. I'll bet they'll be on their best behavior tonight."

"You would think that, but writers and alcohol don't mix, and from what I've heard of their parties, I'm not sure someone won't end up face-first in the punch bowl."

"Relax, sweetie. It'll be an enchanting evening."

Whether or not it would be an enchanting evening I couldn't predict. Bradford would be there, and the grapevine had it that he and Vanessa van Allen had hooked up, and this would be the first time we would come face-to-face in a social setting with our new lovers since our breakup last year.

Oh well, one could hope. But for good luck I crossed my fingers and sent up a silent prayer. Oh, Sweet Jesus, Chief of the Supreme Mystery, please don't let me be the first one in the punch bowl.

****

Vanessa's Doublegate home blazed like a giant, leering jack-o'-lantern. The landscapers had festooned the white brick, three-storied, colonial mansion to the hilt with the newest and scariest Halloween decorations. Warm, yellow light spilled from every window mingling with the music and laughter that could be heard from the open, front, double doors as we pulled up behind a line of cars parked along the street.

"I believe the party has started without us." Preston handed me out of the passenger side, tucking my hand into the crook of his arm, and led me up to the front entrance and into the crowded foyer—where Snow White and her Prince stood waiting to greet their guests.

Vanessa van Allen welcomed us with a light handshake and a demure smile, all the while eyeballing me up and down. "Do come right in." She waved an impatient hand. "Ah, Jolene, Annie Mae said you had a flair for the dramatic." Her drawl was cool and amused, but her amber gaze turned frosty upon my entrance. "And who is this handsome Tonto?"

I ignored her and stole a quick glance at her Prince. Sam Bradford. Blue hypnotic eyes moved over my person in one slow, continuous movement bringing to mind the many times his fingers had taken the same stimulating trail across my naked flesh. I shivered, broke eye contact, and took a deep, steadying breath. Preston's solid arm slid around my shoulders reminding me of his presence and my lack of manners.

"Vanessa van Allen and Samuel Bradford meet my date, Dr. Preston Neally," I said over the increasing din.

The two men shook hands and eyed each other pleasantly, but with a subtle undertone that lightened my mood. Really, this might turn out to be a great party after all. Perhaps Preston had been right in saying this would be an enchanting evening. But first, a tall, cool glass of something intoxicating to ease me into the mood.

"Your parents are here, as are your sisters." Vanessa interrupted my thoughts. "I believe you'll find them over by the book display."

I turned away and scanned the jammed room. Billie Jo, dressed as a Raggedly Ann doll, stood only a few feet away, fanning herself and looking wilted. Her husband, Roddy, costumed as Raggedly Andy, bent close over her with a worried expression. Despite the opened double doors, the cool evening air made hardly a dent in the warm, stuffy house, and I wondered if she too felt stifled by the press of bodies.

As Preston and I wove our way across the room, I caught snatches of conversation:

"...Vanessa has outdone herself with this cookbook. It's sure to be a best-seller..."

"...Peaches Fletcher Noble is surely to be the winner in this year's Romance Writer..."

"...I heard the Terminator is here and ready to slash her latest work."

"...I actually talked with her agent. He wants to see my work!"

"...Firebrand Publications is always on the lookout for fresh, young faces, and voices, of course..."

A woman in a blue feathered costume lifted her glass in a toast with her identically dressed partner as we scooted past and reached my sister and brother-in-law. A passing waiter stopped to offer us a glass of wine, either red or white. I seized a glass of white from the tray, took a sip, and then another. Preston and Roddy shook hands.

I fanned my face with a free hand. "Whew, it's warm for October. Are you okay, Billie Jo? You don't look well.

Billie Jo managed a wan smile. Roddy spoke up. "She's been feeling under the weather for the last few days."

Preston plucked a glass from the tray. "I could have a look at her if we could find a quiet space if you'd like. It would put your mind at ease, so you can enjoy the evening."

Roddy brushed a pale curl from Billie Jo's forehead. "How about it, honey? I'm worried about you, and it won't hurt to have a doctor check you over."

"I'm fine. Stop fussin'," Billie Jo murmured. "I ate something bad, that's all. Give it a rest, Roddy. If I'm not better in a day or two, I'll go see my own doctor. I'm not lettin' Jolene's new boyfriend have a gander at me, so shut up about it."

Roddy did a playful mock salute. "Yes, my dear. I always stand ready to obey your wifely orders."

I spotted an empty chair in the corner of an adjoining room and pointed it out to the others. They were in agreement and we moved our party away from the pressing crowd. Once we had Billie Jo settled in the quieter room, I made an excuse of needing to use the restroom, and went in search of the rest of my family.

And encountered quite a scene, with clowns, kings and queens, witches, goblins, and every kind of costume competing for attention.

In the large library at the back of the house, I found Mama seated at the book display table autographing cookbooks as Daddy watched with a proud smile from his position behind her. He spotted me first and motioned to Mama. She gave me a quick wave and bent back down over the pile of books in front of her. Boxed in by an intoxicated pirate with roving hands, I backed out of the room and into the hall, in hopes of finding Deena and her fiancé, Wheeler County Probate Judge, Ryder Matheson, somewhere in this flock of party animals.

After searching most of the house, I spotted a virginal bride in white lodged between a rugged Daniel Boone and a wilted Thomas Jefferson deep in conversation near the butler's pantry.

"You don't have much of an imagination," I complained to her when I pushed my way to her side. "It's a costume party, Deena, not your wedding day."

"Oh, excuse me, *Sister Dearest*, for not living up to your expectations." She snickered in a playful tone. "You, however, look like a spray-painted Lone Ranger. I'm surprised you haven't dropped in a dead faint from lack of oxygen." Her eyes fastened on my bursting blouse seams. "Your boobs look enormous. It's kinda embarrassing the way the men are ogling you."

I snagged another glass of wine from a passing waiter who eyed my voluptuous display with a lecherous smile. "Yeah, I know, but it's worth it. You should've seen Bradford's face when I walked in." I fanned myself. "The look he gave me almost set my

9

pants on fire! Vanessa wanted to strangle me. That woman definitely doesn't like me which suits me because the feeling is mutual. Where's the groom-to-be?"

Deena frowned. "Fetching me a glass of cold water. And don't change the subject. What about Preston? He's a good man, and I'd hate to see him hurt by all this. Forget Sam and move on. He's not the man for you. Besides, you blew it. Mama says that he and Vanessa are in a serious relationship."

"His body language speaks otherwise." I pouted, rebuffed by her words. God, how I hated to admit Deena was right—I did blow my chance with Sam last November during the Pecan Festival. He'd warned me numerous times that he couldn't accept my "paranormal abilities" and had finally walked away when Scarlett did one of her flashy disappearing acts almost blinding him in the process. Sam doesn't believe in the afterlife, and well, the afterlife follows me around like a shadow. So I let him walk.

Big mistake on my part and I wanted him back—bad. I was a middle-age hairdresser—currently sex-deprived—and I was getting antsy about not getting laid soon. Recently, Preston had started champing like a boar hog in mating season, and that had my attention. I'm not shy about wanting sex, and I wanted sex—and since I couldn't have Prince Charming, Preston was a viable candidate for now.

"Jolene, are you listening to me?"

I flashed a big smile. "Refresh my memory."

Deena waved her hand at the costumed guests. "I was saying how easy it would be for a stranger to crash this party. With all the costumes and masks covering our faces, it wouldn't take much to convince the hostess you were invited. Someone could burst in here and rob us blind, and we'd never be able to identify them."

Again, I surveyed the crowd and spotted Vanessa's mother, Betty, decked out like a star-studded 1940's Hollywood actress. She waved a bejeweled hand at me from across the room, and then turned her attention back to Lady Liberty and her companion. From my viewpoint, most all the invitees were indeed wearing elaborate costumes which included a mask that concealed their identities. They could be anyone for all I knew from this perspective.

"Well, Deena, I hadn't thought of it like that but I suppose you could be right. But then again, isn't that the purpose of Halloween? Dressing up and fooling people? Trick-or-treating and having fun? I don't believe we have to worry about someone impersonating a guest and robbing us. The DA is here. And most of the Whiskey Creek police force. Look over there by the piano." I pointed to a large multicolored bird. "There's the police chief. And the Shakespearean Romeo beside him is the sheriff."

Deena's rosebud mouth quivered with amusement. "Can you imagine someone impersonating Mayor Kent? Or his wife? She's dressed up as Little Bo Peep."

I turned to see the lady in question stroll by on the arm of Superman and giggled at the sight of the plump woman who favored a pink Liberty Bell more than a gentle shepherdess.

"Oh, look." Deena grabbed my arm, jerking my attention away from the First Man and Lady of Whiskey Creek to the fairytale pair making their way toward us. "There's Sam and Vanessa now. You have to admit, Jolene, they do make a handsome couple. Sam looks content, don't you think?"

My heart did a quick step at the sight of Vanessa's hand resting cozily through Bradford's arm. Jealousy kicked my gut like a mule. Damn, I had to make my escape, and fast, if I didn't want to make a fool of myself. Deena had enough to worry about with her wedding drawing close without any added distractions—like me strangling the woman.

"I left Preston cooling his heels in the next room with Billie Jo and Roddy. See you later." I turned and bolted through the crowd. At the door, I turned back to witness the smiling couple engaged in a cozy embrace. My previous confidence took a dive, and my spirits sank even lower. I sat my empty glass on a nearby table and went to find Preston and another glass of liquid comfort.

Chapter Two
Queen of the Vampires

Three glasses of wine later, I was feeling no pain and well on my way to making another life-altering mistake. The combination of jealousy and alcohol had completely stripped me of common sense, inhibitions, and any second thoughts I might be entertaining at the moment. And, at the moment, Preston and I were standing outside in the small, enclosed, moonlit backyard behind a group of prickly bushes that offered a maximum of protection from any interested bystanders who had the same idea.

The girls were about to escape their confines when a familiar voice penetrated the heated haze fogging my brain.

"Stop the theatrics, Cash. I have the proof in my hands."

"Vanessa, give me a chance to explain."

Hastily, I pushed away Preston's hands and started buttoning my blouse. The last thing I needed was my replacement running back to Bradford with tales of me and Preston gettin' it on in her backyard. Hell, I wouldn't put it past her to have us *doing the dirty* in every kinky position her writer's imagination could dream up.

Preston immediately protested my sudden shyness. His fingers plucked again at my buttons. "Ah, Jolene, don't stop me now." He fished a condom from his shirt pocket with one hand, and opened the top button of my blouse with the other. "I've been fantasizing about this moment from the first time I laid eyes on you." The second, third, and fourth button followed.

"Shh," I whispered. "We have company."

Warm hands slipped inside my bra. My world tilted.

"Explain? My royalty statement explains it all. You're fired, Cash. I'm hiring another agent."

"Not so fast, *Vanessa, my dear*. Fire me and I'll be forced to explain to your boyfriend cop that dirty little secret you've been keeping from him. I wonder how he'd react to know—"

Preston's nimble fingers found the bra clasp. I couldn't think clearly. All resistance took a hike as my breath quickened, and a wave of liquid warmth flooded my twinkie pie. I licked my lips and lifted them toward him.

"You wouldn't dare, you fool. I'm not the only one who will lose. Your reputation won't stand another scandal. I'm going to bury you if it's the last thing I do."

"Never say never, Vanessa. I've weathered many storms. I'll weather this one, but the truth about you would kill your career. Think about the lawsuits and get back to me."

The kiss was hot, urgent, and mind numbing, and I gave into the pleasure and the alcohol coursing through my bloodstream. Tomorrow might bring regrets, and of course, a whopper of a hangover, but tonight I was gonna do things in the dark with this man that would make the devil blush.

Giddy-up Silver! Away we go!
****

Later that evening, after Preston and I had returned to the party, I escaped to the upstairs powder room to restore my appearance before Mama and Deena caught a glimpse of me and bombarded me with outrageous indignation for dilly-dallying in Vanessa's backyard. Billie Jo would've given me the thumbs-up because she's been bugging me for months to get back in the saddle again. I suppose I should feel guilty for using Preston in the manner that I did, but I didn't. I felt wonderful after sex in the bushes with a younger man. A weight had been lifted from my shoulders, and I felt like dancing like a silly teenager.

Humming along with the rhythmic music drifting from downstairs, I brushed off the leaves and twigs clinging to my costume, smoothed my hair back under the cowboy hat, retied the mask, and stepped back to survey my work in the mirror. All signs of dishabille had been erased but for the pink staining my cheeks, the sparkle in my eyes, and the huge smile on my lips. Some things can't be disguised no matter how hard you try.

Ready to rejoin the party, I left the bathroom and made my way to the top of the landing where I paused when faint, angry voices on the stairs caught my attention. Thinking to avoid an embarrassing confrontation with whoever and allow them privacy, I sat down on the velvet settee and waited for them to work out their problem or move on.

"Come on Vanessa, I know you want it," a man's drunken voice wafted up the staircase. "You've been keeping me at arm's length long enough. Your boy toy

15

won't mind sharing."

"Purvis Dupree, take your hands off me, you fool. Someone might see us."

Curiosity overcame caution at the anger in the famous author's voice, and I peered over the railing to see a broad-shouldered Victorian dandy embracing Bradford's girlfriend in a compromising embrace. Large hands roamed freely over her body, pinching, exploring, before his mouth crashed down on hers.

Ah, the turned-on dude happened to be Purvis Dupree. Editor and owner of Firebrand Publications, a publishing company out of Atlanta. I'd heard his name bandied about this evening by several of the female writers I'd been introduced to, and I came away with the impression that there was more to the man than meets the eye. He was a lecher—a fact easy to discern if you stood within hands' reach, they'd said, and a crack-shot businessman who wanted to, and here I quote, "take a bite of the multimillion dollar Queen-of-the-Vampires empire," unquote. Yep, those Southern romance writers definitely had some issues to resolve I discerned from the tone of their voices. Jealousy topped the list.

Heat flooded my face as I continued to watch their dance on the stairs. Hey, I'm no voyeur, but curiosity kept me glued to the spot. Muffled cries erupted from the pair, and I stood in indecision, uncertain how to react to the steamy porn show unfolding before me. Captivated, I couldn't look away as Vanessa broke the hold and tried to step away. Mr. Dupree only laughed as he captured her hands behind her back and pressed her body into the wall, raining slobbery kisses across her face and neck.

And then it happened. Vanessa jerked out of the man's embrace, swung back, and delivered a stinging blow to the side of his face. Immediately he crumbled to the stairs, sobbing contritely then begging for forgiveness. The pitiful sight of the deflated man and the petite author gently bending over him, murmuring soothing words much like a mother tending her wounded child, left me stunned and sickened. Damn, the character traits these writers displayed. God, I hoped Mama didn't pick up any of their bad habits while hanging around them. With that on my mind, I silently backed away from the railing and slumped down again on the settee—feeling a tad queasy and confused about the strange scene I'd witnessed.

My picture of the Queen of the Vampires, as her competitors had dubbed her, underwent another change. One minute she's fluttering about her guests like a lightning bug on a search for a mate. Then she lands on some pitiful flower and devours its sweet nectar before moving on to take another bite out of her next unsuspecting victim. First, her agent and then the publishing mogul.

My stomach did a flip as I thought about Mama in the library autographing her cookbooks for the masses. Exactly what was Vanessa's agenda concerning my mother? And what about Bradford? Just as sure as the grass was green in spring, I knew I had to find out more about this woman who held the happiness and prosperity of two important people in my life in her deceptively delicate hands.

****

From my hidden position by the corner hutch in the breakfast area, I could hear Vanessa give the caterer strict instructions to keep an eye on Purvis Dupree until he sobered up. I shadowed Vanessa as she left the publisher drinking hot coffee in the kitchen and into the dining room where she paused to speak with a group of women. From their conversation, I assumed they were part of the local writers group that met in the library every Wednesday afternoon. From there she moved between groups of people, stopping here and there to engage in casual conversation during which she would lift her head and survey the room as if she were searching for someone. My immediate guess would be Bradford.

After several more seconds of chitchat, she excused herself and walked in the general direction of the back library where I'd last seen Mama autographing cookbooks. Suddenly, without warning, Vanessa halted her progress and swung around, again searching the crowd nervously.

Before she could spot me hot on her trial, I ducked behind a large man in a clown costume. So far, my mission to learn more about this woman hadn't turned up much. One thing for certain, this was going to take time and patience on my part, but I was determined to stick it out until her true colors were exposed.

Over the country music and conversation, I heard a cell phone ring and Vanessa's loud "Hello" as she answered the call. "You're here—now? Leave this instant! Wait. I can't talk here." The crisp words were spit out in machine gun fashion. Her tone of voice made it easy to deduce her displeasure at hearing from the caller. Cautiously, I peered out from behind my cover and saw her dart into a room off the hall. In a flash, I skirted around Mr. Clown and followed—my curiosity pushing me forward.

I paused in the doorway, hoping to hear more of her private conversation and heard only the muffled sound of exasperation over the noise in the hallway. If I wanted to snoop, I'd have to do better than this. Pressed against the doorjamb, I poked my head around the entry and saw Vanessa, her back to me, standing in the farthest corner of what appeared to be a small study. A nearby closet offered a great hiding place. With her preoccupied with the caller, I slipped inside the room on silent feet and then the closet, leaving a slit in the door to allow eavesdropping without detection. Through the crack I had a limited view.

As though sensing my presence, Vanessa swung around, her amber gaze sweeping the room. I held my breath in fear of discovery and pulled my face back into the shadows.

"Hold on while I close the door," I heard her say, then footsteps echoed across the hardwood floor, and finally the soft click of a door closing.

"Listen to me good. This is not the right time to make the switch," she continued. "Wait until after the party to lessen the chance of a mistake." A pause. I peered through the crack to see Vanessa sink down onto a plush chair, her face pulled into a frown. "Yes, I know our agreement... Yes, I know all of that, but listen to reason. Sam will know. He's acting strange. I've done what you've asked, but he's suspicious...yes, of course, I understand. You're the boss." Her voice echoed exasperation. "It end's tonight? Yes, yes, whatever you say. I expect to be paid. Handsomely. Yes, I won't keep you waiting."

Vanessa sat in silence for several minutes after

ending the call. She let out a long, audible breath. "Now what am I going to do? I can't let my work be in vain. Somehow I have to stop this from happening tonight." She grabbed up her phone and sent out a text message. "If he fails to check his phone everything we've worked for is gone. The money, the fame, the spotlight. It's over for us."

From the crack in the door, I watched her climb to her feet and make her way across the room. It sounded as if she sniffled just a bit. Seconds after I heard the door open and close, I emerged from my hiding place with the intent of following her. I wanted to, no, had to know what was going on with this woman. Bolting for the door, I pulled it open and charged out into the hall only to crash into Prince Charming—the one person on the planet, other than Mama, who would take one look at me and know exactly what I had been up to.

"Jolene?" His strong hand on my elbow steadied me. "What have you done to Vanessa?"

His words were unexpected. I jerked my eyes to his. "It's not what it looks like."

"She was crying when she came out of this room mere seconds before you," Bradford accused in a manner that set my teeth on edge. I wanted to share my concerns and observations with him but not when he was harboring the notion that'd I'd taken a bite out of his lady love.

"Vanessa is a kind and sensitive soul, Jolene. And she's going through a tough time right now. I wouldn't expect you to understand, but take it easy on her, will you?"

Okay, nix that last thought. "Oh, so now I'm a troglodyte?"

Annoyance crossed his face. "You're making a scene."

"You started it when you accused me of attacking your girlfriend." I sounded like a jealous teenager, but I turned my head to see a big yellow bird and a werewolf staring at us, open speculation coloring their expressions. I flushed under their continuing gaze, twisted free of Bradford's grip, and stalked off in search of Snow White and her mysterious caller.

Chapter Three
My Favorite Ghost

Preston caught up with me fifteen minutes later at the bottom of the staircase. My search for Vanessa had been fruitless. The damn woman seemed to stay one step ahead. I'd combed the upstairs to no avail and was about to check outdoors when my date found me.

His face mirrored impatience. "There you are. I've been looking everywhere for you. I thought you'd like to know that Roddy took Billie Jo home to rest. Also, Vanessa is getting ready to make a big announcement in the great room."

With hardly a blink, I linked my arm in his. "Forgive me, Preston, for being distracted." I forced a weak smile. "I promise not to leave your side for the remainder of the evening."

The tension eased from his face. "Well, that's good news." His eyes brightened with pleasure. "I missed my lady."

I let those softly spoken words go unanswered, my mind tangled with the mystery of the Queen of the Vampires and her mysterious caller to worry about the implication his words evoked. Tonight, I had to stay focused on the matter at hand. Tomorrow would be soon enough to deal with the consequences of the backyard frolic with the smitten doctor.

The first thing I noticed when we entered the great

room was Vanessa clinging to Bradford like a copperhead on a sun-warmed rock. The second thing I noticed was how those golden eyes narrowed with animosity the instant they settled on me. A slow satisfied smile crossed her sultry red lips.

The air sizzled with cosmic radiation. My psychic radar clicked on as waves of intense vibrational frequency rushed at me from the Vampire Queen. Instinctively, I took a step back, gathering my heightened intuitive faculties around me for protection, all the while wracking my brain for any information that would explain the weird sensations assailing my person.

Okay. This was new. My spiritual software hadn't covered human-to-human psychic assault, and I had no clue how to fight something I didn't fully understand. Suddenly, without thought, Scarlett's name floated across my line of vision like a plastic banner trailing behind an airplane.

Ah, the answer to all my unworldly problems. Scarlett Cantrell—my favorite ghost with the sass of a Southern belle, and the finesse of a highly skilled card shark.

As Preston and I moved farther into the room to join the rest of the family, I cleared my physic channel of cosmic static and sent out an emergency SOS in universal celestial Morse code. For extra measure, and to keep my fingers still, I crossed them behind my back and waited for backup.

Which never happened. Scarlett was a no-show. Five minutes passed without one ghostly peep from the Great Beyond. Not even the fluttering of big kick-ass angel wings.

Luckily, by that time, the Vampire Queen had moved to stand in front of a huge stone fireplace that dominated the great room. The strange vibrations abated as she raised her hand and called for quiet. She waited for the partygoers to settle down before she motioned for Mama to join her at the front of the room.

"I would like to thank you, my beloved guests, for joining me on this special occasion to launch what I hope to become a bestseller." She looped her arm around Mama's shoulder. A light applause broke out. "And I'm happy to report that advance sales on *Mama Tucker's Ole Fashioned Southern Good Eats* are experiencing a favorable outlook." Again, light applause broke out. "I received a phone call earlier that leads me to believe that Annie Mae Tucker cookbooks will be in high demand not only here in the South, but all over the world."

Daddy let out a loud catcall, which prompted a frown from Mama. Beside me, Deena grabbed my hand. Tears of pride sparkled in her eyes. I wanted to be as enthusiastic, but Vanessa's mention of an earlier phone call had distracted me. What I had overheard in the study definitely hadn't been about cookbooks. Or could it? I distinctly heard Vanessa say that now wasn't the time to make the switch. Switch what? Cookbooks? If so, now I had more of a reason to investigate Vanessa than ever before. Cheat Mama? No way in hell.

My attention was immediately drawn back to Vanessa when she announced in a light, jovial tone, "...and now that my fourth Dark Enchantment book is in the hands of my publisher, I'd like to announce privately to my friends gathered here at my home, my next anticipated project which is sure to stir a little excitement in the publishing world." Here she paused.

A low rumble of voices sounded across the crowded room. Speculating glances passed among the guests as whispered comments swirled like a small swarm of agitated honeybees. I watched with concern as Bradford's brows drew downward in a frown. He knew all about that project, I was sure of it. And, apparently, he didn't like it one little bit.

Which piqued my curiosity all the more. My gaze focused on his delicious figure, and tried to read between the lines, but his rugged features smoothed out, betraying nothing to the observer. However, that only served to make me more determined to root out the problem between the two.

And it figures Scarlett would choose that particular moment to answer my summons dressed as...um, what? A biker chick? Jeans and leather? Yes, definitely a biker chick with skin-tight jeans and a black T-shirt several sizes too small. Her store-bought boobs clearly visible in spite of the leather vest that strained to contain them. Wow, what was Heaven coming to? Surely, there had to be a dress code enforced in the celestial golden city in the sky.

"What's happening, girlfriend?" She clicked her fingers to get my attention. "Hey, my eyes are in my head, Claiborne."

My head snapped up, startling Preston because he squeezed my hand, and I turned to see a quizzical expression light his eyes. I gave him a quick smile of assurance and waited until he turned his attention back to Vanessa who continued to chat about a sizzling exposé on her life as a Southern writer. Sexual escapades and all. Names included. A no-holes barred look at the cutthroat world of publishing.

Several outraged gasps from the guests captured my attention. Tension mounted like a Friday night football game with out-of-commission restrooms.

"Bitch! You wouldn't dare!" A red-faced Statue of Liberty shouted.

"I'll sue for slander!" Peaches Noble screamed from the back of the room.

"Vengeance is mine sayeth the Lord," an angry male voice reverberated from the crowd.

"Dead people don't tell tales." A furious voice echoed with evil.

Oh, Lordy. Vanessa's writer friends didn't share her enthusiasm for the project. Not that I blamed them. No one likes their dirty laundry exposed to the world. I shot a quick glance at Bradford. His frown had returned.

I don't rattle easily, but the strong words, and hateful glances directed at Vanessa had me rethinking things. I detest violence, no really, and from the looks of the guests, violence simmered just beneath the surface. Vanessa treaded quicksand with this new book. Some mud holes are best left alone. Like this one humdinger of a slush pile.

"Claiborne, I don't have all night, you know." Scarlett snickered, regaining my attention. "You've got two minutes to tell me why I'm here. After that, well, I'm outta here. I have a job to do."

I blinked several times and righted myself. Scarlett was right. I needed her advice, and I couldn't have a conversation with her here in front of everyone. Quickly, I excused myself, an urgent bathroom call and fled the room, Scarlett in tow, and ducked into the nearest powder room.

Scarlett remained quiet as I explained the strange evening to her.

"What do you think it means?" A nervous tingling had started in my inner being. I chalked it up to Halloween overload. That, alcohol and yummy outdoor sex with the doctor.

Scarlett tugged at the stretched neckline of her black Harley-Davidson T-shirt. "I'm not sure, Claiborne, but something's screwy in the cosmos tonight. There's a lot of chatter on the universal network."

I sat down on the toilet seat to relieve my aching toes. Cowboy boots weren't my thing. I prefer heels. "Such as?"

"I'm not at liberty to say, but all the signs point to an uprising among the fallen ones."

I rolled my eyes. "Scatterbrain. That happened eons ago. I'm interested in the here and now."

Scarlett tapped the side of her head with long green fingernails. "Give me a moment to plug into the cosmic starvine." After a minute of silence, she gave me an impish grin. "There's mischief abroad in this house. Twins. One of the twins will lose."

Confusion hit me. Twins? One of the twins will lose? What could that possibly mean? "Are you playing a game with me?" I asked though dry lips, perturbed with the delay. "You're talking in riddles."

She cast me a mean look. "I rarely play games, *dar-ling*. And never with women. This is exactly what I heard. Now, is there anything else? If not, then tootle-loo."

"Well, there is one "

Scarlett didn't wait for me to finish. With a flash, she vanished—leaving me alone with the strange riddle ringing through my thoughts.

The mystery deepened.

I took a long breath, counted to ten, and exhaled slowly, allowing the surrounding stillness to calm my rattled nerves. First things first. Twins. I latched onto that like a hungry tick on a fat, lazy coonhound. Disguised in the crowd of angry guests were twins. That's my first move. Find twins at a Halloween costume party where most of the guests wore masks.

Impossible.

By the time I had returned to the great room the party had broken apart. Preston appeared tired, his face a mixture of anxiety and anger. Mama and Daddy were nowhere in sight. Deena and Ryder had also left. Even Snow White and Prince Charming had absconded. Only a few stragglers remained. No chance in hell of locating twins now.

I sided up next to Preston, linking my arm in his. "I guess this means the party's over?"

"As usual you missed the best part." His frosty tone signaled displeasure. "Should I even bother to ask where you've been? Damn, Jolene, I've spent most of the night looking or waiting for you."

Oh, great day. I smothered the sigh that lodged in my throat. Some men were such babies. Take the tit away, and they pitch a hissy fit until the tit is firmly reinserted in their mouth. Brother. I had too much on my mind to deal with a temperamental man, but he was my date, and I had neglected him. The backyard frolic flashed through my mind. Well, not all the time.

With that pleasing picture planted upmost in my

mind, I slipped an ardent hand under Preston's faux suede shirt. His nipples immediately hardened under my light caress. "I'm ready to head to the house and a warm bed, Tonto." I tweaked his nipples harder with my fingertips. "I'm sure I can make it up to you in some way. Any suggestions?"

Preston answered with a wolfish grin. "Ke-mo-sah-bee, your horse awaits."

The drive home was short and silent, much to my liking. The smile on Preston's face left no doubt what occupied his thoughts. That, too, was much to my liking. Perhaps at some time during the evening, he had seen the illusive twins among the guests. Or had glimpsed Vanessa's mysterious caller. Or overheard some interesting fact that would help me solve this mystery. I could question him outright, but I had learned the hard way that some words can come back to bite you. More precisely, land you in jail. No, I needed Preston to be unaware he was being interrogated. And I'm an expert at extracting information from a distracted man. I have big boobs.

Chapter Four
Deadly Consequences

Late in the afternoon, three days later, Bradford showed up at the salon. I knew he had a stick in his craw the instant he strode through the door with a worried expression on his unshaven face and headed straight for my station. The disturbing psychic vibrations zinged me as he drew near. Weird. Definitely weird.

"I need to speak with you ASAP." His tense voice strained with some unspoken crisis. He gave a quick nod of acknowledgment to my client who stared open-mouthed from my black leatherette stylist chair. Around us the soft chatter of the curious began. New fodder for the grapevine. By tomorrow Whiskey Creek would be abuzz with the Bald Eagle's flight to the abandoned nest. In other words, I'm the abandoned nest and Bradford was sniffing around another hen. Poor Vanessa. Gag.

I flashed him a "give-me-a-minute" smile in his direction as I finished with my client's comb out. Bradford paced nervously until I whipped the cape from around my client's neck and sent her to the reception desk to pay her bill.

Since it was near closing time, and Jane Ross had been my last client, I instructed our receptionist, Holly to lock the door behind her when she left, then steered

Bradford to Deena's office knowing she'd left early for an appointment with her wedding planner. Billie Jo was still out sick, and we would have plenty of privacy since most of the staff would be leaving.

Bradford sank with a sigh into the plush chair opposite Deena's desk. "Thanks for seeing me on short notice, Jolene. I didn't know where else to turn, and you're my only hope."

I shut the door behind me, and settled into Deena's chair—needing the expanse of the desktop between us. Bradford appeared distraught. I wanted to take him in my arms and soothe his ruffled feathers. That would never do. I'd moved on. Three days of luscious sex with another man was a clear-cut signal that I'd moved on.

The disturbing psychic vibrations around him intensified, and a slight buzzing sounded in my right ear. Gnats. It buzzed in my left ear. Perturbed, I peered closer at Bradford and noticed for the first time a pale, pulsing light off his left shoulder. I couldn't make out any details other than a faint rainbow-colored figure hugging close to him. Real close. A nature spirit? Disincarnate entity? And apparently, this citizen of "inner space" had a hold on Bradford's physical sphere because he kept glancing over his left shoulder as if he could discern his invisible companion.

"What can I help you with, Bradford?" I asked, intrigued by this unexpected turn of events, and I wondered if this unusual visit could be related to Halloween night and the weird riddle of the twins. If so, I fully intended to lend my aid. Curiosity had taken a bite, and I was hell-bent on answers. Preston hadn't been any help at all. The only thing he noticed during the night was my more-than-a-mouthful boobs and had focused his energy on how to get into my panties. Well, he'd succeeded in that endeavor, but nothing else. No twins had come across his radar.

Bradford leaned forward. "This confession might shock you, but I've got to put an end to it before I lose my mind." His voice strained on the last words, and a light sweat broke out across his brow.

The rainbow-colored figure glowed brighter with every word, and the slight buzzing sound in my ears grew to a roar. I reached up in an attempt to swat away the disturbance, but the buzzing only grew louder.

"Stop it," I shouted at his invisible companion who continued to pulsate multicolors much like a disco strobe light from the '80s. Now, added to the noise, the rotating lights were making me dizzy and nauseated.

"Jolene?" Bradford's hand gripped my outstretched arm. "Are you all right? Is something wrong? Stop what?" His Southern twang twanged strong with tension.

I swallowed hard and fought back the urge to confide in him, but Bradford wasn't ready for the truth. That's why we were no longer a couple. Samuel Bradford, the pragmatic police detective, didn't believe in the afterlife. If I mentioned a ghost, he'd be out of here like a shot. Supernatural wasn't in his vocabulary. No, I had to handle this with kid gloves to spare him, and me, the embarrassment that comes with my special gift. Really, at times, a curse. Like now.

Out of the corner of my eye, I caught movement. Not physical, but the slight disturbance of air as if a live body walked by. Distracted for a moment, I hesitated, intrigued by this new experience. I could see the effects of citizens of inner space, or departed spirits, move though earth's atmosphere. Cool.

With a shake of my head, I returned my attention back to Bradford. The distraction had given me time to gather my wits. The noise had quieted, and the rainbow-colored figure had dimmed to a pale, silvery beam hovering close to his shoulder.

"Sorry. Didn't mean to shout," I apologized. "I've been having some trouble with my inner ear. A loud ringing that's driving me nuts. You were about to tell me what brings you here and how I can help."

His eyes met mine. He arched a brow shaking his head slightly. "It's about Vanessa," he began.

My smile withered. Christ. My ex-boyfriend wanted advice about his new main squeeze. Damn my freakin' luck. My throat tickled from lack of moisture. I gave a funny little cough to ease the tickling. "I'm not the one to come to for advice about relationships, Bradford," I croaked. God, he looked yummy with a five-o'clock shadow covering his face.

"Oh, no. Don't misunderstand. I'm not here about my relationship with Vanessa. It's another matter entirely."

Thank God for small miracles. "Okay. Well, then, what?"

"It started with that damn announcement Halloween night. A mistake. I told her not to do it but no, she was so full of herself. Not her usual gentle personality." He took a shaky breath. "Later, her mother walked in on us fighting. Betty jumped to the wrong conclusion. I would never hit a woman. Even a hysterical one. And she was. Hysterical."

I felt a quiver of shock. "Oh, my God, Bradford. What are you saying? What did Vanessa's mother witness? Or misinterpret? I know you. You're a pussycat."

Bradford jumped up from his seat and began pacing, wringing his hands. "You wouldn't believe me if I told you. I witnessed it and I still can't believe it." He continued to pace back and forth in front of the desk. The pale beam of light growing brighter with his agitation, the buzzing, louder. Then the dizziness began.

"Sit down, Bradford," I ordered in my most authoritative tone reserved for high-strung employees and wayward siblings. "I can't help you when you're like this."

My harsh tone must've worked because he dropped back into his seat, pushing his hands through his hair in a nervous manner. "Yeah, I know, Jolene. But damn, I'm going nuts over this." He let out a long breath.

"You were saying that Vanessa was hysterical?" I kept my voice level, and steered the conversation back to the problem. "Can you tell me why?"

He glanced toward the window, then back at me. "No, that's the crazy part. Halloween night started out normal. Vanessa was in her element at the book launch. Calm, charming, beautiful. The classical fairy tale princess. Until that incident in the study. She wasn't the same afterward. Something happened to upset her."

A hint of an accusation colored his words, and my hackles rose in self-defense. "Ah, yes, the kind and sensitive soul going through a rough time as I remember. I had nothing to do with your *girlfriend's* meltdown, I can assure you."

Bradford flushed at my tone. "I'm not accusing you of anything, but you were in the study with her, and she was crying when she came out. You have to know what caused the upset. I need your help, that's why I'm here."

The air between us crackled like an electrical live wire. To put some distance between us, and gain some time, I leaned back in the chair and clasp my hands together. Bradford's questioning gaze never left my face, and I felt as if my heart would explode in my chest. He was so close, yet so far away. A moot point. We had moved on with other people. I was with Preston now. Time to let go. A sobering thought.

"I'll tell you what I know, Bradford, after you finish telling me your story, agreed?"

Since the first time he'd waltzed into the salon, a faint smile cracked his lips. "So we're dancing that jig again, huh?"

Bradford was referring back to the time of Scarlett's murder, and we'd been forced to work together to bring her killer to justice. To get what I wanted, I had resorted to blackmail—a strange quirk of mine extremely useful in times of need. A fine tradeoff if you asked me, however, Bradford wasn't as enthusiastic. The same stubborn expression flinted across his face now. But I was winning and that was all that mattered. He wasn't the only one wanting answers. I gave him a quick nod.

"After leaving the study, Vanessa disappeared for a while," he continued. "Maybe fifteen minutes, give or take a few."

Yes, that coincided with my timeframe of the incident. Vanessa had literally disappeared for seventeen minutes. I'd been unable to locate her in the house, but I hadn't had time to search the outdoor area.

Perhaps she'd met her mysterious caller out in the pool cabana, or the garage.

"When she finally did show up, she showed no signs of the earlier upset. Her makeup was perfect, her costume unwrinkled. I didn't buy it, though. No, she did a great cover-up job, but I could see the change. Something about her didn't feel right. Too excited. Too keyed-up."

The switch. Twins. Mama's cookbook. The exposé. Damn, what am I missing? There had to be a connection. A common denominator linking the above.

"That's when she decided to announce her latest project." He shook his head and sighed. "I warned her not to, but she wouldn't listen. Too soon and dangerous."

"Dangerous? How so? It's only a book."

"One would think that, Jolene, but Vanessa's manuscript has the potential to do a lot of damage to a lot of people. Careers ended. Costly divorces. Businesses destroyed. Lives ruined. Even a possible lawsuit for slander. I warned her not to do it, but she refused to listen."

At his words, the pale, silvery beam began to pulse and change colors. The gnats buzzed around my ears. Every time Bradford mentioned Vanessa, the figure reacted. Another clue in the mystery.

"The guests were upset when she announced her plans," I pointed out.

"Angry is more like it."

"Furious."

"Serious threats were made."

"Dead people don't tell tales," I agreed.

"Deadly consequences." Bradford's tone flattened.

"What do you mean?"

"Vanessa is dead. That's what I've been trying to tell you."

Chapter Five
The Rainbow Figure

A wave of cold moved through my hot flesh making me feel as if the blood had frozen in my veins. I clenched my teeth together to keep them from chattering. Goose pimples raced along my arms, as I focused my attention on the wavering rainbow-colored shape clinging to Bradford's shoulder.

Vanessa van Allen.

Good God Almighty. The Vampire Queen had bitten the dust. Crap. Not good.

"Give me the details." My voice shook with disbelief. "There's been nothing on the news."

"That's where this gets sticky, Jolene." He stood up.

Another wave of cold passed through me. "You're a suspect?"

"Not yet."

"You're being vague."

"It's complicated." His deep voice deepened. "I'm not even sure what's going on." He held out his hands in an appeal. "Vanessa's death hasn't been reported to the authorities. Her mother assures me that she's alive and well and attending the Baconton Writers' Retreat."

"For God sakes, Bradford!" I jumped up from my chair to race around the desk to clasp his shoulders. "What the hell is going on? How can she be dead and alive? Holy crap. This is nuts."

Bradford disentangled himself from my grasp, pushing me into the chair he'd vacated. "I need you to be calm."

Calm? Did he say he needed me to be calm? Hell, calm wasn't in my DNA. He knew that. I was a hyperactive paranoid with a dark side that knew how to drive a stick. And I don't mean a stick shift. A broomstick. Those Salem gals had nothing on me.

"Don't look at me that way," he growled. "I know what you're thinking."

"I'm thinking you're an ass," I retorted. "I knew that woman was trouble the moment I laid eyes on her." I pointed my finger in his face. "How you got yourself entangled with her, I'll never understand."

"We're wasting time," he shot back, the muscle in his jaw clenching. "Do you want to hear the rest or not?"

I did. And he was right, of course. Not the time to rehash old hurts. We had to get a handle on matters before they skyrocketed out of control. "Tell me the rest."

"After the party broke up on Halloween night, Vanessa and I went upstairs to change. I had an early flight out of Atlanta in the morning, so I hadn't planned to stay overnight."

So they were lovers. Old news. It hurt to hear it from his lips, nonetheless. I had a new lover. Preston and I had spent the last three days in bed, breaking only to eat, sleep, and bathe. Oh, and change the sheets a couple of times. I'm a stickler for cleanliness.

"Vanessa didn't like that." Here a look of dogged resistance crossed his face. "She expected me to cancel my trip to Wyoming and attend the writers' retreat as her bodyguard. When I refused, she became unreasonable. Not herself."

"Could alcohol have been a factor in her behavior?"

"I don't see how. I never saw her take a drink the entire evening but for the toast to your mother's success."

"Drugs?"

He shook his head. "Not likely."

"Then what?"

"Vanessa began screaming for me to get the hell out of her house. As I was leaving, she launched herself at me, kicking and biting. When I tried to restrain her, she pitched a hissy fit. I thought she was going to hurt herself, so I restrained her the only way I know how. Vanessa was screeching her head off when Betty walked in and immediately drew the wrong conclusion. Vanessa didn't straighten her out. Just cried in her mother's arms."

"Then?"

"Then I got the hell out of there. I figured her mother would have better luck calming her if I was no longer in the picture. Before my flight the next morning I tried to reach Betty, but there was no answer at the house. I finally reached her yesterday morning. She told me Vanessa was fine and scheduled to attend the writers' retreat starting today."

"That makes no sense at all." I was thoroughly confused by his story. "If Vanessa is alive and well, what makes you believe she's dead?"

"Because she's haunting me," he answered in a shaky voice, and threw a quick glance over his left shoulder as if he could see the pulsating light.

My eyes followed his gesture. Sure enough, the rainbow figure still clung to his shoulder like a kudzu vine on a Georgia pine. I hesitated, then took a deep breath. "You don't believe in the afterlife."

"The last three days have been educational."

"How can you be sure it's Vanessa haunting you?"

"I presume you can see her?"

"You presume wrong," I answered. "I can only see and hear what the deceased allows, and your visitor isn't sharing. What makes you believe it's Vanessa? Especially in light of the evidence to the contrary?"

"Because I've seen her. It's Vanessa, all right."

"She's materialized into the physical world?"

Bradford scratched his chin. "Enough for me to make a positive identification. Snow White costume and all."

"She was still in costume the last you saw her?"

"Yes."

"How do you explain Betty's insistence that Vanessa is alive and well?"

"I can't," he said, with a weak smile. "That's why I'm here. I need you to communicate with her until I can track down the truth. This is your area of expertise."

I chuckled. "I never imagined I'd hear that from your lips. You wanting my help with the supernatural. My, how things change."

"Yeah, I never would've believed it myself if not for," here he gave another head jerk over his left shoulder. "This."

His action brought my gaze back to the rainbow figure. Slowly I circled Bradford, all the while focusing

41

my psychic abilities on the lost soul stuck between worlds. At first, I could vaguely visualize a woman's shape, but that soon disappeared as the pulsating light faded away into nothingness.

"Anything?" Bradford asked when I plunked back down into Deena's desk chair.

"If your unwelcome guest is Vanessa van Allen, she doesn't want anything to do with me. I'm going to need some help."

Bradford's face reflected his uneasiness. "I don't want to involve anyone else, Jolene. Too risky under the circumstances. The less people who know about this weird business, the better. Understand?"

I did, but Bradford couldn't know the limits of my abilities. And I wasn't talking about live help. This required the assistance of a certain ghost with experience. Yep. Time for a powwow session with Scarlett Cantrell: Heaven's top-rated female private investigator, and my favorite ghost. If anyone could get to the bottom of this growing mystery, it would be her. Plus, we made a great team. I smiled, anxious to get started, already formulating my pitch to her. And it had better be a good one, Scarlett had made a big deal out of her heavy workload on Halloween night.

"I'm not liking that look," Bradford said. "No outsiders, understand?"

"I heard you the first time. And I'm not thinking about involving my sisters if that's what you're worried about."

"It is," he complained. "Y'all are glued at the hip. You tell them everything."

"Not this time," I assured him. "Deena's busy planning her wedding, and Billie Jo's under the weather."

"What about your mother? Seems like she's been involved before. Your father, too."

"My parents could help, you know. They plan to attend the writers' retreat. Mama's real close to your gal pal, and they could be our eyes and ears. Plus, they don't even have to know why we want the information. It wouldn't hurt to plant a mole in the midst "

"Won't work."

"That's your point of view," I declared, feeling supremely confident in my suggestion. "Mama's incredibly adept at extracting information. At least think about it."

"The answer is no, Jolene. I don't even like the idea of you being involved. If it weren't for the special circumstances, I wouldn't have taken you into my confidence."

The frown on his face closed further discussion, so I dropped the idea of using my parents as moles. Besides, they weren't who I had in mind to begin with.

"Okay, no moles," I conceded. "Just a passing thought. Truly, my ambitions run a lot higher than that. Much higher."

"You've lost me."

Time to explain Scarlett's role in the investigation. Taking a deep breath, I plunged ahead. "Since you're now in the position to fully understand, Bradford, I intend to seek help from another source. One that can reach Vanessa as you and I can't."

"And who would that be?" His voice was calm, his gaze steady.

"Scarlett Cantrell."

"I think not. One ghost is enough, Jolene." He

shook his head as if genuinely concerned with my suggestion. "There has to be another way. Dear God, please let there be another way."

"Scarlett's our best bet. It's either her or you learn to live with your ghostly hitchhiker."

His brow drew together in an agonized expression. "I know I'm going to regret this, but let's do it."

****

Darkness had fallen and Scarlett proved once again that she wasn't at my beck and call. Several hours had passed and the only citizen of inner space in the office continued to be Bradford's shadow friend.

"This is going nowhere," I whined. "Scarlett's not going to show up tonight, Bradford. I'll keep trying, but I may have to enlist Madame Mia's superior connection."

"Madame Mia's House of Psychic Vision on Fifth?"

"You know the place?" I stared at him in astonishment. "I didn't think you'd heard of her."

"I've been in every business in this town at least once. That woman is a fraud. I'm surprised you don't know that."

"Your point of view is off-kilter with this one, Bradford. There's more to Madame Mia than meets the eye."

My first visit to the beautiful psychic had been after Scarlett's demise. Communication difficulties with the netherworld had sent me scurrying straight to the Madame's door. What an eye-opening experience that had been. But I came away with the impression that the striking psychic knew more than she was letting on. And I wasn't just talking about the invisible world. No.

She had her finger on the pulse of the town, of that I was sure, so I made it a habit to seek her out whenever the stars misaligned or the spirits came out to play. The woman definitely had X-ray vision where trouble was concerned. Now might be the time for another quick visit to Fifth Street.

Bradford raked his fingers across his stubbly chin. "I'll have to take your word for that. And since you brought it up, I'd like to apologize for my past behavior toward you regarding your paranormal abilities. I should've supported you no matter how I personally felt about the subject. That's what couples do—support one another."

His words caught me off guard. How long had I longed to hear them? Long enough. Now that the moment had arrived, I felt no pleasure however. Bradford's admission had come at a cost. If it hadn't been for a woman's death, prompting the confession, he wouldn't be here. I sighed, then yawned as weariness crept over me. My stomach growled, reminding me that I hadn't had a bite since lunch.

"I think this would be a good stopping point," he said, ignoring the awkward silence that had sprung up between us. "I'm starving. How about pizza? There's a new joint over on the north side of town that's getting great reviews down at the station." He smiled as my stomach rumbled loudly in response. "I take it that's a yes?"

I grabbed my handbag and followed Bradford out of the office and into the empty salon. We'd made it to the front door when a loud motorcycle roar, and heavy metal rock music thundered. Mesmerized by the display, I stopped in my tracks. Bradford paused too, swinging his head around to look quizzically back at me.

"Scarlett." I shrugged my shoulders. "She's changed her arrival notice again. Kinda loud and funky, but I like this one.

"Huh?"

"Never mind." I threw my handbag on one of the reception chairs. "Pizza will have to wait."

No sooner had the words left my mouth than a brilliant white light flashed. When the spots dissipated from my vision, Scarlett stood before me decked out as before, but for a long, leather duster and a sidearm on her hip to complete her Hells Angels apparel.

"Halloween is over," I said without blinking.

Scarlett's haughty gaze traveled down my palomino-colored pants and top. "Yeah, I could say the same to you. Red heels? Really, Jolene. Ditch the disco era."

"Bitch."

"Whore."

Bradford cleared his throat. "Excuse me for interrupting your exchange, ladies, but the clock is ticking."

Scarlett cocked her head in Bradford's direction. "This is new."

"A recent acquirement," I said. "Totally unexpected, but the reason I sent for you."

"Well, get on with it, Claiborne. As the hunky detective said, the clock is ticking, and I'm on a job. Pain-in-the-ass detainee slipped away while her holding cell was being cleaned and heads are rolling."

"Purgatory isn't very heavenly," I speculated.

Scarlett tapped the butt of her side arm. Sparks

flew. "That's because it ain't. Well, what's the story?"

I motioned my head in Bradford's direction. "See anything usual about him?"

Scarlett moved closer to Bradford, circling him like a vulture around roadkill. "Other than the spirit attached to his aura, no, nothing." She smacked his buttocks with the palm of her hand. "Yummy."

"You're not here for that, Scarlett. Concentrate on the problem."

Scarlett cocked her head. "Your problem is female."

"Is that all?" Bradford frowned. "What about a name?"

Scarlett wagged her head but continued her close perusal of his aura. "No, nothing comes to mind." She poked her fingers into Bradford's aura. The rainbow figure pulsed a bright red, moving out of her reach.

"I don't think she likes that," I commented as the figure darted away from Scarlett's probing fingers, all the while glowing bright red. Bradford shifted his weight as the figure continued to swing about wildly.

"Interesting." Scarlett pulled her fingers from Bradford's aura, and then retreated over to the reception desk. "I think I might need some advice. Be right back."

The resulting flash came unexpectedly, and both of us stumbled back in surprise.

"Are you sure this is the right course of action, Jolene?" A doubtful expression marred Bradford's face. "I get the distinct impression that Vanessa doesn't like Scarlett."

I returned his frown. "Do you have a better suggestion?"

"Perhaps we should call on Madame Mia after all."

"Consult a fraud?" I asked sarcastically.

"I spoke too soon."

"Too late. Scarlett will be right back with help."

"That's what I'm afraid of." His frown deepened. "I don't believe I can take another one of her probing sessions. She keeps pinching my ass, and she even copped a quick feel. God, I feel sexually abused with all that finger probing. Let's sneak out the back door. Besides, I'm hungry."

"Think again, Bradford. It's not wise to piss her off. And it won't hurt you to give her a thrill." I fished out my cell phone. "How about Chinese? The Peking Palace delivers."

Bradford gave an unenthusiastic nod, and I hit the speed dial button and ordered a double portion of my usual selections. With that done, we moved into the kitchen to wait for our food delivery and Scarlett's anticipated return.

Chapter Six
Snow White's Capture

As before, Scarlett's arrival notice sounded, followed by a blinding flash. Thankfully, I had the foresight to cover my eyes. Bradford wasn't as fortunate. He was still rubbing his when Scarlett materialized in front of us.

"Found it." She held up a battered handbook and clipboard. "First, I consulted the list of new arrivals and noticed one failed to report." She pointed at Bradford's aura. "That could be her hitching a ride with handsome." Next, she flipped through the handbook. "Here. The chapter on extracting DEARS."

"Deers?" Okay, so I was curious.

"Yeah. Departed Energy and Reflective Soul." She spelled each letter out. "D-E-A-R-S."

I withheld comment. However, Bradford spoke up. "Do you have a name for that dears?"

Scarlett consulted the clipboard. "Hmm, that's odd. The name has been crossed out and replaced with the initials, C.H."

"And the crossed out name?" Bradford wanted to know.

"Vanessa van Allen."

Bradford stood with his hands jammed in his pockets, his face thoughtful.

"C.H. could be a nickname," I offered, hoping to

spark recognition in his eyes, or something to speed things along. "What about an alias? Or pen name?"

Bradford remained silent, locked in concentration.

Scarlett rechecked the clipboard information. "I've never heard of Heaven making a mistake, but this could be a first. If so, someone's going down. Heaven's administration is fantastically thorough with the paperwork. They don't tolerate typos. Even in Purgatory."

"Vanessa didn't use a pen name," Bradford spoke up. "She wanted everyone to know who and what she was. But it is a lead that I can follow up on. Thanks, Scarlett. I appreciate the help."

She positively glowed with the compliment. "Oh, I'm just getting started, detective. I'm going to extract Miss Mysterious like a bad tooth and return her to Purgatory where she'll answer for her crimes. Stand back, Jolene, this can get real messy according to the manual."

Messy? That stopped me short. After eating, Bradford and I had returned to the reception area to await Scarlett's return. "Let's move into Deena's office. Everybody and his uncle can see us through this plate glass, and I don't need more rumors started about the salon being haunted. You use this place like a second home."

Scarlett giggled at my last remark, but trailed behind us as Bradford and I moved into Deena's office. I shut the door and closed the blinds for extra privacy.

With that done, I settled on the sofa on the opposite side of the room away from Bradford, who stood between Deena's desk and the door. Scarlett hovered close over Bradford's head, poking and prodding his aura. The rainbow figure reacted negatively with each poke, which in turn elicited a jerk or sidestep from him. From my point-of-view, it was comical, but I kept my feelings to myself—seeing how Bradford wouldn't appreciate my sense of humor at the moment.

Scarlett was up to her elbows in Bradford's aura when I remembered the weird riddle of the twins.

"I've got it!" I bolted to my feet and rushed over to them. "Twins! Remember, Halloween night, Scarlett? You know, the message from the netherworld. C.H. could be Vanessa's twin. There was a mix-up. The death angel pegged the wrong woman. That would explain the crossed-out name." I smiled at my awesome powers of deduction.

Scarlett paused with a hard look. "What are you babbling about? I'm trying to persuade Miss Mysterious to join us, and you go and interrupt my concentration."

"What's this about a twin, Jolene?" Bradford's tone indicated his displeasure. "Why didn't you mention it earlier?" He stopped fidgeting when Scarlett withdrew from his aura to turn her full attention to me.

My cheeks burned under their stern gazes. "I meant to, but it slipped my mind until now. So, what about it, Bradford? Did Vanessa or her mother ever mention a sister? Possibly a twin?"

Scarlett whistled. "There's mischief abroad in this house. Twins. One of the twins will lose. I remember the message. One of the twins will lose. That would explain things."

"Vanessa never mentioned a sister." Bradford scratched his stubbly chin. "She's an only child. Sorry to shoot down your observations, but we need to look elsewhere."

I thought about the odd conversation I'd heard in the study. "Not necessarily. Vanessa was planning to make a switch of some sort on Halloween night. I thought—"

"That's what you were up to in the study," he interrupted. "For once, I'm glad you did. Now tell me everything. And I mean everything, no matter how insignificant you think it is."

Hastily, I spilled the beans. I told him about Vanessa's emotional confrontation with her agent, Cash Hitchcock, of course, leaving out mine and Preston's backyard sexcapade. Then the sickening scene on the stairs with a drunken Purvis Dupree, the mysterious phone call, Vanessa's disappearance, Scarlett's strange riddle from the Other Side, and the bad vibrations I'd perceived when Vanessa had finally reappeared after a lengthy absence.

"So you see why all the puzzle pieces fit together," I concluded. "Twins. Switch. C.H. I believe Vanessa switched places with her twin sister, and the death angel knocked off the wrong sibling. Makes perfect sense to me."

"But not to me." Bradford's tone was sarcastic. "And it doesn't rid me of my problem." He made a head motion over his left shoulder. The rainbow figure glowed bright red.

"But I can if you two are done." Scarlett lifted a haughty brow. "But first let me get comfortable." She shrugged out of her leather duster. Bradford's eyes fastened on her magnificent store-bought boobs straining against the soft black T-shirt, nipples hard and standing at attention. No bra! A tinge of jealously coursed through me at his glazed look, and I glanced down at my slightly sagging bust line. Yep, time for a lift. To save costs, perhaps Preston would put together a bundle for me. Boobs, nose, and tummy tuck. Yeah. A midlife birthday present to myself.

Thus rid of any encumbrances, Scarlett dived hands first into Bradford's aura, fishing around like a cat-daddling in Whiskey Creek on a lazy Sunday afternoon after dinner and preachin'. After several unsuccessful attempts, frustration twisted her lovely face, and sweat broke out across her snarling upper lip.

"Damn it to hell," she screeched, emerging half her body into the now pulsating aura, causing Bradford to twist away from her. "Hold still, handsome." She made one jerking grab at the furious red figure. "They don't call me the Georgia Giant for nothing. Oh, and Jolene, you might want to step back. Things are coming to a head."

Usually I don't take orders well, but Bradford's aura had turned a swollen luminous neon blue and showed the signs of a supernova. For extra precaution, I ducked behind the sofa and covered my head with my hands as I'd been taught during tornado drills in elementary school.

I called that one right. A loud sucking noise rose to a crescendo before exploding into an earsplitting pop, and then complete silence. When I peered over the back of the sofa, Bradford stood unmoving in what appeared to be shock, and covered in a fine dusting of white, glittering snow-like material. I couldn't help it, but I giggled at the sight of the abominable snowman with brilliant blue eyes standing dumbstruck in the middle of Deena's office.

And then, out of the corner of my eye, I noticed Scarlett struggling with Snow White over by the bookcase. Incensed, Scarlett whipped out a pair of golden handcuffs and shackled the screeching ghost to the floor lamp. Both were unaffected by the exploding aura. Only Bradford and Deena's office had suffered.

"Okay, the scene is secure." Scarlett glanced over at me and then Bradford. "Y'all can come question the DEARS before I hand her over to the authorities."

Bradford remained frozen in place, only his eyes reflecting the misery he must've been through. I took pity on him, crossed over to his side, and tried to brush the snowflakes from his face. The goo stuck to my fingers like cobwebs, and refused to shake off.

He sneezed several times at my ministrations.

"How do we get rid of this stuff?" I wiped my hands down the side of my silk pant legs, transferring the wet goo to my expensive trousers. Christ. Another dry cleaning bill. Nix the new orange heels down at Second Street Boutique. Damn the luck.

Scarlett waved a dismissive hand. "It'll dissipate on its own. Pay attention. You and Detective Delectable are wasting time. I need to get her back and move on to the next job."

As Bradford and I approached the ghostly figure shackled to the floor lamp, my cell phone twined, and I glanced down to see who was calling. Mama. Damn. What did she want at this hour?

"I have to answer this," I told a scowling Scarlett. "It won't take long, I swear."

In hindsight, the phone call turned out to be a lifesaver. Mama and Daddy had decided to skip the writers' retreat in favor of sun and fun in Florida, and would I be so kind as to keep an eye on the farm for a week or so? Deena was tied up with wedding plans and Billie Jo had the stomach flu, so I was the only sibling left. To speed things along, I agreed, not voicing that I wasn't sure how to manage my growing workload. With Billie Jo out sick, and Deena knee-deep in wedding preparations, I was practically running the salon alone these days. My daughter, Becky, and son-in-law, Jacob, couldn't help as they and my precious granddaughter, Hannah, were visiting Jacob's relatives in Israel. Perhaps my nephew, Bo, could oversee the farm.

With that settled, I hung up the phone and turned my attention to Snow White, who was making goo-goo eyes at Bradford, who in turn was scraping snowflakes from his face, swearing quietly at the insanity of the situation. Scarlett drifted close by, her hand resting comfortably on her sidearm.

I sided up to Bradford. "This is your haunting, so I'll stay on the sideline and jump in only if needed."

Bradford pulled out a handkerchief from his pocket and wiped his hands. "I feel weird, but here goes." Snow White literally glowed when he smiled at her and drew closer.

"Tell me your name," he ordered in an authoritative tone used for questioning criminals.

"You know my name, Sam," she cooed. "Why the pretense? I've always been Vanessa to you."

"Do you have a twin sister with the initials C.H.?"

"What's wrong with you, Sam?" She pulled at her restraints. "What's this about? And why has *that* dreadful woman handcuffed me to this lamp? Where am I?"

Bradford's confused gaze locked with mine. "She doesn't appear to understand what's happened to her. Now what?" He shoved the wet handkerchief into his rear pocket.

"Explain to her what's happened," I directed. "It's common that most ghosts have holes in their memory immediately after their death."

"It's true," Scarlett added. "My mind was like Swiss cheese after my untimely demise. I don't know what I would've done without Jolene."

At first Snow White refused to believe that she was now a citizen of inner space. Actually, she pitched a hissy fit and turned bright green. Recalling the last incident, I backed off for good measure and used the opportunity to scout the kitchen for Lizzie's secret cookie stash. Ghostbusting makes me crave sweets.

Snow White had settled down when I rejoined the group. Still shackled to the floor lamp, she seemed to accept her unusual circumstances as truth and had returned to a more normal shade of ghostly.

"Is she still insisting she's Vanessa van Allen?" I asked Bradford.

"Yes." He shook his head. "She remembers the book launch party on Halloween night, but after that, nothing."

"Did you question her about the mysterious call I overheard in the study?"

"She insists she was talking with her editor, Clarissa Howard. They were discussing changes to the manuscript. That's all she can recall."

I opened my mouth to point out the obvious, but Bradford held up a hand to silence me. "Yes, I've thought of that. C.H. Clarissa Howard. Scarlett's checking on that now, but I think it's a waste of time. This woman is a dead ringer for Vanessa, and I believe her."

I surveyed the room and noticed for the first time, Scarlett's absence.

"Don't worry, Jolene. She'll be right back," Bradford assured me. "However, we do have a problem."

"What's that?"

Bradford pointed to a quiet Snow White. "She and Scarlett have a mutual dislike for one another."

"That's because the diva element is eternal. Scarlett is the ultimate Dixie diva. Vanessa comes in a close second."

"So what are you saying?"

"Dueling diva ghosts." I shook my head in dismay. "Our lives just became a whole lot more complicated. Why can't Scarlett just return Snow White to Purgatory without all the fuss?"

"Because I'm not going anywhere until my manuscript is in the right hands, and I'm staying until that's accomplished," Snow White piped up from the floor lamp, her voice resonating. Her golden brown eyes glittered with malice in the muted office light. "Count on it."

"See what I mean?" Bradford's tone had a sharp edge.

I nodded, "Yeah. What's your plan?"

"Haven't got one."

"Well, I do."

"Care to enlighten me?"

"As you know, Vanessa is scheduled to speak at the writers' retreat. I know from Mama that most of same people from Halloween's book launch will be in attendance. They've decided not to attend, so you and I are taking their place, thus allowing us to track down the woman impersonating Vanessa." Here I paused, fastening my full gaze on the shackled ghost. "Or find out the identity of Snow White. Either way, we must find the body and the crime scene before the killer can get away. No body, no crime."

Chapter Seven
The Baconton Writers' Retreat

Most people entertain the notion that women from the South are countrified and enjoy Mother Nature's bountiful hand. I can't speak for my fellow belles, but in my case, nothing could be further from the truth. I detest the country. I'm a small-town girl who appreciates the sights and sounds within the city limits. No outdoorsy stuff for me. I don't camp. I don't hunt. I don't fish. And I don't eat anything unless it comes from the local grocery store with an identification sticker saying chicken or beef.

I say this because the Baconton Writers' Retreat squatted smack dab in the middle of nowhere. Way out in the country. Way out of my comfort zone. No drugstores, no convenience stores, no mall, no boutiques, no sign of civilization anywhere. Just dusty red roads and trees. Lots of trees. Actually, a dense forest located about twenty miles from town.

Baconton Lodge sat back deep in that forest of pines and wild pecans as old as the state of Georgia itself—a rustic two-storied structure complete with a social hall, a lounge, a restaurant, and a several private rooms. Smaller cabins made of the same weathered logs were set in a circle around a picturesque lake connected by a winding path through delicate dogwoods and Cherokee roses. A perfect hideaway for an author who wanted complete privacy, or one who didn't want to be found.

And my perfect vision of hell.

Bradford didn't share my feelings. The instant we pulled off the narrow clay lane and parked his pickup under a towering loblolly pine, that looked to house a city of sparrows, he whistled. "Ah, the peace and quiet of the country. Man, this is the best-kept secret in South Georgia. I bet the quail hunting is off the charts. Too bad I won't be here long enough to sample the pickings. Well, let's go check in."

My heels sank into the soft ground the instant I climbed out of the truck cab, suitcase in hand.

"I told you to ditch those things." Bradford came around to the passenger side to take my bags. "I hope you packed better shoes. Preferably flats or boots."

Scarlett peered over my shoulder. "You're wasting your breath, detective. Jolene ain't parting with her heels."

"You talk too much," Snow White complained from over Bradford's left shoulder. "If you can't shut up then leave, you scatterbrained nitwit."

Scarlett gestured to the handcuffs dangling from her hand. "How would you like to try on my bracelets again? Don't forget who's in charge here, missy."

"Both of you pipe down," Bradford commanded. "We work together as a team, understand? The sooner we crack this mystery, the sooner everyone can go their separate ways. Until then, don't be seen or heard, got it?"

Scarlett arched a brow, but remained silent, her features composed in deceptive acceptance. Snow White, as I continued to call her, fluttered her eyelashes like a besotted idiot, and nodded. Talk about a scatterbrained nitwit.

With ghosts in tow, we headed up the gravel path between jewel-colored perennial flowers, their delicate petals perfection in the early morning sunlight, and red ginger lilies reaching up to capture a buzzing bee's interest. Somewhere close by in the lush forest, a pair of mockingbirds fussed over their nest, squirrels chirped, and the distinct serenade of cicadas concreted my earlier vision of country hell. Peace and quiet, my ass. It was louder than a two a.m. tornado siren.

Now once I stood on the shaded wraparound porch, with a row of oversized rocking chairs with colorful cushions and hanging ferns, my aversion shifted slightly, and I found myself reconsidering my earlier prejudice. The lodge offered respite from a busy lifestyle, and I could see how the artistically minded would flock here for privacy.

Passing through double log doors, my gaze was immediately drawn to a spectacular center staircase dominating the main lobby. A piece of art straight out of a brilliant architect's mind. Made from local pines, intricately carved forest animals scampered playfully up the massive banisters to the second-floor landing.

The rest of the lobby followed the hunters lodge theme. The floor and walls were pine, the simple furniture in browns and greens, with vases of vibrant wildflowers sprinkled throughout, and mounted on the walls were the heads of deer, boar, and wild fowl. If I didn't know that I was in South Georgia, I would've thought I'd traveled to the Alaskan backcountry.

Colorful braided rugs scattered about gave the lobby a warm, inviting feeling. On the far, opposite wall, flanked by tall, wide windows, a fireplace promised warmth during the cold winter months. Now all it needed was snow-covered mountains in the background to become Bradford's idea of paradise.

We went directly to the desk where an older woman smiled a warm greeting when I gave her Mama's name. Amelia Goldenrod, her name tag read, appeared to be an exact replica of the flower she was named for. Petite and flowerlike, her short, frizzy yellow hair sprigged in all directions, and dancing brown eyes that smiled with an energy and directness that immediately put one at ease. I liked her on sight.

"Welcome to the Baconton Writers' Retreat, Mrs. Tucker." She beamed in my direction. "You and Mr. Tucker are in the Flannery O'Conner cabin. Most of the attendees have arrived and are preparing for the opening workshop.

Bradford merely nodded, but I could tell from the frown that he was still harboring doubts about our assumed identities. Really, at times the man could try the patience of a saint waiting for the rapture. We'd spent most of last night arguing the pros and cons of my plan. Bradford didn't believe we'd be able to pull it off, but I had faith we could. Sure, assuming my parents' identities had its drawbacks, especially if we ran into someone we knew, or who knew my parents, but it would land us in the desired location. And I doubted that anyone would pay us much mind. Mama wasn't in the big leagues, and not notable. From what I'd observed at the book launch, Vanessa's acquaintances hadn't given Mama any recognition. Besides, we'd keep to the background, thereby limiting our exposure to the players. Since Bradford didn't have a better plan,

I'd won the argument, and here we were at the mini-conference.

"Thank you, Mrs. Goldenrod." I returned her infectious grin. "My husband and I are thrilled to be here. I understand Vanessa van Allen has arrived?"

The desk clerk punched several keys on a small computer. "Yes, she checked in early. You'll find her in the Margaret Mitchell cabin." Here, she cast me a shrewd look. "However, I believe Miss van Allen has requested privacy, and here, privacy is respected." As the spiel continued Scarlett materialized behind the woman's back and peered over her shoulder at the computer screen.

"Vanessa van Allen co-authored my wife's cookbook. They're friends of a sort." Bradford's frown melted into a smile sure to captivate any female.

Mrs. Goldenrod's face didn't flinch at his sugary tone. "Then I'm sure Miss van Allen will let her know when she's free to receive visitors. Now, if you'll follow me, I'll show you to your cabin." She handed me a packet. "Your itinerary."

Silently, we followed her out of the lodge and down the pathway to the group of identical cabins surrounding the lake. The Flannery O'Conner cabin was indeed at the end of the row, butting up against the dark, lush forest that promised a symphony of night sounds to wake the dead. Good thing I'd brought along a big supply of sleeping pills.

Mrs. Goldenrod unlocked the door, and we followed her inside. "As per your instructions, Mrs. Tucker, I stocked the bar with whiskey and peanuts for Mr. Tucker." She hurried over to a small bar just off the kitchenette and opened the cabinet doors to display the mentioned items. "Housekeeping will change the sheets and towels only if you request it. Ring the office and we'll see to it. The kitchen is stocked with fresh local foods. If you require any additional foodstuffs, you'll have to fetch it yourselves. The Internet password is listed in your itinerary. Well, if there's nothing else you need, I'll excuse myself so you can get to work."

After the woman had shut the door behind her, I again surveyed the cabin with dismay. Good Lord, I'm in trouble. The small room was filled with furniture too heavy for the size of it—especially if the occupants were above average in height and weight. Not that Bradford and I were fat. No, but we were, as I said, above average. The double bed tucked over in the corner appeared to have come out of a dollhouse, and the only other soft surface was a love seat that wouldn't be a sleeping option at all unless you were a leprechaun.

That meant Bradford and I would have to share the bed. Tight squeeze. Good or bad? Not sure I wanted the temptation. Even after three days of glorious sex with a younger man.

Bradford had the same uncertain gleam in his eyes when I turned to face him.

"Sorry for the tight quarters. I guess I didn't think this through."

His brows flickered a little. "As usual."

Snow White materialized over his shoulder. "This is unacceptable, Sam. I demand better accommodations." Her mouth puckered. "And we can't all sleep in that poor excuse of a bed."

"You ninny." Scarlett's tone matched her mood. "The bed is for them, not us. We're way past that earthly function."

"Over my dead body will they share that tiny bed," Snow White shrilled as her anger intensified. Bradford's aura pulsed blue under her assault.

"Exactly," Scarlett purred, stretching her arms over her head provocatively as Bradford's eyes bugged. "Now, you're getting with the program. Shall we leave these two alone?" She winked at me suggestively. "I'm sure Jolene would appreciate a little privacy with Detective Delectable."

I stepped toward the minuscule bathroom. No way was I gonna be sprayed with exploding aura.

"Enough of the squabbling, ladies," Bradford's voice cut through the sizzling atmosphere. "I need to speak with Vanessa, or her imposter, without raising suspicion. Any ideas? "

"We know she's here," Scarlett said, with a sultry smile. "In the Margaret Mitchell cabin. We start there. It's the second bungalow from the lodge."

"How are we going to handle this?" I asked Bradford. "Are we going to confront her?"

"No. First, we need to make a positive identification. If it's truly Vanessa, then I'll shift my investigation to the imposter. I need to identify her and find her body if possible. There's still a murder to solve."

Snow White materialized beside Bradford. "I'm Vanessa van Allen. The woman in that cabin is the imposter, I'm telling you. I'm the real deal."

"We'll see about that, missy." Scarlett snorted. "Everything about you is false."

"Like those silicone basketballs on your chest?" Snow White snickered. "Not much originality there."

"Enough!" Bradford bellowed, his face red with anger. "Find a way to get along or get the hell out of here."

The room fell into silence as we all surveyed the other. Snow White faded back into Bradford's aura, leaving the three of us in the small room. Finally, Scarlett seemed to pull herself together and give a quick nod in Bradford's direction. "What's your plan, Boss?"

"Like I said, we need to identify the woman checked in as Vanessa van Allen."

"How do we do that without confronting her?" I questioned.

"Carefully. Now let's get moving. And try not to draw attention to yourselves."

I didn't budge. "In broad daylight? No way. Mrs. Eagle-eye Goldenrod is sure to catch us, and I'm not in the mood to go to jail. Not even for you. Come up with a better plan."

"I could scout out the cabin with none the wiser," Scarlett offered. "If she's there, you can come up with another plan. If it's empty, then you could proceed with a search."

Bradford shook his head impatiently. "This is my case."

"And this is my ass on the line," I added. "Besides, I need to change my shoes. Scarlett will be back before I can dig them out of my suitcase."

He gave in with a grunt, and Scarlett disappeared in a flash. Hurriedly, I retrieved my suitcase from beside the bed and dug around until I located my brown flats and a pair of comfortable jeans. I had just slipped them on when Scarlett reappeared.

"The cabin is empty. I observed the woman hiking

in the woods."

"Odd behavior for her, wouldn't you think." I joined Bradford at the door. "What about Mrs. Goldenrod?"

"In the kitchen stuffing her face," Scarlett replied. "I did a quick recon of the area, and all the other attendees are occupied."

With no further discussion, we slipped out the door and headed for the Margaret Mitchell cabin.

Chapter Eight
The Break-In

"Now what?" My voice intensified as I grew more anxious. We'd been poking around the cabin for a way in and thus far had found our efforts blocked by locked windows and front door. I was ready to call it quits and head back to our cabin for a bite to eat.

"Keep your voice down," Bradford commanded in a strong whisper. "We don't want to draw unnecessary attention to our activities."

We were hunkered down under the back window of the cabin behind a boxwood bush. We'd been unsuccessful in breaking and entering, and I was beginning to seriously question our investigative abilities. The woman would be returning before long, and our time had just about expired.

"Don't you have a pick or something?" I mumbled to Bradford's back. "I thought you guys were trained for this sort of thing."

Bradford removed the window screen, placing it down beside me, then gave a forceful push on the window frame. It slid open a fraction, then stopped. "It's stuck. Help me, Jolene."

Together we gripped the window and pushed. Nothing. The window remained partially opened.

Bradford's gaze swept down the length of my plus-size figure. "I don't suppose you could squeeze through this opening?" A teasing grin twisted his mouth. "Take one for the team?"

My heart constricted at his shining eyes, and for a moment I remembered happier times. Sadly the moment vanished when the window suddenly sprang open on its own.

"What's taking you guys so long?" Scarlett's tone was contemptuous. "We need to get in and out of here. Quick. The woman won't stay away forever."

I wasted no time with a reply but heaved myself over the windowsill and into the room. Bradford followed. The layout of the cabin was identical to ours, but for the overly Southern belle influence. White lace everything. Curtains, bedspread, dollies, and fluffy pillows. Local landscapes dotted the walls and offered the only splashes of color to the room. Oh, and Vanessa's belongings were scattered everywhere. The bathroom shared the same fate. Towels littered the floor and makeup spilled from a cosmetic case—covering the marble vanity top.

"Lord, what a pig," I declared from the bathroom. "Looks like a bomb went off."

"Or someone beat us here," Bradford's voice came from the main room. "This place has been searched."

I stuck my head out of the bathroom. "What do you mean?"

"I agree with Detective Delectable," Scarlett remarked from above. "Someone went out of his way to cover his tracks, but he was definitely here. See how the pictures aren't quite straight?"

Slowly, my gaze traveled the room. I saw what she meant. To the casual observer it appeared that the occupant was indeed a slob, but overlying that

69

impression was the distinct markings of a slow, methodical search. But for what? Jewels? Cash? I shook my head. That didn't seem plausible here in this backwoods location. Even the Vanessa of my acquaintance wouldn't be that stupid.

"What could he be after?" I mused aloud.

"Or she," Bradford added.

He was digging through a pile of papers on an antique lady's desk, his blue aura turning slightly purple. Without much ado, Snow White materialized beside him.

"Perhaps the imposter has absconded with my manuscript." Her velvet eyes heightened the translucence of her face and neck. "That could be the key to this mystery."

"You don't mean that piece of trash you announced on Halloween." I shot her a twisted smile. "And I do mean trash."

Snow White's brow rose a fraction. "Trash makes the bestsellers in my profession, my dear. Of course, you don't know anything about my intricate world."

Just as I started to respond with another stinging zinger, my cell phone shrilled from my back pocket.

Ignoring the scowl on Bradford's face, I whipped out my phone. Deena. Dang. I forgot we were shopping for her wedding dress today. For the tenth damn time.

"Hey sis," I answered. "Sorry I'm not there, yet. Flat tire," I lied. "Can I reschedule?"

"I'm running out of time, Jolene," Deena's teary voice cracked over the line. "I haven't found the perfect dress, plus the country club phoned this morning to tell me they've overbooked the clubhouse. Now I'm out a prime venue. What am I going to do? Please, Jolene,

I'm depending on you."

Deena's panicked tone had me backtracking. Instead of helping my sister with her upcoming wedding I was scouring the countryside looking for Vanessa van Allen, or an imposter with her face. Even thinking it gave me a headache. Hurry, put on your thinking cap, woman. How can you be in two places at one time? Investigating or dress shopping? Former boyfriend or sister? How could I choose? Either way I was screwed.

Bradford's pissed expression made the decision for me. "Listen, Deena, run out to the country club and personally speak with the manager, Gloria. She's one of my best clients and will get to the bottom of the mix-up. I'll meet you at the dress shop in two hours." With that, I hung up and returned the phone to my back pocket, my eyes glued to Bradford's face.

"I have to do this," I said at his continuing silence. "I'll be back as soon as I can. Really, you don't need me for this. Scarlett is the best at what she does. Trust me."

"Seems I don't have a choice." His face softened as he withdrew keys from his jean pocket. "I hope you can drive a standard shift." He tossed me the keys. "Leave the way we came."

I pocketed the keys and had moved over to the window when the front door knob rattled stopping me in midflight. Bradford made a motion of silence. Snow White ducked back into his aura, and Scarlett lounged confidently across the bed, her eyes shining with glee. Bitch. I shot her a bird just because and turned my attention back to my leader. The knob rattled again, and the soft murmur of voices could just be heard outside the door.

Bradford's brow creased in concentration before pointing to the closet. I wagged my head in acknowledgment and crept silently in that direction. No such luck. The front door swung open freezing me to the floor. Outlined by the warm sunlight streaming through the doorframe stood a bear of a man. Red hair and beard. Mean eyes. Thin lips. On his chest a silver star. And in his meaty hand, a sawed-off shotgun pointed directly at me.

"Busted," came a sugary voice from the bed. With my hands in the air I couldn't shoot her another bird but, by God, at the next opportunity I was going to do a little ghostbusting of my own.

****

Greenwood County Sheriff Cleaster Snellgrove turned out to be colder and harder than Stone Mountain on a frosty winter morning. Added to that was Mrs. Goldenrod's displeasure at finding the couple registered in the Flannery O'Conner cabin making themselves at home in the Margaret Mitchell cabin. It took several minutes of heavy explaining to get the sheriff to holster his weapon and allow us to drop our arms, although his hand rested in close proximity to his massive sidearm. Scarlett, who flittered around the grisly sheriff like a pollenating bumblebee, was downright disgusting. A dark flush stained her cheeks, and every once in a while, she would touch his sidearm and squeal with orgasmic delight. He, on the other hand, remained ignorant of the provocative ghost clinging to his side.

"I ought to kick you off the premises this instant," Mrs. Goldenrod scolded. "This sort of thing is strictly prohibited." We'd been shuffled outside before she closed and locked the door, and now we were standing on the front porch doing our best to appear contrite, and ignore Scarlett's lustful play.

"As I said earlier, Mrs. Goldenrod," Bradford began in his nicest tone. "We were passing by when we heard a crash inside the cabin. The front door was unlocked, so I assumed the worse. We only meant to assist Miss van Allen. No harm intended."

The head registrant raised her eyebrows. "Miss van Allen reported hearing noises inside her cabin. That's why I called the sheriff," she voiced. "Appears to me that you're lying, Mr. Tucker."

Bradford's gaze impaled me. Let me handle this it seemed to say. Although I wanted to deck the woman, I clamped down on my response and remained subdued.

"Is it possible for me to speak with Miss van Allen?" Bradford continued in a calm tone. "I'm sure she'll be happy to clear up this misunderstanding once she realizes that my wife and I were only looking out for her welfare. We are after all personal friends, right, honey?"

I smiled in acquiescence. "The best, my dear." Gag.

Mrs. Goldenrod relaxed her stance. "I believe that would be the wise course, Sheriff. If Miss van Allen can vouch for these two, then I'll drop the matter."

Sheriff Snellgrove tipped his cowboy hat at her. "As you say, dear lady. I'm here to serve."

Sandwiched between Mrs. Goldenrod and the country sheriff, we returned to the main lodge in search of Vanessa, who at last sighting, was sharing tea with another writer in the lounge.

Of course, she wasn't there.

But surprisingly Cash Hitchcock was. He informed Mrs. Goldenrod and the sheriff that Vanessa had suddenly gone into town for an unnamed errand. I didn't buy it for a minute. The weasel's slimy smile indicated he had more information. Problem was we couldn't question him without raising suspicion. That would come later. After we'd extracted ourselves from the sticky situation in which we found ourselves.

Thankfully, Mrs. Goldenrod had other pressing matters and had by that time grown tired of us. After a stern warning from Snellgrove to stay out of trouble, he left, leaving us to our own devices.

Minus Scarlett, who'd disappeared along with the sheriff, we silently made our way back to our cabin for a quick powwow.

"What is Vanessa's former agent doing here?" I questioned the instant the door closed behind us. "And why the subterfuge? What's his game? He's hiding something, Bradford. I know it. He knows Vanessa's secret. Remember? The one she's keeping from you?"

"Drink?" Bradford turned from pouring a whiskey at the liquor cabinet. He held out a glass of the amber liquid. When I declined, he downed the liquor and poured another.

"Well?" My voice had a bite. "Your thoughts, please."

"All in time, my dear. We'll have our answers in time."

"Aren't you the patient one?" Unable to corral my nervous energy, I pulled a water bottle from the small fridge, and continued to mumble under my breath as I fished out a container of something green.

"It's all about pacing, Jolene. Slow and steady.

That's the plan. When I'm ready, Cash Hitchcock will talk."

With spoon and container, I joined him at the small, yellow table. "Appearances seem to verify that Vanessa is indeed alive."

"If true, then we must identify my friend."

"Funny that everyone but us is able to connect with this woman."

Bradford nodded his head. "We need solid proof that the woman is indeed Vanessa van Allen and not an imposter. I'm not convinced that it's Vanessa."

"DNA would be solid proof."

"My sentiments exactly. That's why I'm returning to the cabin."

"And what am I supposed to do in the meantime?" I scooped the remaining goo into my mouth.

Bradford set his empty glass on the table. "You're going into town, my dear. Deena's waiting on you, and when you're finished with wedding plans I want you to swing by Vanessa's house and pick up a DNA sample."

I slid a glance at him. "You're kidding?"

"It's the only way to positively identify her. If we obtain a hair sample from Vanessa's house and the cabin, then compare them."

"And how am I supposed to accomplish this? I don't believe her mother will readily hand over Vanessa's hairbrush to a complete stranger."

"I'm sure you can come up with something, Jolene. You're a resourceful woman."

Resourceful. Great. Just the compliment a woman wants to hear. Before I could waste any more valuable time on vanity, my cell phone jiggled. Geez. Deena again.

"Don't panic, I'm on my way." I reached for my handbag.

"Don't bother," came Deena's prompt answer. "Something's come up. I can't explain but I rescheduled with Mona for tomorrow morning at ten. Be there, please." The line went dead before I could respond.

"Appears I'm not needed in town." I placed my handbag and phone on the table. "Unless you want me to head over to Vanessa's to collect that DNA sample."

Bradford glanced at his watch. "Let me check in at the station. I want to see if there's been any reports of missing persons, or deaths, namely Vanessa's. We'll decide our next move then."

I left Bradford on the phone and went into the bathroom for a quick shower. Thirty minutes later, I emerged squeaky clean and in a better frame of mind. Truthfully, I was relieved that wedding dress shopping had been postponed one more day because I dreaded the chore. Oh, I loved my sister, and would do anything for her, but Deena had morphed into Bridezilla. We'd shopped the entire state of Georgia for a wedding gown, and nothing, or no one pleased her. Every minor setback required tears. Lots of them. Really, I couldn't understand all the fuss and had gently mentioned elopement. Which had been immediately axed. Oh well, so much for sisterly advice.

Bradford was stretched out shirtless on the bed when I entered the main room.

"Um, you smell like lemons." His lazy smile ignited my senses. A warm flush began at my toes, creeping up my limbs to settle south of my waistline. My twinkie pie zinged with anticipation. Geez. That wouldn't do. My hormones were firing off like a nuclear reactor.

I diverted my eyes, hoping to head off the natural direction of my thoughts. "What's the word from the boys in blue?"

"Nothing." Sounds from the bed indicated Bradford had sat up and slung his long legs over the side. "Everything's quiet. No missing persons or homicides. Actually good news, but for the mystery hanging over my head. God, this is driving me nuts."

I lifted my eyes to see him sitting on the side of the bed, his hand ruffling through his wavy hair. Still shirtless, the muscles rippled across his broad chest, quickening my pulse, and I couldn't look away. Alarm bells blasted out a warning, and I knew with a certainty that one touch would bring me back into his bed. Hell, one sizzling look and my panties would be off.

"Jolene?"

"I heard you." Get a grip. "I agree. We need to pin down Vanessa."

Bradford stood up and grabbed his shirt. "We'll both head into town tomorrow. You meet up with Deena, and I'll head over to Vanessa's house. I spoke with her mother while you were in the shower, so she's expecting me. For tonight, we'll hang around here. There's a cocktail party and dinner in the main lodge. Hope you packed something nice. I'm going to take a shower."

Scarlett hadn't returned by the time Bradford and I were ready to leave. Apparently, Snow White had settled down for the night, for his aura had faded into nothingness. A calm peacefulness blanketed the cozy room. If one weren't tuned into the netherworld, they would only see the surface as normal. I, on the other hand, felt the fluid reality take a subtle shift. Somewhere out there in the great beyond karmic payback gathered forces, and I knew with a certainty that tonight I was gonna get my ass kicked.

A Dead Pig in the Sunshine

Chapter Nine
The Ghostwriter

Writers are kooks. Intelligent, but bat-ass-crazy. And the bunch surrounding me were the cream of the crop. Poster children for the dysfunctional. And some people think I'm crazy? They should get a gander of this gang of tipsy misfits.

Like I said on Halloween, writers and alcohol don't mix. The atmosphere of the cocktail party had the dizzy excitement of the Kentucky Derby—beautiful clothes on beautiful people all racing to be the first one at the finish line. The room was jammed with much of the same crowd from Vanessa's Halloween party. Vanessa hadn't put in an appearance, yet, but I recognized Purvis Dupree immediately. The lecherous publisher had cornered some sweet, young, unsuspecting female over by the bar. From the roving position of his meaty paw on her curvaceous hips, and the stargazed expression of the girl's face, I deduced the man had sealed the deal, and the young writer would soon be signing her first book contract.

Peaches Noble echoed the sentiment in my ear. "I hope she enjoys the ride. Those royalty checks come with a high price." I caught the sweet whiff of bourbon, and the smooth aroma of warm caramel and toasted vanilla made me think of Daddy and Mama's pecan pie.

"I'm sure I don't know what you mean." I laced

my voice with just enough curiosity to encourage her loose tongue.

The romance writer shrugged. "How do you think I got my start?"

"Really?" I gushed. "You? I don't believe it."

"Believe it. Common in my time."

"And Vanessa knows all about it."

She downed the rest of the amber liquid from the tumbler in her hand. "Every last degrading detail." She lifted the empty glass. "Late night and too much liquor. That's when we met. At a romance writers conference years ago. Roommates. God, we sat up all night talking. She hadn't sold a thing yet, poor kid. But I had, so when she asked me to look over her work, I did. Couldn't write squat." She gestured to the bartender for another drink.

Interesting. "I don't understand. If Vanessa can't write, then how did she come to write the bestselling Dark Enchantment Vampire Series?"

Peaches leaned closer. "That's what I'd like to know, my dear. My money's on a ghostwriter."

Another unfamiliar term. "A ghostwriter? Sounds like a dead writer out for hire." I laughed.

She didn't share my humor. The bartender plopped down an amber-filled tumbler on the bar. Peaches's long fingers wrapped around the glass. "A ghostwriter writes material for someone else who is named as the author. Good money for a good writer."

"Does the ghostwriter receive any credit for the work?"

"Depends on the buyer. With Vanessa, definitely not."

Loud, boisterous laughter temporary distracted my

train of thought. I glanced down the bar to meet Bradford's concentrated stare. His slight nod signaled his success in obtaining valuable information. I parroted his signal, and returned my attention to Peaches, who was detailing the perils of an inflated ego. When she paused to slurp her drink, I shifted the conversation back to ghostwriting. "Any ideas who Vanessa could've hired to write the Dark Enchantment series?"

Peaches cocked an eyebrow. "What's your interest in all of this?" Her words were slightly slurred. "Who are you? A reporter? Because you're definitely not a writer."

"Annie Mae Tucker. Vanessa co-authored my cookbook. We met at the Halloween book launch."

Her icy gaze swept over my sapphire silk sheath clinging to my voluptuous curves. "I thought you were older. Much older." Her gaze settled on my perky boobs hiked high with the latest steel torture contraption meant to help us older gals deny gravity.

I gulped a mouthful of frozen Margarita—regretting the vanity that had prompted me to make an unwise wardrobe choice. Christ, my brains were hogshead cheese. I was impersonating my mother, not a middle-age hairdresser with relationship issues. "It was a costume party. I came as my mother." That would have to do for an explanation.

"Not a writer. A spy." Peaches slapped her tumbler down on the bar. Several heads swung our way at the commotion, including Bradford's. He cast an appraising gaze across the bar. "Vanessa sent you to spy on me. More dirt for her book."

"No, no," I tried to assure her. "I'm not Vanessa's spy."

My explanation fell on deaf ears. Peaches Noble spun on her heel and stalked off to a group of women I didn't recognize.

"Peaches give you the ole heave-hoe?" A gruff female voice sounded in my ear, and I turned to look into amused green eyes clear from the fog of alcohol.

She stuck out her hand. "Maylene Lovett. And you are?"

Her hand was warm, her smile friendly. "Annie Mae Tucker," I lied. The die had been cast, so I had to stick with it. Can't switch boats in midstream.

"Ah, yes, you're the *Mama Tucker's Ole Fashioned Southern Good Eats* author."

I dropped her hand and studied the book critic. A dead ringer for the stereotypical librarian. About my height, five-foot-seven give or take an inch or two, thin body with arms and legs to match, dark hair pulled into a bun, glasses strung on a silver chain around her thin neck, and an oversized print dress that didn't quite fit. If not for her beautiful dark-lashed, green eyes, she would've been entirely forgettable. But not with those emerald orbs. Mesmerizing.

"And you're the Terminator."

Her eyes twinkled. "Call me Maylene, Annie Mae. And not to worry, my dear. I seldom review cookbooks. However, with Vanessa's name on your work, I just might be convinced to break the rules."

I took a long pull of Margarita. "Is that a good thing?"

"They don't call me the Terminator for nothing."

I considered her words, pondering how best to proceed. Another long pull from my glass. Daddy says just put your hook in the water and see what comes along to nibble at your bait. "I would welcome your input, Maylene." I threw out my line. "Vanessa van Allen speaks highly of you, as does Peaches Noble."

"Hah, those two tremble at the mention of my name." Tiny nibble.

"Gave them bad reviews?"

"Nothing they don't deserve. Those historical bodice-rippers Peaches turns out by the dozens make me vomit. She gets bad reviews because her books are bad. And the Queen of the Vampires suffers from the same malady."

"The public loves them."

"Yes, as long as breasts are bared and sex runs rampant, the books sell. But that doesn't mean they rate five stars. No, I write 'em as I see 'em."

I cast my line deeper into the waters. "What do you think about Vanessa's newest project?"

"More trash."

"You're not worried about how she will portray you in the book?"

"No, why would I? What have you heard?" Nibble, nibble.

"Oh, nothing of great significance." I finished the last of the margarita. "Vanessa did remark offhand that she was dedicating a whole chapter to your illustrious career."

"Vanessa should tread carefully with her words, or she may find herself dangling at the end of a lawsuit, or worse. I intend to stop the publication of that book."

Wham! A largemouth bass had taken the bait. Now to reel her in. "Peaches had an interesting opinion to share about Vanessa."

Maylene didn't say anything, but her smile

returned.

"It involves a ghostwriter," I prompted her.

Still nothing from the Terminator, so I continued, "Peaches believes a ghostwriter is responsible for the Dark Enchantment Vampires Series."

Maylene cocked her head in Peaches's direction. "That would explain it. Vanessa's earlier work was more formulistic. Thus, the bad reviews. Now, the voice is much more complex. A certain genius I've never seen in her earlier work."

"Any ideas on who that mysterious writer could be?"

"That is an interesting question, Annie Mae," she replied. "Of course, there's no proof that the theory is correct, but if it's true, I'm going to expose Vanessa for the fraud she is and stop her cold in her tracks."

"What do you know about her editor, Clarissa Howard?"

Maylene's face clouded. "Only that she was an exceptional writer before she turned editor. Wrote several good romances, but not on the same level as the Dark Enchantment series. I can't see her being the ghostwriter."

"No one else comes to mind?"

She gathered her purse from the bar. "No, but thanks for the info, Annie Mae. You can be sure I will find out, though."

I had one more question for the book critic. "If you don't mind me asking, Maylene, what brings you all the way out here?"

Chuckling, she waved her hand toward the occupants in the room. "The same as them, my dear— to bury an axe in Vanessa's head."

Chapter Ten
Not a Freakin' Pig in Sight

Vanessa van Allen waltzed into the crowded lounge with a handsome, distinguished man on her arm just about the time the tequila I'd consumed kicked in. Through the fog hazing my brain, I perceived a subtle shift in the cosmic atmosphere and turned to see Snow White emerge from Bradford's expanding aura.

Damn, where's Scarlett and those heavenly handcuffs? From the furious look of the dead diva, trouble was making its way toward the author, and all help was needed to stop trouble in her ghostly tracks.

A quick psychic radar sweep detected only one departed soul in the immediate atmosphere, and she was circling Vanessa like a vulture on the scent of death. My personal trouble-making denizen of hell had completely abandoned her post. Probably still drooling over Sheriff Snellgrove and his massive sidearm. Horny ghost.

I slid up next to Bradford at the end of the bar. "We have trouble, and who's the guy?"

"I know, and I don't know."

"Well, whatdaya think? Is it Vanessa?"

His beer glass hit the bar with a thud. "Sure looks like her."

"I suppose you should go over and say hello."

"Too many people around her. She knows I'm

here."

"Yeah, she does." I watched Snow White pulse red as she circled her twin. "Your other gal pal isn't drinking the Kool-Aid."

Bradford swung his gaze around to meet mine. "The dead one?"

"Yeah, she's as confused as the rest of us. Like looking in a mirror."

"So how do we proceed?" He took a long swig of beer. To the casual observer, he appeared at ease, but I knew different. Bradford was cocked like a tricky hammer on a revolver.

I shook my head. "I haven't a clue, but we sure could use Scarlett's help in hogtieing Snow White to the juke box. I'm thinking of leaving before she explodes again."

He chuckled. "Vanessa wouldn't like that. She's gussied up real nice in that fancy dress."

I frowned at the compliment. Bradford hadn't said a word about my wardrobe but to complain about my heels. I tampered down the rising jealousy with a picture of Preston laying butt naked on rumpled bed sheets. Buns of steel. Oh, yeah. A rush of endorphins flooded my bloodstream, and my good mood returned.

"You stay here, Jolene." Bradford drained the last of his beer. "I'm going to speak to Vanessa and her new boy toy now that the crowd has thinned."

As he started off in that direction, I latched onto his arm. "Not without me, detective. I need some up close and personal eye contact with the twins."

"Okay, but keep your mouth shut. Let me do the talking. See if you can tap into the Universal Mind for guidance."

I let that comment slide. Keeping my mouth shut and my senses open might glean some information from the living and the dead, and since I'm pretty good at multitasking I should be able to observe the twins in action.

As we drew near the couple, those golden snake eyes settled on me with the same intense cosmic radiation of Halloween night, and I knew I faced the same woman now. No mistaking the pout gracing sultry red lips ripe for smacking. And boy did I want to smack her good. Taking a deep breath and holding it while I counted to ten, I relaxed and concentrated my psychic powers on the twins. Snow White immediately disengaged her perusal of Vanessa and fastened herself to my left shoulder, closest to Bradford.

"I swear to God it's me," she breathed into my ear. "But how can that be? If I'm dead and she's alive, how can I be in two places at once? I'm Vanessa van Allen, I swear it. I'm the author of the Dark Enchantment Vampire Series."

Get the hell off my shoulder.

While Snow White continued to spout her trivial drivel in one ear, I cocked the other to pick up Vanessa's response to Bradford's greeting. "...so delighted to see you, Sam *dahling*. I'm surprised to see you"—she paused to focus those snake eyes on me—"and Jolene here. I imagined you to be on your new job in Wyoming."

Shock held me immobile. My breath caught in my throat at the unexpected news of Bradford's leaving Whiskey Creek. Damn him. Damn his secrets.

Bradford patted me on the arm, but his gaze never left Vanessa. "I was worried. You seemed off

Halloween night."

Her twinkling laughter sounded false. "Sam, *dahling*, as you can see I'm fine and fully recovered from the book launch." She turned to the man at her side. "Michael has been keeping me company, haven't you, *dahling*?"

The man held out his hand to Bradford. "Michael Halsey. Pleased to make your acquaintance."

"I vaguely remember this man." The words breathed into my ear.

Bradford returned the handshake. "Sam Bradford, and this is Jolene Claiborne."

I nodded acknowledgement but kept silent, my gaze riveted on the couple. It took a few seconds for me to register Snow White's words, but when I did, I did a double take.

You know this man? From where?

Snow White vacated my shoulder for a better position to study the man. Ghostly fingers trailed through dark, wavy hair and around his ear. "Blood ties."

As in a family connection? Brother? Cousin?

Goose bumps crept up my arm as Vanessa watched me, her eyes narrowed with undisguised hate and suspicion. With my psychic radar distracted by the evil twin, all cosmic communication halted. Again, perched on my shoulder in a state of quivering excitement, Snow White kept my ear hot with a steady stream of gibberish I couldn't understand. A flash of black in my peripheral vision unbalanced my equilibrium and upset my stomach. Jolted by the violent assault, Snow White buried herself deep into my aura. Bile splashed into my mouth, and for a split second, I tasted an evil too horrible to contemplate. Tuning into the angel frequency, one of the many new tricks Scarlett had taught me, I scoured the energy waves for the source of the assault, but perceived nothing.

Get the hell off me!

"You feeling all right, Jolene?"

Bradford's voice slurred as it penetrated the cloying fog, and I blinked rapidly to restore blood flow to my brain. "There's a bug in my crawl."

Bradford caught the look. "Probably just hunger. Excuse us, Vanessa." He placed my hand on his arm. "Nice meeting you, Mr. Halsey."

Not waiting for a reply, Bradford pulled me to his side and strode quickly out of the bar and into the lodge restaurant. The hostess seated us in a booth by the window, took our orders, and left with the menus. Bradford waited until she was out of earshot. "Okay, what's up? You look terrible."

"Your dead gal pal is rootin' around in my aura." I fidgeted in my seat, but Snow White remained firmly attached to me. "See if you can convince her to scram. I feel like hurling."

Bradford looked aghast. "Good Lord, I'm living in the Twilight Zone."

"Welcome to my world." I continued to fidget as my unwelcome guest contorted in every shape imaginable. "Christ, where the hell is Scarlett and those handcuffs?"

"Learn anything interesting?"

"According to Peaches Noble, Vanessa can't write squat. She believes a ghostwriter wrote the Dark Enchantment Vampire Series. Maylene Lovett agrees."

Bradford had no knowledge of ghostwriting, so I

quickly explained, pausing only when the waitress delivered our drinks and salads.

"What else did you learn?" He picked up his fork and rolled a tomato in dressing before munching on it.

"Well, as a book critic, Maylene sees a completely different voice in Vanessa's later works. A certain level of genius Vanessa never showed in her earlier novels. I think we need to look into it."

"Anything else?"

I dragged my fork through my salad, then laid it down, still nauseated. "Michael Halsey may be related to Snow White."

Bradford's brow creased in question.

"Snow White feels a blood tie with him," I explained.

"I'll do a background check." He pulled out his cell phone from inside his Western blazer and placed a call to the Whiskey Creek police department. I sipped my tea as he communicated his request to Officer Diamond Presley.

"So when were you going to tell me about your new job in Wyoming?" I questioned in a heavy voice when he pocketed his phone.

"I guess now would be a good time." His eyes were darker than sapphires.

"When are you leaving?"

"Soon. I'd like to be settled before the heavy snow falls on the mountains."

"You love the mountains and cold winters," my voice caught.

"Yes, I want to live in a town I've never lived in before. I want to meet new people and experience different cultures. The South is beautiful, but my heart is in the West."

We shared a smile. "You would love it out there, Jolene. The wide-open spaces and towering mountains stretch into forever. The air is clean and crisp and refreshing."

"My family is here."

"And you have a new boyfriend. A doctor, right?" He picked up my limp hand and made silly little circles across my palm, sending a familiar shiver of awareness up my arm.

I cleared my throat, pretending not to be affected. "Yeah, a plastic surgeon."

"He seems like a nice guy."

"He is."

"Does he know about your ghost buddies?"

"Not yet, but soon." Round and round his fingers stroked a sensuous fire, scrabbling my thoughts.

"Are you happy with him?"

An instant squeezing hurt as the memory of our breakup flashed before my eyes. Bradford had walked away. Reuniting with him meant leaving my family and friends for the wilds of Wyoming. Bradford was fun and passionate and blew my panties off. But Preston offered security in my hometown where I'd spent my entire life and built a thriving business. He was kind and gentle and a man with a slow hand in the bedroom. Dependable and stable.

Bradford tipped my chin up. Our eyes met. "Vanessa was just a passing thing. A rebound relationship. I never got over you. I still care—a lot."

"Things change, Bradford. People change."

"You haven't answered my question. Are you happy with him?"

The arriving waitress with a loaded tray saved me from answering. The steaks smelled wonderful, and I forced myself to eat. Hopefully, the food would stay down as I now had a splitting headache. Although the other patrons in the restaurant couldn't see my swirling aura, it continued to manifest itself on me physically—much like my first boating excursion on the choppy waters off the Georgia coast.

The symptoms parroted seasickness. Christ, I had to ditch Snow White and soon if I didn't want to lose my supper here in the restaurant. Best to return to our cabin and coax the diva ghost out of hiding.

I pushed my plate away. "Get me outta here, Bradford."

One look at me had him on his feet. "Bad food?" He signaled for the check and helped me from the booth.

"No. Your friend won't settle down." I clamped my hand over my mouth and reached for my handbag.

Not waiting for the check, Bradford slammed down a couple of bills on the table and ushered me toward the door. "Keep the change," he told our waitress as she headed our way.

We made it to the door. Unfortunately, so had the rest of the group from the cocktail party. In front of the packed door, Vanessa and Michael were waiting for the hostess to seat them. Together, they blocked the only exit.

"Please allow us to pass." Bradford's voice was tight with anxiety. "Jolene isn't feeling well."

I glanced at the door. Anxious faces peered at me. Probably didn't want to be the recipient of my undigested supper. "Let 'em through," Maylene Lovett ordered. The crowd parted just enough for us to squeeze through.

Bradford gave a quick nod of thanks at the book critic and made for the opening with me pinned to his side. However, a strong pull on my arm broke Bradford's hold and spun me around to face Vanessa's angry countenance. "A word please—"

I barfed down the front of her red silk dress.

"Ahhh, you fat cow," she screeched, and stepped back, her hands thrown upward. "You did that on purpose." Livid at the slimy, smelling liquid and chunks of red meat dripping down her torso, she delivered a stinging slap across my face. Dizzy from all the action in my aura, I landed unceremoniously on the floor, jarring my teeth into my skull, and immediately sensed Snow White slip from my rocking aura. Now free of her and my supper, all traces of sickness vanished. Gazing up at the stunned, murmuring onlookers, I flashed my best smile and lifted my hand to Bradford.

He set me on my feet and smoothed the front of my dress down over my hips. "Are you all right?"

"Never better," I chirped. "Just what the doctor ordered."

Hoots of laughter sounded from the crowd. Vanessa's head snapped around to appraise the offenders before zeroing in on me. "I'll get you for this, bitch." The woman's mouth twisted in disdain, and her snake eyes grew cold and dark with a knowledge I couldn't read.

"Now wait a minute, Vanessa," Bradford piped in, "no call for insults or threats."

I clenched my fists. Those were fightin' words. I allowed my gaze to slowly traverse her slight, stinky form. At five-foot-seven and one-hundred and sixty pounds, this fat cow held the advantage, but since I was a Christian woman, I let the insult pass. "I'm sorry, Vanessa. I'll pay to have your dress cleaned."

Vanessa wanted no part of my Christian charity. "Oh, you'll pay all right, I'll see to it." Her fists clenched, and for a second I thought about slugging the bitch. Instead, I remembered Jesus's response when he was confronted with the possessed man in the tombs. Tossed that devil demon into a herd of pigs, he did. Well, I wasn't Jesus, and not a freakin' pig in sight, so I made for the door.

The crowd parted as Bradford and I exited the restaurant. In silence, we crossed the lobby and strode out into the cool autumn night. At the cabin, I brushed my teeth and changed into lounging pajamas. As soon as I came out of the bathroom, Bradford disappeared inside with pajamas which were new because he slept in the nude. In the kitchen, I made a pot of coffee and fished around for snack foods to appease my empty stomach.

The cupboards yielded a sweet treasure, and I grabbed up the bag of powdered donuts, poured a cup of coffee, and settled at the table to indulge. I had eaten two and was dunking another donut into my coffee when Bradford emerged from the bathroom. He quirked an eyebrow at me while he stashed his clothing into his suitcase, and I did the same at his blue plaid peejays.

He joined me at the small kitchenette table and plucked a sugary donut from the package to pop it into his mouth. I poured him a cup of coffee, added cream and sugar, and pushed it across the table.

"Not exactly a successful night."

He took several sips of coffee to wash down the donut. "Not true. We know more now than yesterday."

"We're no closer to the true Vanessa van Allen." I popped another donut into my mouth. "And speaking of your gal pals, the dead one hasn't come home. Your aura's clear."

"Yeah, I know. I hope it stays that way."

"Did you learn anything new at the cocktail party?"

"Not a peep from Cash Hitchcock. He acted as if he were still Vanessa's agent."

"Then Vanessa didn't follow through with her threat to fire him." I shook my head. "He's lying. I know it. Something stinks in the woodpile."

"Yeah, Snow White's body." Bradford downed the last of his coffee. "I have to tell you, Jolene, this is the craziest situation I've ever been involved in. I don't know how you stand it all the time. The ghosts, I mean. I'm still not certain I'm not having a nervous breakdown."

I laughed. "I've been having one since Scarlett bit the dust. Don't worry. This is probably a one-time thing for you." I drained the last bit of coffee and set our cups in the sink. When I returned from brushing my teeth, Bradford was still at the table.

"How are we going to handle the sleeping arrangements?" His eyes burned into mine.

My gaze traveled to the small bed. "It's not like we haven't slept together."

Bradford's brow rose. "And how does your boyfriend feel about you sharing my bed?"

"I'm not sharing your bed, dumbass," I returned dryly. "And we're only sleeping, not having sex."

"He doesn't know you're here with me, does he?"

The question caught me off guard. Truthfully, it never occurred to me to ask Preston's permission. We were only dating. Yes, we'd had sex, glorious sex I might add, but what does sex have to do with anything? A man's ball and chain, I ain't. Never again.

Bradford read my silence and gave me a gentle smile. "Don't worry, Jolene. Come to bed. You're safe from my advances, trust me."

He, I trusted. Myself, not so much. Every solid inch of muscled skin hiding beneath those silly blue, plaid peejays were forever burned into my memory. Every delicious, hard inch.

Chapter Eleven
Ghostly Madness

I awoke to sunlight streaming through frilly yellow curtains, and the familiar sensation of Bradford's pecker poking me in the back. A delightful shiver of wanting shot through my bloodstream almost setting me on fire. I clamped my jaw shut to still the moan rising in my throat as past memories of our lovemaking flooded my brain cells. Mistake. Liquid warmth flooded my twinkie pie, and before I could stop myself, I turned around to face him, and maneuvered my body to fit his.

My heart thundered when his eyelids fluttered, then slowly opened to peer into mine. A slow smile spread across his face as his pecker spoke to his brain. "Good morning, sunshine," he whispered, then leaned in closer, his nose touching mine. Softly his breath fanned my face. Coffee and donuts. Briefly I wondered if my breath held the same hint of our late-night snack or had morning breath arrived with the sunrise.

He pressed a tender kiss on my nose before moving his mouth passionately over mine. Pleasure radiated outward, and my limbs became rubber when his hand traveled beneath my T-shirt nightie. The gentle tug on my panties brought the first awareness that we were approaching the point of no return, but I had no desire to stop the enviable outcome to his search for my treasure chest.

Stop!

Don't!

Think of Preston!

Don't!

A loud pounding on the door halted the silent battle warring in my head. Startled, I reached for my panties and bolted out of bed, rumpled and frustrated, and ran for the bathroom. Through the door, frantic mumbling resonated from the front of the cabin. Mrs. Goldenrod. Something must've happened. Hastily, I slipped on my panties and bathrobe and rushed out into the main room where a jean-clad, bare-chested Bradford listened to a harried Mrs. Goldenrod. "I'm not imagining anything," she declared. "I know what I saw, Mr. Tucker."

"What's going on?"

Two sets of eyes fixed on me. Bradford spoke first. "Vanessa is missing."

"She's been kidnapped," Mrs. Goldenrod gushed, wringing her hands. "A disturbance was called in, and when I went to check on her, I found the cabin trashed and splattered blood on the floor. Miss van Allen and her briefcase are missing!"

Butterflies assaulted my stomach. "Good lord, Bradford, what the hell is going on?"

Mrs. Goldenrod's eyes glinted suspiciously. "Bradford? You registered as Annie Mae and Harland Tucker. Perhaps you should tell me what's going on?" Suddenly her gaze shifted to the door and she took a step backward. "Wait a minute. Y'all broke into her cabin." Another step. She grabbed the door handle.

"Stop," Bradford ordered in his authoritative manner. "I'm Detective Samuel Bradford from Whiskey Creek, and I'm here in an unofficial capacity."

He fished his badge out of his back pocket.

Her hand dropped to her side. "I believe you'd better start explaining. Sheriff Snellgrove is on his way, and I'm sure he'll be interested in your story." Here she turned to me. "And I suppose you're a police officer, too?"

"This is Jolene Claiborne, and she's here at my request." Bradford cut me off before I could answer. "I speak for us both."

Bradford's intense gaze quelled my impulse to deny that assumption. If he wanted to explain, then let him. Words failed me at the thought of another murder.

"I believe now would be a good time for you to get dressed, Jolene. I'll accompany Mrs. Goldenrod to Vanessa's cabin to await the sheriff." Bradford plucked his shirt off the back of the chair. "You can meet us down there."

I dressed in record time, pulled a brush through my tangled curls and anchored them behind my neck in a makeshift bun, applied light foundation to cover my bruised jaw, lipstick to my swollen lips, thanks to that missing she-devil, mascara, and blush for a dash of color. Not great, but it would have to do. A natural beauty I'm not.

When I arrived outside of Vanessa's cabin, I noted the opened door. Bradford and Mrs. Goldenrod were nowhere in sight, so I assumed they must be inside. I eased through the door and surveyed the trashed cabin—clothes scattered everywhere, overturned furniture, and the coppery scent of blood—a smell you never forget.

I spied Bradford and Mrs. Goldenrod hunched over a small pattern of blood drops just outside the bathroom door. They both glanced up at my entrance.

"Be careful not to touch anything, Jolene," Bradford cautioned. "This is a crime scene."

Mrs. Goldenrod strode to the door. "I'll wait for the sheriff on the porch and keep out any wondering guests."

I stared at the blood, frowning. "Vanessa's?"

Bradford snapped to his feet. "Forensics will determine that." From his front shirt pocket, he withdrew a small notepad and pencil and began to sketch a basic drawing of the cabin.

"I assume you're collecting evidence?" I questioned as he continued to jot down items on his notepad.

"No. The evidence technician will take care of that, assuming the sheriff's department has one. I left my phone in the cabin, and since we don't have a camera to document the scene, this is the next best thing for my personal investigation." He paused to fix his stare on me. "When the sheriff arrives, we'll be conducted from the crime scene and questioned. This is out of my jurisdiction. You need to join Mrs. Goldenrod outside. I don't want you implicated in any way."

A sudden movement from my peripheral vision drew my attention away from Bradford. The familiar Snow White costume flashed past me in a frantic dance across the room, bouncing from wall to wall. I drew in a deep, fortifying breath. "Your shadow friend has returned acting rather erratic. She appears to be lost. Perhaps you should call her and see if she responds to your voice." I backed toward the door not willing to have another possession episode.

Bradford groaned. "I don't believe I can stand

much more of this ghostly madness. And where in the hell is Scarlett?"

"I believe she's with Sheriff Snellgrove. She has a thing for his sawed-off shotgun. Go on, call Snow White, she's making me dizzy."

He gave me a wry grimace. "When we get back to the cabin, I want you to make an appointment with Madame Mia. I'm desperate."

"Sure thing, boss, but for now, give it a try."

Bradford pocketed his notepad. With a comical expression covering his face, he whispered Vanesa's name several times with no response.

"Louder," I advised.

"What about Mrs. Goldenrod?"

"Chance it."

Bradford did as I had instructed, and Snow White materialized at his side.

Her ghostly energy flashed rainbow. "I saw myself again."

Bradford fished out his notepad. "Where and when?"

"In the graveyard."

My stomach did a flip. "What graveyard?"

"The one in the forest."

Bradford and I exchanged puzzled glances. Bradford scribbled on his notepad. "What were you doing there? I mean Vanessa."

"Arguing with that man."

"What man?" we asked in union.

Snow White froze. "Gotta go. He's coming," she screeched and dove head first into Bradford's aura.

Bradford staggered a step back at the sudden impact and dropped the notepad and pencil to the floor.

As I bent down to retrieve the items, a voice boomed behind me.

"Well, slap my mammy and call her Sammy. Somehow, I knew y'all would return to the scene of the crime. Put your hands up real slow, now."

With a slight of hand, I pocketed the notepad and pencil in my bra. Bradford winked an acknowledgement, and as I stood upright, we both raised our hands in the air and turned to face Sheriff Snellgrove.

****

I don't blush easily, but the sight of Scarlett dry humping the sheriff's sawed-off shot gun sent blood rushing to my cheeks. "Holy moly." Bradford's whispered words brought a smile, and I glanced over at his stunned expression. Got a good looksee at my horny ghost gal pal, did he? Good. Now he'll understand my daily dose of Zanny to keep me sane and functioning in this wacked out invisible world.

I cleared my throat. "I think now would be a good time to give it a rest."

My words had the necessary effect. Sheriff Snellgrove tilted his head and furrowed his brow, but Scarlett ceased her outrageous behavior. However, when her glazed blue-green eyes met mine, I could see she had achieved satisfaction.

With a slow languor, Scarlett detached herself from the robust sheriff and drifted over to the bed.

She yawned. "Time for my beauty sleep."

I huffed. "Time for you to get to work." Bradford shifted beside me, but I ignored him.

"Exactly," Snellgrove said. "Y'all got some explaining to do, Detective Bradford, Miz Claiborne.

But first, put your weapon on the floor, detective."

Bradford did as ordered. I wasn't packing, so I remained focused on Scarlett who continued to gaze at me with a silly, satisfied smile.

"Miz Claiborne, you wait outside with Miz Goldenrod," Snellgrove ordered. "I'd like to have a private word with Detective Bradford."

I gave Scarlett the evil eye and made for the door. Once outside I skirted the nervous head registrant and strode to a towering magnolia offering privacy from nosey ears. Scarlett and I needed a chat session. I had hoped that Snow White might join us, but she remained firmly attached to Bradford's aura. At Scarlett's arrival, I turned my back on Mrs. Goldenrod.

"I won't waste any time on your not-so-nice activities, Scarlett. We've a new crisis to deal with."

"I'm aware of that."

The cool morning breeze brushed against my fevered cheek. "Anything to report? Or were you able to peel yourself away from temptation?"

"Jealous?"

"Redheads aren't my type."

Her ghostly sigh rattled the waxy leaves. "More for me, I say."

"Get on with it, Scarlett. What do you know?"

"Well, Purgatory is in an uproar over that screwed-up arrival list. Heads were rolling when I took out of there—fast."

"Nothing new?"

"Well, yeah, but you won't be happy. Vanessa's name is back on the list."

The sights and sounds of early morning wrapped around me allowing Scarlett's announcement, and the implications, to wash over me. Could the splattered blood be Vanessa's? A shy morning sun spread its yellow rays across the still waters of the pond. The treetops stirred with the gentle fingers of a warming breeze, and from the branches sprang the melodious chirping of songbirds. Had to be. It was her cabin.

"What about C.H.?" I wondered aloud.

"Crossed out."

"So Snow White is definitely Vanessa van Allen?"

"According to the list."

"The list was wrong before, Scarlett."

"Snow White insists she's Vanessa. I believe her."

I stared at the mirror-surfaced pond. "We need to speak with her. She observed Vanessa arguing with a man. Do you know of a cemetery in the vicinity?"

"There's a small one in back of Mount Zion Missionary Baptist Church. Been abandoned for years."

"Can you show me?"

"Now? The sheriff won't be happy if you disappear. And ole eagle eye has her sights on you."

From a distance, a train whistled. I lifted my gaze from the pond to the opened cabin door. Bradford wouldn't be pleased, but what other choice did I have? "I might not get another chance if I wait. You'll have to distract her."

"Not. She's coming this way." Scarlett faded into the branches of the magnolia.

I swung around at the sound of approaching footsteps. Mrs. Goldenrod's brown eyes glittered with suspicion. "The sheriff sent me to fetch you, Miz Claiborne."

Frustrated at my derailed plans, I stole a fleeing glance back at Scarlett tucked within the sheltering branches of the magnolia tree. "Wait for me here until I return."

"Excuse me?" Mrs. Goldenrod shot me an anxious glance. "I'll do no such thing."

I shrugged, allowing Mrs. Goldenrod to believe I'd been speaking to her. Scarlett winked an acknowledgement, and I strode back to the cabin, uncertain how to answer the sheriff's questions as Bradford and I hadn't had time to synchronize our stories.

Snellgrove met me at the door and steered me to the small kitchenette table. I took the indicated seat, all the while swiveling my head to locate Bradford.

"He's keeping my deputy company." Snellgrove eased into the chair opposite me, his smile never making it to his eyes.

Every sense on high alert, I kept my mouth shut, and my gaze locked on his. I'd been through this a number of times and had learned to reveal as little as possible about anything. Give just enough to appear cooperative and then fake the rest.

"Why the pretense?"

"Excuse me?"

"Come on, Miz Claiborne, cut the crap. Answer the question."

"Clarify the question, Sheriff, and I will." Breathe. Breathe. Stay cool.

"I want to know why you and Detective Bradford checked in as Annie Mae and Harland Tucker. Why the pretense?"

Truth this time. "We were concerned for Miss van Allen's safety. My parents decided to skip the retreat. Their absence afforded us with an opportunity to keep an eye on Vanessa."

Snellgrove curled his lip. "Is that what you were doing in here earlier? Keeping an eye out for Miss van Allen?"

"Yes, Detective Bradford was concerned for her safety. There were several veiled threats spoken against her on Halloween night. Not too many people are in favor of the book she's writing. It has the potential to ruin lives."

Thankfully, a lone deputy entered the cabin with a large, black box I recognized from previous crime scenes. The crime scene technician. Sheriff Snellgrove stood up and strode over to the man giving me time to gather my forces. If only I knew what Bradford had told him? What to do? What to do? I dropped my head into my hands and prayed like hell for reinforcements to rescue me from any further questioning.

"Sweep the area, Jack." I heard the sheriff directing his man. "Look for the obvious."

And not so obvious, dummy. Every investigator knows this.

"And not so obvious," the sheriff added.

Okay, so he's not a dummy. I'd better stop assuming he's clueless and pay attention to this good-ole-boy. Heavy footsteps alerted me that he was headed my way. I lifted my head just as he stopped beside the table.

"You're free to go, Miz Claiborne, but keep yourself available for further questioning."

I stood and faced him. "I'm returning to Whiskey Creek today, but will happily return at your request."

He dug his notepad out of his front pocket and repeated my phone number. "Correct?"

"You may reach me at that number or at Dixieland Salon."

Sheriff Snellgrove snapped shut his notepad and shoved it back into his pocket. "See that you don't leave the area, Miz Claiborne. You and Detective Bradford won't be in the clear until Miss van Allen is found safe and sound. Remember that." He directed his gaze to the splattered blood drops. "I'd be praying if I were you. This doesn't look good."

Chapter Twelve
My Ass Is on the Line

I found Bradford pacing the floor when I returned to the cabin. He flew to my side as I strode through the door.

"How'd it go?" His voice reflected his mood. Tight. Concerned. Worried.

I willed my muscles to relax. "I told the truth."

"What! For God's sake, Jolene. The truth?"

"Yes, the truth minus our other worldly visitors. That we're concerned for Vanessa's safety." I slanted a reproving look. "What about your story?"

His aura flickered as he sank down into an overstuffed chair. "Pretty much the same. Vanessa's well-being. He put in a call to the chief."

"How'd that go?"

"Could've been worse. The chief is still sore at my leaving, but he vouched for me and assured Sheriff Snellgrove that I'd be around until this incident was cleared up. I have to be in his office in an hour."

At the mention of his leaving, I shifted my gaze from his and dodged around him. The last thing I needed was him seeing how much I wanted him to stay. Determined to hold my own, I dug around in my purse until I found my phone. Two voicemails. One from Deena. Of course. And the other from Mama.

"I'll get my things together as soon as I return

these calls," I told him without turning around.

"Take your time. I'll finish packing and start loading the truck."

Deena's frantic voice left no doubt that another crisis had struck in her never-ending nuptial plans. I punched in her number and got her voicemail. Leaving a message promising to meet her at the bridal shop by ten, I then listened to Mama's message. Apparently, my parents had decided to check out timeshares and would be home in a couple of days. Not having a lot of time to talk, I sent her a text message relaying my support. With that out of the way, I repacked my suitcase and cosmetic case. Bradford wasn't back by the time I'd finished, so I hauled myself and my luggage to the truck where he was waiting for me. I threw my suitcase and cosmetic case in the backseat with his.

"I left our contact information with Mrs. Goldenrod," he said, as I slipped in the front seat beside him. "She's decided to close down the retreat for a couple of weeks until this blows over. The other guests have to make other accommodations. I heard several making plans to return to Whiskey Creek since Snellgrove ordered them to stay in the area."

"Before we leave, I need to fill you in on a couple of new facts." I scanned his aura for any sign of Snow White. Yep. Still sticking to him like glue. "Scarlett finally gave me a condensed update on Vanessa."

Bradford perked up. "Yeah? What? Good news I hope."

"This riddle just keeps getting weirder every day. C.H. has been crossed off the list and Vanessa's name is back on it." I buckled my seat belt. "I don't know what to believe."

"Nothing's changed." Bradford fired up the engine. "We've got to find Snow White's body and locate the missing Vanessa if she's still alive."

"The blood could belong to someone else."

"True. I want to check out the cemetery Snow White mentioned at the crime scene."

"Mount Zion Missionary Baptist Church. It's been abandoned for years but it's the only one in the vicinity according to Scarlett."

Bradford backed the truck onto the dirt road leading out of the forest and shifted into drive. "Any chance she's available to show us?"

I shook my head. "She's gone to only God knows where, but it's somewhere close by. Should we try to find it ourselves?"

Bradford glanced into his rearview mirror. "Now's not a good time."

I glanced at the passenger side mirror. No tail. "Now's the best time." The soft strands of a classical guitar from the CD player filled the cab as we crept along the dusty road leading to the main highway to Whiskey Creek.

Finally, Bradford spoke. "My ass is on the line, Jolene. I've got to return to the station and give the chief a rundown on my activities. You, too, have obligations waiting. We'll reconnect later today and compare notes and decide how to proceed. Hopefully, by that time, you can make contact with Scarlett, and Snow White will come out of hiding with more information to share. Agreed?"

I agreed to his plan and fell silent for the remainder of the trip into town. Bradford dropped me off at my house on Pineknoll, promising to call later. Glad to be home, I unpacked before fetching my cat, Tango, from the vet. After settling in back home, I showered and changed and drove over to the salon to check on business before my scheduled meeting with Deena. Perhaps she'd hadn't left for the bridal salon yet and we could ride together.

I entered Dixieland Salon amid a babble of women's voices and marched up to the reception desk where Holly had just hung up the phone. The familiar smell of chemicals washed around me like a warm summer breeze. Ah, home sweet home.

"Is Deena in her office, Holly?" I gazed around the packed reception area. By the looks of things, business was hopping. Hopefully, Billie Jo would be over the stomach flu in a couple of days.

Holly swept back her overly long bangs. "She left about five minutes ago for her appointment. She wanted me to hurry you along if you stopped in. Oh, and your book is full for tomorrow. You will be back, right?"

"Yes, indeed. What time is my first appointment?"

"Althea Davis at seven sharp. A perm."

After a quick chat with each of my employees, I ducked out of Dixieland and headed down Love Avenue for Gail's Formal Wear. I parked next to Deena's green Buick and entered the exclusive boutique to find my sister flittering about like a wounded butterfly. "No, no, not that style, Angie. No lace." I heard her anxious voice say as the sales clerk spread out a beautiful wedding gown for her approval.

"Stop harassing the help, Sister Dearest," I said as I came up behind her. Deena swirled around to grasp me in a bear hug.

"Oh, Jolene, thank God, you're here." Her eyes

watered as they bore into mine. "I'm overwhelmed by all the details. Please tell me you're not leaving again!"

I did my best to soothe my sister without making promises I couldn't keep and steered her attention away by oohing and ahhing over the variety of dresses the sales clerk had selected. With tearful emotions under control, I watched Deena model each dress, giving her my honest opinion of each. Finally, after an hour, and gentle coaxing, Deena choose a simple A-line gown of ivory satin with no embellishments. That would come in the form of pressurized carbon. Ryder had gifted Deena with a spectacular diamond necklace with matching earrings. Lucky girl.

We left the boutique for the café next door. Since the weather permitted outdoor eating, we chose a table on the patio. After ordering, I launched the conversation away from wedding plans. "I guess our parents have decided to buy a timeshare in Florida."

Deena's forehead wrinkled. "I spoke at length with Mama last night. She told me that Daddy is smitten with the golf courses. He's talking about selling the farm and buying a condo."

I laughed at her outrageous expression. "Are you against them moving away? We've wanted them to sell the farm for a while now."

"Well, it's not that I'm against them moving, but Ryder sprung some surprising news on me yesterday that has me worried."

Deena paused as the waitress arrived with our iced teas. Several seconds passed after she moved out of earshot before she spoke. "He wants to relocate to Atlanta." Her voice cracked on the last word.

"Well, what do you want?" I tried to sound casual

with my insides quaking at the news. First, Bradford was leaving, and my parents were thinking of leaving Whiskey Creek, and now, Deena. Not a cheerful prospect, and I was not okay with this.

"I hate the thought of leaving here, but his mother has recently been diagnosed with lung cancer, and his father is having a hard time coping with the situation." She gave a tiny, melancholy sigh. "He's an only child and feels compelled to be there."

"They could relocate here," I suggested.

"Medical care is better there."

That much was true. Whiskey Creek had a great hospital and qualified doctors, but not compared to metropolitan Atlanta. The best state-of-the-art medical facilities congregated around the capital. His mother stood a better chance of beating the disease there, and it would be easier for Deena and Ryder to relocate than his parents. There was only one thing to do to help my sister.

I took a long sip of tea. "You should go. Atlanta is a great city with loads of opportunities. And you'd be closer to Summer. You've done nothing but complain since she and Mike relocated to Buckhead after their wedding last month."

"Being closer to my daughter is definitely a plus, but what about the salon? How will you manage without me?"

"It'll be hard, but Billie Jo and I can manage. You do what's best for you and Ryder."

"Speaking of Billie Jo, I'm worried about her. This stomach flu is lingering too long."

"I'm sure everything is fine, Deena. Stop fretting. Call and check on her while I run to the restroom?"

"Good idea." Deena withdrew her phone from her purse.

Five minutes later when I returned to the table, our food had arrived and Deena was finishing her call. By the looks of her expression, I figured that our younger sister hadn't shaken off the bug. Deena confirmed my suspicions.

"Billie Jo isn't any better. She has a doctor's appointment this afternoon. She promised to call as soon as she has any news."

We ate in silence. Like me, Deena was preoccupied with her own thoughts. The waitress cleared our dishes and brought coffee and chocolate cake for dessert. I devoured the luscious treat while Deena picked at hers.

"So, what's going on with you, Jolene?" She quirked a curious brow. "You've been acting particular, even for you, the last couple of days. You're never available when I need you, and you've rescheduled most of your appointments. I know you and Preston are hot and heavy, but I thought he went to LA for a conference."

I opted for the truth as Deena could smell a lie a hundred miles away. A fluke in her personality to her advantage. That's how she caught her former husband cheating with Scarlett. But that's a long story and told elsewhere.

At the end of my tale, Deena sat stone-faced. "I don't believe it. I swear to God, Jolene, I don't believe it."

"Believe it, sis. It's all true."

"What are you going to do?"

"It's Bradford's game. I'm only along for the ride."

"Jolene, why can't you just leave the dead alone?"

114

I threw up my hands in exasperation. "I don't go looking for them, Deena. They find *me*!"

Deena drained the last of her coffee. Her chocolate cake remained untouched. "So how soon is Sam leaving Whiskey Creek?"

"When this mess is cleaned up."

"How do you feel about it?"

"Like a knife plunged straight into my heart," I answered honestly.

"Do you love him?"

"He haunts me just as much as the dead."

"Do you love him, Jolene?"

I let out a long breath. "I don't know what love is."

Deena huffed. "Well, you'd better figure it out and soon, sis, or you'll regret it for the rest of your life. Love doesn't come easily."

I answered with an indulgent smile. "It did for you."

Deena's bunched shoulders relaxed. "And I want you to have the same, Jolene. Don't let Sam leave alone. Take a risk."

"Whiskey Creek is my home," I argued. "My family and business are here."

"And mine. Yet, you advised me to leave home and family."

I could only shake my head futility. After a few seconds of shared silence, we allowed the subject to drop and summoned the waitress for the check. After promising to call with news about Billie Jo, we went our separate ways. Me out to the farm, and Deena to an appointment with the florist.

Chapter Thirteen
A Dead Pig in the Sunshine

Later that evening the phone rang. Thinking it might be Deena with news of Billie Jo's doctor's visit, I grabbed up the receiver to hear Bradford's husky voice. "I'm on my way over. We need to talk.

I hastily agreed, leaving a barrage of questions unspoken. That would come later, after Bradford unloaded his mind. To keep my hands busy, I put on a pot of coffee, then set the table with cups and saucers, cream and sugar, and a platter of pastries I'd picked up at the bakery. I tend to munch when I'm nervous, bored, or anxious. Bradford's troubled tone had me climbing aboard the nervous train with an anxious load.

The sound of his truck pulling into the drive had me at the back-kitchen door. I switched on the outside porch light and swung open the door at his approach, Tango at my feet.

"I made coffee," I said as a greeting. Tango yowled when he spotted my guest.

Bradford slipped past me without acknowledgement to pull his cowboy hat from his head and settled down onto a kitchen chair. Silently, he placed his hat upside down on the table, and waited for me to join him. He bent down to pet Tango who had continued to purr for attention. I poured two cups of steaming coffee before sitting down, remaining quiet, allowing him the time to gather his obviously swirling thoughts.

"You won't believe the day I've had." He gave me a sour look when he straightened in his chair. "A day from hell."

With my full attention focused on him, I nibbled at a pastry. I knew this man, intimately, and he needed a listening ear, not a hyperactive chatterbox.

"First thing, the chief read me the riot act. Sheriff Snellgrove made me out to be some kind of pervert. Told the chief that the evidence suggested I was stalking Vanessa." He sipped his coffee. "Wouldn't even listen to my explanation." Heavy sarcasm laced his words. "Threatened to call Mayor Boswell out in Wyoming and effectively kill my career.

"Then he ordered me to stay out of Snellgrove's investigation." He huffed. "Like that's possible with Snow White playing havoc with my life. And now the other woman is missing. Possibly dead. Damn, I wish I'd never met Vanessa van Allen. A complicated piece of humanity. She's turned my life upside down." His aura flashed an ugly green, then faded into nothingness.

I set my cup down ready to ask my first question. "What's our next move?"

He did the same with his cup. "Question Snow White. I need to know about the man she observed arguing with Vanessa. Any chance of getting Scarlett to make an appearance?"

"Depends on her mood." I skidded my chair back and climbed to my feet. "But first I'd like to fish around in your aura. See if I can locate Snow White. That is if you don't mind. Maybe we can do this without Scarlett."

Bradford heaved a heavy sigh. "Okay, but keep it simple. No repeats of intergalactic explosions. I don't believe I could stand it."

I laughed out loud as the picture of him standing in Deena's office covered in white, sticky goo resurfaced. "Keep your fingers crossed."

Bradford sat straighter in his chair as I approached him. With delicate fingers I probed his aura, all the time gauging the ever-changing colors for any sign of danger. After several minutes of examination. I pulled my fingers free and stepped back.

"Tell her to come out of hiding, Bradford," I suggested. "Tell her she's safe."

"Safe? Safe from what? She's dead."

"Just do it."

He did, and she popped out like a toaster pastry surprising us both. Bradford jumped up from his chair, knocking it over in the process, and tripping me as I tried to step away. Sitting on my kitchen floor with my cat yowling with excitement, Bradford gawking down at me, and Snow White perched over his shoulder, had me laughing. For the first time since this craziness had started, all my concerns and expectations flew out the window. The Universe with all of its wonderful surprises continued to amaze and inspire me.

"I'm glad you think this is funny." Bradford reached down for my hand.

"Well, it is, if you think about it," I replied as he hauled me to my feet. Once on solid ground I scanned the kitchen for Snow White and found her seated at the kitchen table as if it were the most natural thing for a ghost in her position to do. She offered us a grim smile.

"I suppose you would like an explanation," she

said. "I mean about the man."

Bradford and I joined her at the table. "That would help to clear up this mess," I told her in a gentle, caring voice.

Her energy field blinked several times. "I see a light. I don't want to go."

"The man?" Bradford's tone echoed impatience. "What about Vanessa and the man in the cemetery?"

She began to fade. "Red hair. Big gun."

"Sheriff Snellgrove?" We yelled in union as she became almost transparent.

She nodded back at us without speaking, then disappeared back into Bradford's aura.

"I don't believe it." Bradford pushed his hand through his wavy hair. "She must be mistaken. What connection could Vanessa possibly have with the sheriff?"

"Good question," I responded, my attention focused on the barely perceptible spot in Bradford's aura. "I'm not sure, but I believe Snow White will be moving on shortly."

A streak of orange fur burst out from beneath the table with an angry yowl and streaked for the den. Goose bumps peppered my body as Tango's unexpected departure startled me.

"You perceive correctly."

Scarlett's otherworldly voice sounded from the closed pantry. A second later, she walked through the door into the kitchen swinging a pair of shiny gold handcuffs in one hand. The spot in Bradford's aura flashed a muted red before dying down again to a mere dark, blue spot.

"I'm here to fetch her." Scarlett floated over to

Bradford's side, handcuffs clanging. "Her time on Earth is over. Her case is solved, and the Powers That Be are cracking down on wayward DEARS."

"Solved? How so?" Bradford's bloodshot eyes spoke of extreme tiredness.

Scarlett retrieved her prisoner from his aura. "This is Vanessa van Allen." She snapped the golden handcuffs on a silent Snow White. "She and I will be on our way. Until the next time, Jolene."

"Wait!" I exclaimed before the dueling divas could vanish back into the netherworld.

Scarlett shot me daggers. "What is it, Claiborne? I have orders to complete."

"The body hasn't been found—"

"Nor the missing woman," Bradford added. "How can you say she's Vanessa van Allen without proof?"

"I don't need proof," Scarlett said. "Only orders to drop this spirit off in Purgatory. I can't afford to buck the authorities on this one." She pointed a manicured finger at Bradford. "Your ass isn't the only one on the line, Buckaroo. Any more screw-ups and I'm transferred south, and barbeques aren't my thing."

My chair scrapped across the hardwood floor as I pushed to my feet. "Can you make a detour before heading home?" I had a destination in mind that might pan out a lead. Speculation, of course, but a lead.

"Mount Zion Missionary Baptist Church," Bradford declared. "Well, Scarlett, ready to rattle some chains?"

Scarlett narrowed her eyes. "Is that a challenge or another one of Jolene's suspicious plottings?"

Bradford nodded. "This might be a good time to hone your investigating skills. What I've seen doesn't impress me."

Guessing what might ensue after Bradford's provocative statement, I traced Tango's path across the kitchen to the den entryway, wanting no part of the coming fireworks. Scarlett's trigger-happy temperament had followed her into the afterlife.

"We'll see about that, cowboy." Her mouth curved into a triumphant grin. "Saddle up that pony in the driveway and follow me."

****

Mount Zion Missionary Baptist Church had seen better days. White paint peeled from its old wooden clapboard siding, the failing roof showed signs of imminent collapse, and the front steps sagged in the middle—not to mention the encroaching forest with evil designs to smother the grand old lady with its creeping vines and evergreen trees.

I shivered as I stood in the small clearing, my ears tuned in to the subtle sounds of night-prowling beasts of the pine forest. In the muted light of a full moon, I pulled the Pink Panther, my .38 special, from its holster and tucked it in the front of my jeans for a quick draw if needed and stepped closer to Bradford.

"There's nothing to be afraid of out here, Jolene," Bradford said as I inched closer. "Maybe coyotes or wolves."

"Great." I strained to pierce the murky darkness surrounding me. "With my luck, we'll run across Bigfoot."

"The cemetery must be around back." Bradford's flashlight beam made a wide arc, its silvery light revealing a small pathway around the church.

"You're correct," Scarlett piped up. "Just follow

me, and be careful of snakes."

Bradford took the lead, and I followed close behind, my gaze glued to the ground. If it moved, I screamed. Which irritated Bradford. Dumbass. What'd he think he'd get with a city gal out in the woods after dark? A pioneer woman, I'm not. Finally, after the tenth time of ordering me to quiet down, I suggested, in a strong voice, he shut up or give me a piggyback ride.

He shut up.

The bone yard was in worse shape than the church. Here, the forest was close to completing its takeover mission. Most headstones were toppled over, and the ones standing upright were covered in knee-high grass and vines. Massive ancient oaks towered above, their heavy branches threatening to scoop up an errant intruder.

I plowed to a stop. "I think I'll wait for you here." We were standing on the pathway just behind the church where the light of the full moon shone brightest. "You go on ahead and see what you can find. I'll search the immediate area."

We agreed upon a signal, and Bradford disappeared among the headstones, leaving me alone with my psychic radar stuck on high. For several minutes I stood frozen, my ears like parabolic mics, picking up every hoot owl, snapping twig, and rustling undergrowth. The air about me was turbulent with noise. To calm myself, I cupped the Panther in one hand, the flashlight in the other, and attentively stepped forward. When nothing earth shattering happened, my confidence grew, and I ventured into the shadows until I'd explored the back of the church, finding nothing.

Ten minutes later I was ready to call it a dead end

and head for home when an ear-splitting scream rent the night air. I dropped my gun and flashlight and scampered for the moonlit clearing, avoiding the eerie graveyard. The dead come to me, not the other way around. Not one toe was I placing in the dead's domain. Cross my heart and hope to die.

Bradford found me cowering in the moonlight.

I latched onto him like a hungry gatorbug. "What the hell was that?" I continued to scan the landscape for any moving shadows.

"We found her, Jolene." His voice shook. "God, it's not pretty. The wildlife also found her."

"She looks like a dead pig in the sunshine with that half-baked smile."

"Christ, Scarlett, what a horrible thing to say," I accused. "And who is she? Snow White or Vanessa?"

Scarlett jerked the golden handcuffs. "My prisoner here." Snow White reacted by flashing an unearthly green at the words.

"Who screamed?" I could only guess. Bradford retrieved my gun and flashlight and handed them over to me.

"Her." Scarlett jerked the handcuffs. "Well, now that you have the answers you need, I'll be shoving off with my prize."

"Not yet, Scarlett." Bradford swung his flashlight beam deep into the graveyard. "I need you to accompany us to the crime scene."

Not. "If you're including me in that us, then no way." Cross my heart and hope to die.

Bradford dropped a hand on my shoulder. "There's something you need to see, Jolene."

"Take a picture with your cell phone."

"It's the murder weapon, Jolene." His voice hardened. "I've seen it many times before. Hard to miss a pink revolver with pearl grips."

I felt like a lightning bolt hit me. The Source of that inner Knowingness kicked in, and a dreadful uneasiness settled in the pit of my stomach. I knew. Just as sure as the sun would rise in the morning, I knew without seeing the murder weapon that Mini Pearl had taken a life. And my fingerprints were all over it.

Chapter Fourteen
It's Mini Pearl

Staring down at the mangled, half-eaten body lying face up behind an old headstone gave me the sense of an outer body experience. The Snow White costume had been ripped and torn away by the scavenging forest creatures. The cracked headstone with splatters of blood, the bloated corpse with part of the mouth ripped away, and the white teeth exposed in a taunting smile with Mini Pearl clasped in the victim's hand. The wind whistled through the tall grass and trees spreading the stench of death. God, how I hated that smell.

Twice I swept the flashlight beam across the grisly scene, imprinting the ugliness into my memory to be recounted I'm sure hundreds of times in the days ahead. Bradford's hand was strong, firm, protective, but still I shivered.

"Can you identify the gun?"

"It's mine." My breathless voice faltered as my gaze roamed over the pink gun with pearl grips. "Not another like it in the States. Custom made. I had Mini Pearl engraved on the barrel. I thought I'd never see it again."

My mind flashed back to the day I'd discovered my .32 caliber snub-nosed revolver stolen from my car. I'd arrived out at Pineridge Plantation to conduct tours of the antebellum mansion for the annual fall Whiskey

Creek Pecan Festival. Increased activity from the re-enactors arriving could be heard, so I followed the sounds around past the back terrace and into the rose garden. During my absence, my wallet had been emptied and Mini Pearl taken.

And used in the commission of a crime. Just as I'd feared.

"I hate to break up a tearful scene, but I have to get back to work." Scarlett jangled the handcuffs for emphasis. "As soon as I deliver Miss van Allen, I'll be headed to England to bag a knight."

Bradford addressed his question to a tearful Snow White. "Can you tell me who did this to you?"

"I did this to myself," she whispered.

"Suicide? I doubt it."

"The gun is in my hand. I must've done it." A mournful sigh echoed on the night wind.

"Things aren't always what they appear to be," Bradford assured her. "I suspect the other woman is responsible."

"That makes the most sense," I agreed. "Now if we can link them together. I still believe the other woman is Snow White's twin sister."

"Please stop calling me Snow White, my name is Vanessa van Allen."

"That is yet to be proven," I replied to the tearful spirit.

Bradford pulled his phone from his front pocket. "Time to call the authorities."

"Are you nuts?" I snatched the phone from his hands. "We need to get our asses out of here. We can't call the cops!"

"I am the cops, Jolene. Now give me the phone."

Bradford held out his hand.

"Snellgrove will bury us under the jail." I pitched his phone into the undergrowth as far as I could. "Let's go before someone catches us here."

Bradford directed his flashlight beam into my face, blinding me. "You shouldn't have done that, Jolene. Now hand over your phone."

"It's in the truck."

"Then I'll make the call from there."

"What if Snellgrove is in cahoots with the other woman? Snow White did say she saw them together here in the cemetery. What if he killed Snow White to keep some secret?"

A voice broke in. "If you're finished with speculation, then let me add that you're way off course. Sheriff Snellgrove is above mere murder."

I snickered at Scarlett. "And you would know this how?"

"I've spent time with him."

"You mean his gun, don't you, Scarlett?" I bunched my fists. Overloaded on adrenaline, I was ready for a fight.

"Knock it off," Bradford ordered. "Let's get back to the truck. I need to call this in."

I took one last look at the distorted body. "I see I can't talk you out of this, but if you're determined to bury us then, at least, let me dispose of Mini Pearl. No one has to know it was here in the first place." I bent down to retrieve my stolen gun.

"Don't touch anything," Bradford barked. "Your gun was reported stolen. It's a matter of record. It may lead us to the perp."

Every fiber of my being screamed for me to grab

the gun and hightail it out of there. From past experience, I knew the authorities would connect me to the murder weapon and arrest me just because they could. Once that happened it was all over but the crying. Damn. Damn. Damn the luck.

Reluctantly, I followed Bradford, and the divas, as I'd started calling them, back to his truck and handed over my cell.

Bradford called his chief and explained the situation. From the one-sided conversation I deducted his boss was none too happy to be hearing from his lead detective. By the time Bradford ended the call I had a pounding headache and butterflies had taken up residence in my stomach.

"Well, it's done." His voice was resigned. "The chief will head this way once he makes the call to Snellgrove. He ordered me to stay put."

"We'd be on our way back home if you'd listen to me," I reasoned. "An anonymous call would've done just as well."

"You don't get me, Jolene. I'm a *cop*."

The chill in his tone warned me to back off. To alleviate the building tension, I climbed out of the truck and paced back and forth until the shrill of a siren pierced the silky black night.

****

The night dragged on forever. My dire prediction of imminent arrest never panned out. Luckily for us, Sheriff Snellgrove did things by the book. Of course, it didn't hurt to have Chief Nichols of the Whiskey Creek Police Department looking over his shoulder. I came clean about the gun, and one of the sheriff deputies verified the stolen gun report. Although the crime scene was in Snellgrove's jurisdiction, he listened openly to Bradford's superior and, after taking our statements, allowed us to leave. Bradford protested, wanting to help in the investigation, but both men threatened to lock him up if he didn't remove his physical presence from the cemetery.

However, we were still prime suspects in the case.

I for one, couldn't wait to leave the forest behind for the comfort of my bed. Drained from the intense headache and tension of the discovery, I rode home in a zombie-like state, emerging only to say goodnight when Bradford dropped me off at home.

I slept like the dead and awakened late. Hurriedly, I dressed for work, ate a quick breakfast, grabbed my brown bag lunch from the fridge, and dashed off for the salon. My luck held as the news of our discovery hadn't broken yet, and my morning passed without the gossip grapevine tangled around my neck.

At noon, I stopped for a bite and a chat with Deena, who just happened to be warming soup when I stepped into the kitchen.

"What's the news on Billie Jo?" I pulled a peanut butter and jelly sandwich from a brown paper bag. "She had a doctor's appointment yesterday. How come we haven't heard from her?"

Deena took the steaming soup from the microwave. "I just got off the phone with her. She's on her way over from a follow-up with her doctor. She has some news to tell us in person."

I put down my sandwich without taking a bite. "How did she sound?"

Deena paused to give me an anxious glance. "Not happy."

Holly pushed through the door interrupting our conversation and strode over to the refrigerator and pulled out a soft drink. "For Mrs. Wheeler." She exited as fast as she entered. Several times we were interrupted by employees grabbing soft drinks and snacks then returning to work. I used the time to eat my sandwich and Deena her soup. We settled back down at the table with sweet iced tea to wait for Billie Jo.

Five minutes passed when our youngest sister finally pushed through the door and sank down into one of the chairs, her face white beneath the tan. Concern nipped at my spirit as I eyeballed her real good. She'd lost weight since Halloween, which wasn't a good thing as Billie Jo was petite and lightweight to begin with. Her usually brilliant green eyes lacked their former luster, and her short blond hair had lost its shine.

I got up and poured another glass of sweet tea. "Drink this, Billie Jo. It'll perk you up a mite. You look wilted."

Billie Jo took a sip. "Thanks, sis, I'm okay, just shocked at the news."

Deena leaned in closer to Billie Jo. "What did the doctor find? It's the stomach bug that's making the rounds, right?"

"That's part of it." Billie Jo took another sip of tea. "They found something else while doing tests."

I sat down opposite her. "Is it bad?"

"Well, it's how you look at it, I suppose." She fretted with her glass. "I'm still in shock. And God, what will Lynette think? She's graduating from high school next year."

"Does Roddy know?" Deena asked.

"He knows," Billie Jo answered in a neutral voice.

"Enough of the doom and gloom," I said. "Just tell us what's wrong with you. The rest can wait."

"I'm pregnant."

Deena leaped to her feet and wrapped her arms around Billie Jo. "Congratulations, sis. What wonderful news."

Billie Jo patted Deena's arm without much enthusiasm. "Good for who? I'm knocking on forty and have one kid graduating high school. I'm not sure I want this." Tears welled in her eyes.

"How does Roddy feel about it?" I kept my voice neutral to assure her of no judgment for her feelings as I'm a staunch believer in a woman's right to choose.

Billie Jo withdrew a tissue from her purse. "He's thrilled." She dabbed her eyes. "But I'm the one who has to give up my job to have this kid."

"Why would you have to quit working?" I probed gently. "A lot of women continue to work until their due dates."

"Doctor's orders," Billie Jo said. "She feels the long hours on my feet would be too hard on a woman of my age, and could possibly increase the chances of a miscarriage. Not complete bed rest but no working either. How will you and Deena manage without me?"

I raised my eyes to Deena. With her relocating to Atlanta, and Billie Jo out on maternity leave, the salon would become my sole responsibility. My thoughts flashed to Bradford and Wyoming. If I left with him, what would happen to the salon? It would close, that's what.

Close Dixieland Salon? Never.

Tears welled in my eyes.

Deena read my mind. Her face crumpled. I shook

my head to warn her to keep quiet and smiled wide for Billie Jo's benefit.

"We would manage fine." I flashed a huge smile. "This is wonderful news, Billie Jo. Really, it is. Roddy has always wanted a son. And Mama and Daddy will be pleased with the news. A new addition to the family. What better outcome to the stomach flu."

We all had a good laugh and then a good cry like we used to do growing up on the farm. Bonding with my two sisters over the years had made us an inseparable trio, but times were changing. Fast. Life gets in the way of the best-laid plans. That's what Daddy says, and he's never wrong about matters of the heart. Daddy. He and Mama were possibly moving on, too. My daughter, Rebecca, her husband, Jacob, and Hannah, my three-year-old granddaughter, were visiting his family in Israel. What if they decided to stay?

The family tree was branching out.

"What are you thinking about, Jolene?" Deena's voice broke my thoughts.

I brushed tears from my cheeks. "Trees, my dear. I'm thinking about trees."

Chapter Fifteen
Snow White's Escape

Several days passed with no word from Bradford. Daily I checked the news for any mention of Snow White's discovery, but the case seemed to have dissolved. No word from Sheriff Snellgrove and his investigation. No word from Scarlett or the victim. No word on the missing woman posing as Vanessa van Allen. I suppose I should've been more grateful for the peace and tranquility that comes with ordinary life, but I needed closure—and answers.

Mama and Daddy had returned from Florida, and were happy to learn they'd be grandparents again. Although they didn't say, I could tell they were anxious to be off again. Apparently, the farm had lost its appeal, and they were getting on in years. I could see the handwriting on the wall. Sooner, than later, they would head south to warmer weather and greener golf courses.

Business at the salon continued to be steady, and I decided to hire a barber to take Billie Jo's place. Since my talk with Deena, I began taking over more duties as salon manager. My workload increased, but it filled the hours of the day. Preston had called several times since returning from his conference to say he couldn't break away to see me. Which was fine with me as I was too tired at the end of the day for romance. Or sex.

A subtle shift in the atmosphere greeted me on the

fourth day. As soon as I awoke from a fitful night of sleep, my psychic radar went on full alert. Tango sprang from the bed with a hiss and shot out of my bedroom to disappear down the hall. Although the physical world remained unchanged to the untrained eye, the vibrational field of the angels buzzed like an angry swarm of killer bees.

Animals can detect the disturbance, especially cats. They have a special link to the netherworld. Tango, a hyperlink. He never failed me. I scanned the bedroom for any disincarnate entities. Streams of yellow sunlight filtered through the frilly blue curtains. The air stirred, and I tensed as my plane of consciousness expanded. The room warmed as fibers of flowing energy rode the sunbeams through the windows. Spirals of light danced on the waves of energy building throughout the room. Carefully, so as not to disturb the fluid reality, I slipped out of bed and assumed the lotus position on the floor as Madame Mia had taught me. Breathe in. Breathe out. Open your mind to the possibilities. Again and again I practiced the ancient art of meditation until I connected with my higher level of awareness.

I opened my eyes to my celestial visitor and gave a heavy sigh. "Christ, it's you. How'd you escape?"

Snow White raised a hand from which hung the golden handcuffs. "Truth will set you free. I'm here because I know who I am, and I'm not leaving until I tell you my story."

I struggled to my feet and strode for the bathroom. "Give me a minute, nature calls."

When I emerged from the bathroom, dressed in jeans and blouse, Snow White lay across my bed.

"Okay, I need my morning fix." I left the bedroom,

went into the kitchen, and started a pot of coffee. Snow White followed. She floated over one of the chairs when I turned around with the cream and sugar.

"You don't seem especially interested in my story," she accused with a pout.

"Oh, I'm interested, just getting comfortable for the tale, Vanessa."

"I'm not Vanessa."

That didn't surprise me. "Heaven got it wrong, again. I can see how they screwed it up though, you're a dead ringer for her." I set the cream and sugar on the table.

"That's how I got mixed up in this plot."

"So, you're her twin sister?" I fished in the cabinet for a mug.

"Not even close. We bear a remarkable resemblance, but share no DNA."

I poured coffee into the mug and sat down at the table. "What a fluke. Why don't you start at the beginning, miss? What is your name?"

"Halsey. Careen Halsey from Hawkinsville, Georgia."

"Ah, C.H. Now I understand. Start at the beginning, Careen."

She sighed. "It's a sad story. My parents divorced on my second birthday. I'm the youngest of three. After my father split, my mom had to work two jobs to keep a roof over our heads and food on the table." Her voice quivered.

"Your father didn't pay child support?"

"He died in a car accident seven months after the divorce. My older brother Michael became a surrogate father of sorts."

"Michael Halsey?" I'd heard that name before. Recently. Where? Think, Claiborne. Careen's voice recaptured my attention.

"Michael always tried to protect me from the harshness of our circumstance. Mother married and divorced five times. Each marriage brought its own special brand of baggage. To escape I made up stories. Elaborate ones. I wrote my first book at ten. At nineteen I wrote the Dark Enchantment vampire fantasy trilogy."

I thumped the table with my fist. "You wrote that? How'd Vanessa get her slimy hands on it?"

"I ran into Vanessa at the annual Romance Writers' convention in Atlanta. Late one night in the lounge. We'd both had a bad day. My pitch never made it off the ground, and Vanessa was having agent problems. We became acquainted over Jell-O shots. That's when I shared my ideas for a vampire fantasy romance. She loved the idea and encouraged me to tell her all about it. She then offered to read the first manuscript. Of course, I was thrilled, so I consented."

"Wait a minute," I interrupted. "Vanessa was a published author at that time? I thought the vampire trilogy put her on the bestseller list."

"It did, but at the time of our meeting, she'd published several romance novels with Firebrand Publications. She was an up and coming writer. To have her interested in my work renewed my hopes of becoming a novelist."

"So you handed over your work?"

"Oh yes. I was young and naive."

Tango appeared in the doorway, golden eyes gleaming, and the tip of his tail twitching with interest. "Don't stop, Careen. I'm listening." I got up to fill his bowl with kitty crunch and returned to the table.

"The next morning, Vanessa shows up at my room with the manuscript and her critique, promising to help me improve as a writer."

"So she came through with her promise?"

"Yes, she seduced me with dreams of stardom." Careen's ghostly sigh gave me goose bumps. "It came with a price."

"Your life?"

"Yes, my life. Vanessa convinced me to keep our association secret. Slowly, over the months she revealed her plans. Evil plans. I see that now." She gave me a shamefaced look.

"Go on," I encouraged. "I'm not here to judge you, only listen."

"Vanessa wanted her name on my work. She pointed out that I was an unknown. Agents and publishers weren't interested in unknowns. I bought the lie because I'd received so many rejections I feared I'd never break through that wall. All I wanted was for people to read and love my stories. Vanessa promised to make it happen. We would share the financial rewards, and I could help out my struggling family. When I agreed, she laid out the rest of her plan."

"There's more?"

"Please try to understand why I fell for her." Her face mirrored her despair. "Since we shared a natural resemblance, Vanessa offered to pay me a lot of money to impersonate her at functions she didn't wish to attend. We spent months refining my appearance and speech to mimic her. When we'd perfected my transformation, I made my debut. At first, it was fun, and I loved the attention. The Dark Enchantment trilogy

137

was on the NY bestsellers list for months, and money poured in. But then she began demanding more of my time. After a while, I found myself living Vanessa's life while she disappeared to only God knows where. Slowly, I became Vanessa van Allen."

"What about your family during this time? How did you explain this to them?"

"They never knew. The times Vanessa returned to her rightful place, I would return to Hawkinsville and take up my previous life. When Vanessa wanted to switch, my family believed I was off to a temporary job out of town and I resumed her identity."

"So you fully integrated into Vanessa's identity?"

"Yes, little Careen Halsey from Hawkinsville, Georgia ceased to exist. Even her mother couldn't tell the difference. To all intents and purposes, I was the famed Vanessa van Allen."

"And then things changed?"

Tango's meows intermingled with the ticking of the grandfather clock in the den. My stomach rumbled. I ignored it, waiting for her response.

"One day I received a phone call from the south of France. Vanessa had the brilliant idea of writing a book about her life, exposing the double-handed publishing underworld. I refused to cooperate. Why tick off our money source? Oh, she didn't want to hear that. She wanted another sensational bestseller, and threatened to expose our arrangement. She was coming home to reclaim her life, and I would return to being little Careen Halsey from Hawkinsville, Georgia."

"And that's bad? You'd be free to write under your own name." I failed to understand her logic. "You're an excellent writer according to my sister, Billie Jo."

"Ah, but you're wrong. We deceived the world with our arrangement. No decent agent would touch me. Oh, I could self-publish and make a mint, but my reputation would've been shot, my family shamed. I couldn't allow that. You know, Southern pride and all that nonsense."

I understood completely. "You mentioned siblings,"

"A brother, Michael, and a sister, Alice."

"Michael Halsey...Michael Halsey." I paced around the kitchen trying to recall when and where I'd heard that name before. "Describe him."

"Tall, dark brown hair and mustache, slender build. Attractive."

"That's it," I exclaimed, stopping mid-step. "Vanessa's escort at the cocktail party the other night. At the writers' retreat. Remember?"

Careen began to fade. "Gotta run. That bitch is after me again!"

"Wait!" I cried. "She can help us."

"Ha. She'll return me to that hell hole. No, I'm not going back until I settle the score."

"But where will you go?"

"Sam's."

Back to Bradford's aura. No way. I hesitated, then plunged ahead. "Go to Dixieland Salon. Hide there. In the pink room. I'll deal with Scarlett and meet you there."

"Dixieland Salon?"

"Yes, the one on Love Avenue with a pink awning over the front door. You can't miss it."

Luckily for Careen, she skipped out in the nick of time for Scarlett arrived on my next breath. Minus the

139

fireworks.

"Okay, Claiborne, I know she's here." Her eyes glowed green fire. "Or been here. Start the dialogue and be quick about it."

"I'm sure I don't know to whom you refer." I stepped over to the sink and pulled down my bottle of Zanny from the windowsill. Geez, I'd better get another refill.

"I'm in no mood for bullshit."

I downed a pill. "Such language. Really, Scarlett, Heaven doesn't seem to be having a positive effect on you." Hopefully, I could stall her and give Careen a head start.

The barometric pressure in the kitchen fell. A cold chill swept across the space, causing my teeth to chatter, and Tango to make a mad dash for the den. I plopped back down in a chair and gave her a mean look. "Knock it off, Scarlett, you're scaring the cat."

"Your pussy is not my concern."

My eyebrows rose in mock distress. "There's Zanny on the windowsill if you need it."

She chuckled with a dry and cynical sound. "Your feeble attempts at stalling are a dead giveaway, Jolene. Give her up."

I climbed to my feet with my dirty coffee mug and opened the dishwasher. "Check out the house if you must. I have an early appointment." With that, I turned my back on her and went to dress for work. The resulting lightning flash indicated I'd poked a mad skunk with a sharp stick.

****

Scarlett beat me there. When I pulled my Mustang around to the rear, the back door was blown off its

140

hinges and lying on a grassy patch off the walkway. How she did it, I'm not certain, and I really didn't care. First order of business was to take away another one of her nine lives. My blood pressure skyrocketed as I burst from my car and scampered inside to halt any further destruction.

The facial door suffered the same fate. I struggled to breathe. Crap. How am I going to explain this to Deena? Or Roddy? Because Billie Jo's husband would have to repair the damage ASAP.

"Get your filthy hands off me." Careen's enraged voice echoed from within the facial room. "Jolene granted me sanctuary."

"You're going back to Purgatory." Scarlett's voice rang with authority. "Now stand still so I can cuff you."

I took a deep breath and burst into the room. "Unhand her, Scarlett and get out of my salon. In Jesus's name."

An unearthly quiet settled over the room. Scarlett dropped her hold on Careen, and spun around to face me. Now free, Careen crept to the far corner of the room, her brown eyes huge in the filtered light from the doorway.

"You would use that name on me?" Scarlett's beautiful features mirrored her pain. "How the mighty have fallen."

"You provoked me," I reasoned. "And look what you did to my salon. How am I going to explain it?"

"That's not my problem. Why don't you tell Deena the truth and let her come up with a logical explanation? She's good at storytelling."

I considered it. "Won't work. Just so you know, Deena's gonna have my ass, and you're gonna be barred from the salon."

"Take back what you said. Dixieland Salon is my second home."

True. After her demise in this room, the clients and staff developed an aversion to it. Claimed it was haunted, and wouldn't step a foot inside. To counter the stigma, and to stop rumors of a haunting, I turned it into a lovely sitting room to Scarlett's specifications. I even used it on occasion. The soft pink walls, combined with a flower print chintz loveseat with lovely matching pillows, and a multicolored area rug offered respite during a busy day.

"I have to take her back, Jolene."

I lifted my gaze to hers. "Bradford and I are the prime suspects in her death. She has info that can clear us, and I'm going to do everything in my power to keep her here. Surely, there's something you can do to help us."

After a moment's pause, she said, "You have three days. After that, she agrees to return peacefully with me. And, she's restricted to this space."

"Here in the salon?" Not good. The salon already had a reputation of being haunted. Thanks to Scarlett.

"In this room, only," Scarlett clarified. "Oh, and Jolene, the Powers that Be don't like interference from mortals. You're taking a big chance here. Tread carefully."

"Your terms are agreeable."

"I'll be back in three days to retrieve my prisoner." With that Scarlett vanished from the facial room, leaving a red trail of cosmic dust.

Three days. Not a long time to solve a murder.

Chapter Sixteen
The Reappearance of Madame Mia

"Jolene, this has to stop."

Deena lifted her gaze from the busted rear door to me. Heat crept up my neck and face at her horrified expression.

"I know." I wrung my hands to keep them busy. "How are you going to explain this to the insurance company?"

"Well, I can't tell them that your invisible gal pal from hell had a hissy fit, now can I?" Deena's voice grated out her frustration. "I swear to God, Jolene, you need to get professional help. This ghost thingy is out of hand. And I'm not happy about the one still in the facial room."

"I'm sorry, sis, but what else could I do? Bradford and I are in trouble. Careen is our only link to the crime. I had to give her sanctuary."

She held up a hand to silence me. "Don't explain. Just get her out of there."

"Three days, Deena. I promise."

"Whatever." She withdrew her phone from her handbag. "I'll take care of the damage, but you're going to tell Mama."

I gnawed my bottom lip. "Uh, let's leave Mama out of this. She'll overreact and blame me."

"Too late. She's meeting me here in twenty

minutes to discuss the reception. Oh, and FYI, Daddy's dropping her off. I'm sure he'll have something to add to her lecture. And it is your fault."

I grabbed my head and groaned. "I'm getting a headache."

"Suck it up," Deena advised. "We'll be explaining this one all day." She tapped the crystal of her wristwatch. "The staff and clients will be arriving any minute. I'd better get Roddy over here." She punched several buttons on her phone and headed inside.

I followed behind catching snatches of her conversation with our contractor brother-in-law as she tried to explain the situation. At the facial room, I paused to check on my ghostly guest. I had plenty of questions to ask Careen, but at the proper time. At the moment I had pressing issues to address as the jiggling front doorbell signaled the morning rush had begun.

Grabbing my apron from the dispensary, I turned the corner to see a beautiful, dark-haired woman in a stunning white silk sheath standing at the reception desk. Great day in the morning, help had arrived.

"Madame Mia, how nice to see you again." I rushed over to her and held out my hand. One didn't embrace the exotic psychic. Messes with her aligned wavelengths, she claimed.

She touched my outstretched fingers. Dark, unfathomable eyes gazed into mine. "Ah, Jolene, darling, I rushed over as soon as I received your message. I hope I'm not too late."

Because I'd never placed a physical phone call to her, I knew she referred to the Universal hotline available to all enlightened souls. Unbeknownst to me, I'd placed a person-to-person psychic call for help, and she'd received the summons.

Voices emitting from the rear of the salon alerted me that the staff had arrived. Deena emerged from her office, and seeing me with a client, indicated that she would deal with the staff. Not wanting to be overheard, I steered Madame Mia to Deena's vacant office.

"Have a seat." I closed the door behind her. "My situation requires discretion."

"I'm here to help, my dear." Her low throaty voice washed over me like warm bathwater, and I relaxed into its purposeful seduction.

My front pocket vibrated. Bradford. I answered immediately. "I know Snow White's true identity. Madame Mia is here with me now in Deena's office. Get over to the salon ASAP."

"On my way," he answered and disconnected the line.

While I waited for Bradford to arrive, I explained the situation to Madame Mia, beginning with Halloween night and ending with her arrival several minutes ago, stopping only to answer her questions.

"Oh what a tangled web we weave, when we first practice to deceive," she murmured as my voice trailed off. "Sir Walter Scott. An ancestor of mine."

Okay, so she's weird. Aren't we all? I lay claim to witch DNA—on my daddy's side. Way back to the Salem witch trials in 1692. Poor soul lost her life over an independence of mind and an unsubmissive character. A family trait Billie Jo and I proudly display.

Bradford arrived minutes later. He strode through the door with his hat in hand, gave a nod of acknowledgement in the psychic's direction, and relaxed down in the chair beside me. I breathed in the familiar scent of his woodsy aftershave and had to quell the impulse to climb onto his lap and snuggle close like in times past. He pulled a sheet of folded paper from his inside blazer pocket. "The body has been positively identified as Careen Halsey from Hawkinsville, Georgia. The news will be released today at noon."

"Hello to you, too," I said, a little huffed at his casual manner. He been out of touch for four days and not even a "howdy-do"? He could at least explain why he hadn't returned my calls or answered my texts.

Bradford answered my sarcasm with a heart-melting smile that burned its way down to my twinkie pie. "Sorry, Jolene, for my lack of manners." He turned to Madame Mia, who sat in her chair like a regal queen. "Jolene speaks highly of you, Madame."

She inclined her head. "As she does of you, Detective."

I glanced at my watch. "Look, I don't have much time, so let's get on with it." I turned to Bradford. "I know all about Careen Halsey. She showed up this morning, and is right now ensconced in the facial room."

"How?" Bradford began but I stopped him.

"Let me finish," I said, and for the next several minutes I relayed my earlier conversation with Careen.

"Everything leads back to Vanessa." Bradford rubbed his chin. "We've got to find her. She's the key to this case."

"Any leads?" I questioned.

"None that I've been able to uncover."

"Perhaps I could help."

Bradford and I both regarded Madame Mia. The back of my neck tingled. A sure sign of good luck.

"What do you suggest?" Bradford's voice echoed his doubts of her authenticity and honesty.

The psychic lifted a hand to brush ebony strands from her flawless ivory cheek. "A reading, of course. Tonight, at my house. A storm is brewing." She gave him a sultry smile. "The spirits love to play in the rain, detective. They'll tell us what we want to know."

Bradford sighed with exasperation. "I'll pass. I've had enough of ghosts and spirits."

"Have you got a better strategy?" When he didn't answer right away, I stood to my feet. "We accept, Madame Mia."

The ravishing psychic rose to her feet, smoothing the white silk over her knees. "Midnight. My usual fee, of course."

"Midnight it is." I gave Bradford a backward glance as I escorted her out into the reception area. At the front door, she lightly touched my hand. "I sense something evil is at hand. Please be careful, Jolene. Don't trust the ones closest to you."

I swallowed hard as she dropped my fingers, pushed through the door and out into the morning sunlight, leaving her signature lilac scent behind. With her strange warning ringing in my ears, I retraced my steps to Deena's office where Bradford waited. Time for a strategy planning session with the hunky detective. It's all about strategy.

****

The private chat never took place. Mama and Daddy landed right about then and things went south from there. Not only did my parents arrive, but Roddy and a couple of his construction boys to rehang the doors. Add to the chaos, a disturbed staff and curious clients, and then to add insult to injury, funky noises started up in the facial room. Deena flipped out and started crying, and of course, Mama blamed me.

At some point in the madness, Bradford sneaked out of Deena's office and hightailed it back to sanity. He did, however, send me a text that he'd pick me up around elevenish for our midnight rendezvous with Madame Mia. Lucky me.

When the afternoon rolled around, I was more than ready to pull my hair out one kinky, dark blonde strand at a time. The only highlight of the day happened when Hattie Sanford came in for a chemical relaxer.

A gracious African American woman of seventy plus years, Hattie Sanford was a longtime client, and the great aunt of Ellie Malone, my former nail tech. Ellie had quit Dixieland Salon to open up her own business after she hooked up with her own personal limitless bank account named Ryan Herrington. My sisters believe I'm responsible for nudging her out the door when I accused her and Ryan of helping his father exit this life. Turns out I was wrong. Word around town was she and Ryan were happy newlyweds.

"Good afternoon, Mrs. Sanford." I draped her thin shoulders with a leopard print plastic shampoo cape. "How's life treating you these days?"

"Jesus has been good to me, Miss Jolene." She flashed a white, toothy smile. "Leroy and I are celebrating our fifty-second wedding anniversary this week. Ellie is throwing us a shindig down at the Moose Lodge."

I pulled out her client card and set it on my workstation. "I hear she and Ryan are doing well."

"Doin' fine. She's openin' another nail salon in

Nashville and another in Adel. The good book don't like proud saints, but I'm a braggin' about her. Her brother too. He owns Mack's Limousine Service. Doin' good, he is. Had a VIP in his limo the other night."

"Oh?" I continued applying base cream to her scalp. "Not many of those in this area."

"Can you keep a secret?" Her eyes met mine in the mirror expectantly, practically begging me to agree. "Got to promise."

Not at all interested, but not willing to hurt her feelings, I decided to humor her. "I promise."

Her toothy smile reflected in the mirror. "That lady writer and her fancy boyfriend."

Great balls of fire, she had to be talking about Vanessa van Allen. Had to be. No other well-known female author in these parts. A lead at last. Bradford will be over the moon when I dump this in his lap. Calm down. Get more info. I let my smile widen a mite. "Quit kidding with me, Hattie. You can't possibly mean Vanessa van Allen took a ride in your nephew's limo?"

Hattie beamed. "None other."

"I'm impressed. Did Mack say where he drove them?"

"No, but I could find out if you want."

"And you're sure it was Monday night?"

Her eyes reflected her curiosity. "What's your interest in this, chile? Nothin' but a car ride."

How much to say? The truth? Lie? Not to her, I wouldn't. I leaned in closer, so not to be overheard. "Vanessa is missing."

"Mack ain't involved." Her gentle brown eyes grew round as saucers.

"It's complicated, but the police suspect Detective

Bradford and I had something to do with her disappearance. We didn't, but any information Mack could provide could clear us of suspicion. Did Mack mention the man's name or describe him?"

"Not a peep."

I jotted down my cell number on my business card and handed it to her. "Call me at this number when you get the information."

She pocketed the card. "If I can get 'em to talk."

"Please, try Hattie," I pleaded. "It could be a life and death situation."

I finished Hattie's hair and picked up the tab. A small price to pay for vital information. Plus it gave her extra incentive to call me with any additional info she could coax out of her nephew.

Deena left early. At closing, the staff scattered like ants on a church picnic leaving me to finish up the laundry. Usually Holly's job, tonight I sent her on her way with the rest of the crew. I wanted the place to myself to finish a conversation with the resident ghost.

When I cracked open the rehung facial room door, a thin stream of light pushed back the darkness. I switched on the overhead lights, flooding the corners with florescent light. Careen transposed forlornly over the loveseat, her lovely eyes huge with sadness.

"I've got to get out of here." Her voice broke the silence. "Please release me."

I stepped into the room and seated myself in an old wooden rocking chair I'd picked up at an estate sale in Macon. "You know I can't, Careen. We have three days to solve your murder. Do you know who took your life?"

"Yes, and I'm going to have my revenge on her."

It came to me. "Vanessa van Allen. I should've guessed sooner. Now all we've got to do is find her and the evidence that links her to your murder."

"I can find her if you'll help me get out of here."

"I would if I could, Careen." Our gazes met and held.

"Do you sincerely mean that?" A spark of life flared in her lifeless eyes.

I gave her a questioning look. "Yes, Careen, I do. Why?" My sense of sympathy heightened.

In hindsight, I should've realized Careen's intentions in time to stop her, but a languorous sensation possessed me, and before I could voice my objections, she slipped into my aura like a horny rooster in a henhouse.

Chapter Seventeen
The House of the Rising Sun

After spending hours unsuccessfully trying to coax Careen from my aura, I gave up, stuck my finger down my throat and flushed my late afternoon snack down the toilet. Temporarily free from nausea, I showered and dressed in a long, flowing black skirt, black silk turtleneck, and black boots. To keep my unruly locks tamed I fashioned a chignon at the back of my head, then hung silver dangle earrings in my ears to complete my ensemble.

Ready to face the unknown at Madame Mia's I settled down in the den to watch TV until Bradford's expected arrival. I was half dozing when Tanya Graham of WXYB Channel Ten news caught my attention.

"The body of the unidentified woman who was found in the Mount Zion Missionary Baptist Church cemetery has now been positively identified as Careen Halsey of Hawkinsville, Georgia."

I sat up in the recliner dislodging Tango from my lap. Disgruntled, he protested with a loud meow and jumped down to the floor and began cleaning himself.

"Greenwood County Sheriff, Cleaster Snellgrove, reports that the next of kin has been notified." Tanya Graham's soft voice continued, "The body has not been released for burial as this is an ongoing investigation. Sheriff Snellgrove went on to say his office is following several leads connected to Miss Halsey. Two citizens of Whiskey Creek have been questioned and released in connection with her death. If you have any information pertaining to this case, please contact the Greenwood County Sheriff's office at the number on the screen."

The number scrolled across the bottom of the television screen.

"In other news, a missing person's report has been filed on well-known erotica romance writer, Vanessa van Allen." A picture of Vanessa van Allen flashed on the screen. "Her mother, Betty van Allen of Whiskey Creek, last spoke with her daughter Monday morning, and nothing seemed amiss. Miss van Allen was attending the writers' retreat at Baconton Lodge. On Monday morning, a staff member found the cabin ransacked and blood in the floor. Miss van Allen hasn't been seen since. A kidnapping is suspected. A five thousand dollar reward is being offered for information that leads to the author's whereabouts. If you have any information, please contact the Whiskey Creek Police Department or the Greenwood County Sheriff's office at the numbers on the screen."

The numbers scrolled across the television screen.

I glanced down at my watch. 11:15. I hit the power button on the remote and climbed to my feet and headed into the bathroom to brush the cat hairs from my clothing and freshen up. I had grabbed a bottled water from the refrigerator when a knock sounded at the kitchen door.

"You feeling okay?" Bradford asked when I swung open the door to admit him.

"Not really." I sank down into a kitchen chair.

"You should see a doctor."

I swallowed back the rising bile in my throat. "You're right, Bradford. As soon as this mess is cleared up I'm going to seek professional help. I can't take this anymore."

"You don't mean an M.D." He swirled a finger around his ear. "One of those head doctors who take on nutbags like us."

I cracked a smile. "Yeah, something like that. But honestly, before we leave could you use your manly influence with Careen and see if she'd hitch a ride with you? I'm sick of her."

All efforts failed. So with my ghostly passenger firmly entrenched in my aura, I gathered my handbag and followed Bradford out to his pickup for the short drive to Fifth Street.

"Any updates from Hattie Sanford?" Bradford asked once we'd turned onto Eighth Street. "Her nephew could provide a vital lead if he'll cooperate."

Lightning flashed in the distance, and I turned from the window. "Hattie wasn't even sure she could get Mack to talk, but as soon as she does, she'll give me a call." Thunder rumbled. "Madame Mia's storm is coming."

"I'm not good at waiting."

Duh. "Tell me something I don't know." Left on Sixth. The historic district. Old money. The old Maco mansion needs TLC. Overgrown grass and weeds, broken windows, and peeling paint. Much like a sad, old crippled man. Someone ought to buy the place and renovate. It would fetch a fortune in resale. As we passed the old place, a flicker of light briefly flared in one of the back windows. Probably some homeless soul seeking refuge from the approaching storm.

"The lead could grow cold." His tone reflected his frustration.

"Can't rush progress." Right on Fifth. Madame Mia's restored Victorian mansion came into sight. Warm, golden lamplight spilled from the front porch light.

Bradford parked in the driveway and killed the engine. He turned to me, draping an arm over the front seat. Fingers brushed my shoulder. "I'm not one hundred percent certain we're doing the right thing, Jolene. I just don't trust the woman."

I pushed open the passenger door. "Then trust me. Come on, let's do this."

Together, we climbed the wooden porch steps. The front door opened. Madame Mia posed on the threshold in a stunning white satin pantsuit that set off her dark beauty to perfection. Always white. I'd never seen the mysterious psychic in any other color. Another odd character quirk.

"Everything is ready." She stepped back, motioning for us to enter.

Nothing had changed since my last visit. The inlaid wood floors in the foyer shone underneath the scattered colorful woolen rugs, and the huge, ornate chandelier high above my head twinkled with a thousand tiny pinpoints of light shaped like candle flames. A crystal vase filled with snowy roses sat in the center of a round antique marble-topped rosewood table.

Madame Mia led us to the small parlor at the end of the hallway where she conducted her readings. Bradford and I seated ourselves at the lace tablecloth covered table while Madame Mia dimmed the overhead chandelier.

"Ah, what's going on?" Bradford asked with a slight hesitation as a flash of lightning lit up the room, followed by a clap of thunder.

"Mood lighting," the psychic supplied, as she took her seat beside me. "I will now light the candles. Spirits seek the warmth and light."

Along with the candles on the round table were a bowl of fruit and several slices of homemade bread. I knew from previous visits the natural foods were an offering to attract spirits.

"Now join hands," the psychic instructed.

Bradford balked. "Not until you tell me what you're doing."

Dumbass. I sighed with impatience and nausea. "It's a séance."

"Oh, no." Bradford stood to his feet and backed away from the table. "I don't believe I would care to participate."

"Careen Halsey." My patience took another dive. "Remember your dead gal pal? Pull up your big boy panties and sit down."

In the flickering candlelight, I couldn't read Bradford's expression, but he resumed his seat, however, stiffly, and grabbed my hand.

Only the sound of the approaching storm filled the parlor. Our clasp hands made the symbolic circle. Madame Mia began her soft chant in a foreign language. Bradford's hand tightened on mine.

"Spirits of the past, move among us. Be guided by the warmth and light of the world and visit upon us. We bring offerings of bread and fruit." More foreign chanting. "Spirits of the night, seek the warmth and light of the candles. We seek your guidance among the lost ones. We seek the whereabouts of a woman. Vanessa van Allen is lost. Help us seek her. Speak."

The soft chanting grew fainter. Madame Mia stiffened, then relaxed.

"The woman you seek is not among us," a man's voice spoke through the psychic.

"She's alive?" Bradford murmured in my ear.

I nodded, then addressed the spirit. "Does she walk of her own free will?"

"The woman you seek walks of her own free will," a woman's voice came through.

Madame Mia stirred, and I knew from times past that thin veil between the two worlds weakened, and I had to act fast. Bradford started to speak, so I crushed my boot heel on his foot to shut him up. "Where is she?"

"Seek the house of the rising sun."

House of the rising sun? What on earth? Baffled by the riddle, but determined to have answers, I gave Bradford a quick shoulder shrug, and asked one more question as Madame Mia blinked her eyes several times. "Where is the house of the rising sun?"

The pounding rainfall answered back. Madame Mia slowly opened her eyes.

"The spirits love to play in the rain."

Bradford rolled his eyes at me, and I motioned for him to knock it off. As long as I had this cursed gift, I needed my relationship with the psychic to continue on good terms.

Madame Mia blew out the candles and turned up the lighting. When she resumed her seat at the table, she stared hard at me. "I see you've picked up a hitchhiker, Jolene. Funny I never noticed it before now."

"Yeah, do you know anything about removing dead weight from human auras?"

She waved a ringed finger in my direction. A waft of lilacs filled my nostrils.

"Jolene, darling, of course I do." She pushed back her chair and came to stand behind mine, all the while chanting her foreign mantra. For several seconds her bejeweled hands circled my head, and Careen materialized in Madame Mia's vacated chair.

Bradford blinked in obvious surprise, and I gave a sigh of relief at having my personal space all to myself once more. Madame Mia directed her attention to Careen.

"So this is the woman found in the cemetery?"

I nodded my head. "Yes, Careen Halsey. And she's going to help us find Vanessa. Who, I might add, is her killer."

Bradford turned to me, his expression hinting at impatience. "This is the first I'm hearing about your theory. Any evidence?"

"Only her testimony." I cocked my head at Careen. "She can help us find the evidence."

"The first order of business is to locate Vanessa van Allen," he countered. "She has a lot to answer for, including Careen's murder if we can prove it. Do either of you have any clue what and where the house of the rising sun is?"

"I do."

Three pairs of eyes settled on Careen.

"The House of the Rising Sun is from House of Secrets, Book Two in my Dark Enchantment series. The House of the Rising Sun is Queen Lada's lair in Transylvania."

"Romania?" I wondered aloud.

"Deep in the Carpathian Mountains," Careen supplied.

"What does a fictional vampire queen's lair have to do with finding Vanessa?" Bradford's jaw tensed.

"Perhaps Vanessa had a home away from home that she dubbed 'The House of the Rising Sun,'" Madame Mia suggested.

"Makes sense to me," I said. "Bradford?"

His brows pulled into an affronted frown. "This is a first for me, ladies. I'll have to defer to your expert knowledge."

"Perhaps there's a clue in the second book that will lead you to Vanessa," Madame Mia again suggested.

"Possibly." I thought back over the months when Billie Jo had raved about the book. I drew a blank, not remembering anything of importance in our conversations. The books were hard-core erotica, I'd learned from my sister. And bestsellers. Hmmm. Strictly for investigative purposes I decided to download the book on my e-reader and see what I could find.

Chapter Eighteen
The Ghost Hotel

At three a.m. I shut off my e-reader not finding anything of value for the investigation, and just plain wore out from the high-voltage sex scenes in Book Two, House of Secrets. From one standpoint, I could see how it had become a bestseller because everyone knows that sex sells—however, for me, a little mystery goes a long way. Just point me in the right direction and let my imagination take it from there. Not only were there too many vivid sexual descriptions, but the manner of the telling left much to be desired.

Trash.

I kept my thoughts to myself as Careen had reattached herself to my aura and could hear every word. Plus, voicing my disgust for her work wouldn't serve my purposes well. I turned off the light and tried to sleep.

When the alarm buzzed at 7:00, I rolled out of bed like a slug and stumbled into the bathroom for a shower. Refreshed, I dressed in a light print dress and heels for work and went into the kitchen for coffee and cereal. The phone rang as I poured my second cup. Caller ID indicated the call I had hoped for had come through. Bradford would be thrilled for another lead to Vanessa's whereabouts.

"Good morning, Hattie, I'm glad you called."

"Mack finally agreed to talk to you." Her voice crackled over the line. "No police."

Oops. Bradford wouldn't be happy to be excluded from the questioning, but what else could I do? To force the issue might shut Mack up good and tight. No, best to go it alone.

"Jolene, you there? You hear me say, no police? Mack don't want no police snoopin' around. His clients expect discretion."

"Yes, I heard you, Hattie. No police. What time?"

"Now."

I glanced down at my watch. 8:30. Barely enough time before my first appointment at 9:00. "I'll be there. What's the address?"

"618 Athens Street."

I disconnected the line and grabbed my purse off the counter, scooted out the door and into my Mustang. As I drove to the outskirts of town, I gathered my thoughts and rehearsed a couple of questions that posed no threat to Mack's business. First, Vanessa's destination. Second, a name or description of her male passenger. Best to keep it short and simple. Bradford and I could take it from there.

I passed the new mall out by I-75 and turned onto Athens Street and drove down until I spotted Mack's Limousine Service in a small, white, relatively new building on the corner and parked in the small parking lot. I pushed open the door and stepped into the air-conditioned lobby, surprised at the upscale décor. Evidently, Mack's Limousine Service was doing well in our small community. Before I could take another step, a tall, handsome African American man in an expensive black suit stepped out of the side door and held out a hand.

"Miz Claiborne?" His mellow baritone, combined with his rock hard body and the even whiteness of his smile, dazzled me. Damn, pick-your-tongue-off-the-floor gorgeous.

I swallowed hard and took the outstretched hand, gazing up into velvety chocolate eyes that seemed to devour me. "Yes, and hopefully you're Hattie's great-nephew, Mack Sanford?"

He squeezed my hand. "Yes, I'm Mack. Aunt Hattie failed to mention the beauty of my inquisitor."

I giggled like a schoolgirl and completely lost my train of thought, my brain zeroing in on one of the high-voltage sex scenes I'd read earlier. Heat crept up my face as I stood frozen in Zombie land. Thankfully, Mack had the good sense to drop my hand and step back.

"I understand you have some questions regarding a recent fare?"

"Yes, last Monday." I answered in a less than steady voice, embarrassed at my attraction to this much younger man. Geez, get a grip old woman.

"Let's go into my office." He pointed to the door from which he'd exited. "It's private."

I followed him into his plush office and sat in the chair opposite his desk. After he'd settled himself, he knit his hands together. "You're interested in my VIP client, I understand."

I relaxed, regaining my composure. "If that VIP is Vanessa van Allen, then yes, I'm interested in her and her male companion."

"Care to tell me why you're interested?"

"Sufficient to say that it's a life and death

situation."

His face grew serious. "Aunt Hattie mentioned she was missing, but I never witnessed any behavior that would indicate a problem. Miss van Allen was pale, and her arm was in a sling, but she and her companion were both fine when I dropped them off at the old Maco mansion. Her gentleman friend tipped me a hundred bucks."

Chills skittered up my spine as I remembered the brief flash of light in the back part of the house as we passed by last night. Great balls of fire! Vanessa was right under our thumb. I had to get this information to Bradford ASAP. But first, I had a few questions that needed answering. "Where and when did you pick up Miss van Allen and her companion?"

"Baconton Writers' Retreat. Early Monday morning. About five."

"Do you have her companion's name?"

He shook his head. "No name. Young, brown hair and moustache, slender build, expensive suit."

The description fit two men. Michael Halsey and Cash Hitchcock. Since Michael Halsey was the last man I'd seen her with, I'd bet my tip money the mysterious companion was none other than Careen's brother. What's the deal? What could he possibly be up to? Did he know about his sister's death when he took up with Vanessa? Revenge? Lust? Blackmail money? Lots of unanswered questions. "How did they pay?" I asked, hoping for a credit card receipt.

"Cash."

"So you have no record of the fare?"

Mack cast me a shrewd look. "What fare? My limo never left the parking lot."

Hmm. So that's how it was. Under the table cash transaction. Illegal, just like the cash tips I fail to report to the IRS each year. Standard practice in my line of business. I'm a firm believer in keeping some things to myself. Cash is one of them. Well, no need to ask if Mack would talk to Bradford. In light of the information he'd just given me, that wasn't happening. I thanked him and made my way back to my car.

Once I'd cleared the lot and was back on Athens Street, I hit Bradford's contact button on my cell. It went straight to voicemail. I left a message and started for the salon. As much as I wanted to head straight for the Maco mansion, I had no idea what was transpiring behind the scenes, and The Lone Ranger I ain't. If Vanessa needed rescuing, she'd have to wait for Bradford, because I had no inclination to place myself in unnecessary danger for her sorry ass.

****

Mama and Billie Jo dropped by around noon. Deena and I were in her office eating pizza from the café next door when the office door opened, and they strolled in armed with shopping bags. Billie Jo dropped her bags on the sofa and headed straight for the pizza.

"That smells delish," she gushed, and scooped up a large piece, and stuffed it in her mouth.

I set my half-eaten piece on a paper plate and wiped my fingers on a napkin before rising. "Would you like something cold to wash it down? Mama?"

"An iced tea sounds nice for both of us. No sugary soda drinks for the expectant mother." Mama reached for a paper plate. Billie Jo just nodded, unable to speak with her mouth full.

I left the office and stopped by the reception area to

chat with several acquaintances waiting for their stylists, then over to the desk to speak with Holly about my next appointment. "When Mrs. Benson arrives, please see that she's shampooed and draped for a chemical service. Also, if you have time, please restock the retail shelves. They're getting low."

Holly gave me the thumbs-up gesture and reached for the ringing phone. With the salon running smoothly, I made my way to the kitchen at the back of the salon. As I drew abreast the locked facial room door, I paused. No sound. Good. Careen hadn't been happy to be unhinged from my aura this morning, but I'd finally convinced her that I'd pick her up at the end of the day. A lie. Not only a lie, but a whopper. Tomorrow her parole ended with Scarlett's return, and until she was on her way home, she'd stay put. Bradford and I could handle matters on our own without either one of them. They were free to disappear forever into the sweet-by-and-bye.

And speaking of Bradford, why hadn't he returned my call? I'd been sitting on pins and needles all morning itching to share my info with him. I could try again, but my phone was in a drawer at my workstation. To retrieve it meant wading through talkative staff and clients, and I didn't have the time to spare. I glanced down at my watch. 12:05. No, best to wait on him.

I fetched two iced teas from the kitchen and returned to the office and a lively conversation on baby names. The predominate choice being male.

Mama glanced over when I closed the door behind me. "What do you think, Jolene? Graham or Creighton? Which one do you like?"

"Neither." I placed the iced teas down on the

coffee table in front of the sofa. "I'm partial to Raleigh or Tucker."

"Raleigh Hazard." The name rolled off Billie Jo's tongue. "Tucker Hazard. Hmm. Also not bad. Hey, thanks, sis."

Mama gave me a wide smile. "I like Tucker Hazard. It incorporates both family names in one."

"So I assume you believe it's a boy," I addressed my question to Billie Jo.

"Roddy insists it doesn't matter one way or the other, but deep down I know he wants a son. What man doesn't?" Her eyes clouded with doubt.

Knowing a sure-fire way of changing the somber mood, I picked up one of the many shopping bags to peer inside. "So, what did you buy for the baby?"

It worked. Billie Jo took the bag from my outstretched hand and dumped the contents onto Deena's desk and began chatting happily away as she held up each item for our oohs and aahs. From the items displayed, Billie Jo too, had her heart set on a son. With the mood significantly lighter the next fifteen minutes sped by before the intercom buzzed with Holly alerting me that my next appointment was ready and waiting in my stylist chair.

I excused myself and left my sisters and mother planning the new nursery, and greeted Mrs. Benson. Once I had her permanent wave finished, I rolled her hair and sat her under the dryer, and grabbed my phone out of the drawer. Making my way to the kitchen, I checked my voice mail to find a message from Bradford saying he wouldn't be available until this evening around nine and would drop by my house then.

On my way back to my station I paused by the

facial room door to press my ear against the panel. Silence. For a split second, misgivings set in. Had Careen somehow slipped out without my knowledge? But how? Scarlett had set a cosmic barrier to prevent her prisoner from escaping. Hitchhiking in my aura had been the only way she'd escaped before. Had some unsuspecting victim wondered in accidently and unwittingly provided Careen with an out? I doubted it—however, indecision froze me to the spot.

I rattled the knob. Locked, and I had the only key in my apron pocket. My hand closed around the hard object. Yep, still here in my pocket. I fingered the key, fighting the overwhelming urge to enter. I withdrew it from my pocket and slipped it into the lock.

"Don't do it, Jolene," Deena's voice whispered in my ear. "Remember your warning?"

I swung around to peer into my sister's impish face. "Good timing, sis. I almost visited disaster on my own head. God, I'll be glad when this is over."

"When do you think that will be?"

I grabbed her by the arm and steered her into the empty kitchen. "You didn't say anything to Mama or Billie Jo, did you? I mean about me helping Bradford with his investigation?"

"Absolutely not." She let out a muffled sound of exasperation. "There's enough going on without adding another problem. Do you believe we'll ever be able to use the facial room for something other than a ghost hotel?"

"I'm thinking of asking the Catholic Church to come in and bless the shop," I answered honestly. "That is as soon as Careen is on her way home."

"Any idea of when that will be?"

"Tomorrow."

"Today would be better."

"Scarlett won't be back until tomorrow."

"What time?"

"I don't know, Deena. Scarlett hardly checks with me with her comings and goings. We're at her mercy."

Annoyance crossed her face. "Atlanta looks better and better every day."

"You know, dead people live in Atlanta, too," I reasoned.

Her expression indicated I'd grown two heads and a tail. "I swear sometimes I believe you need to be institutionalized."

"At times, I do too." I gave her a sisterly hug, turned on my heel and waltzed out the door and back to my station where Mrs. Benson waited for her comb out.

The rest of the day passed in a blur. Every thirty minutes I'd check my phone for any new updates from Bradford, and by closing I craved a ten-gallon bucket of Margaritas to put a lid on my anxiousness. After waiting for the salon to empty out, I once again pressed my ear to the facial room door to hear a faint rustling coming from within. Assured that Careen remained in her pink prison, I locked up the salon and drove home free from any encumbrances.

Once home, I showered and changed into black jeans and T-shirt, made a light supper and spent some time in my home office paying bills and answering emails from long distance friends and family.

Finished with obligations, I picked up the phone and punched in Billie Jo's number. Earlier today, I hadn't been able to pick her brain about a certain book with Mama's big ears tuned into every word.

Billie Jo answered on the first ring. "Hey, I was just gettin' ready to call you. Something's up so spill it."

I choose my words carefully, not wanting to place any unnecessary strain on her delicate condition. "I finally broke down and read one of Vanessa's Dark Enchantment books. I don't see what all the fuss is about."

Her heavy sigh echoed over the line. "You're lying, but I'll bite. How can I help you?"

I dove in. "I'm confused about Queen Lada's lair."

"The House of the Rising Sun?"

"Yeah, that's it. What's so special about an ordinary castle in the hills?"

"Nothing's special, Jolene, that's what makes it extraordinary."

"You lost me."

Billie Jo heaved another sigh. "The Queen of the Vampires resides in an ordinary dwelling under the noses of the local townspeople. Queen Lada hides in plain sight."

"How does the name, House of the Rising Sun, fit in the story?"

"Damn, Jolene, use the brains God gave you." Billie Jo huffed. "The morning sun bathes the Queen of Evil's dwelling in light. Sunlight kills vampires. The subtext suggests she's looking for her final exit or, and this is where Vanessa's brilliance shines through, Queen Lada is seeking redemption for the evil she's perpetuated. Hence, *House of Secrets*.

I thought about this for a moment surprised at my sister's insight into the literature and what this could mean in my search for Vanessa van Allen. And I have

169

to admit, I still couldn't grasp the concept.

In my silence, Billie Jo's aggravation echoed over the line. "All of this is explained in the first book, Jolene."

"The first book?"

"Yeah, the first book, *Twisted Kiss*."

I groaned. "I don't believe I have the stomach to read another. This stuff makes my insides quake. How do you stand the vulgar sex? Mama would stroke out if she knew you read this garbage."

"Seems I'm not the only one, Twisted Sister," Billie Jo pointed out. "And this baby owes his or her existence to Book Three: *The Last Awakening*."

"Information I don't need, Billie Jo," I explained. "Keep it light and simple is my mantra."

"So now that we've had a book club meeting, how about telling me why all the questions about the Dark Enchantment Vampire Series? And don't waste my time with anything other than the truth. I'm not an invalid with this pregnancy."

I considered her request and decided to share my latest adventure with her. Of course, not until she promised to keep our parents in the dark. With a solemn promise, I spilled my guts, ghosts and all. Billie Jo loved it and complained about being kept out of the loop. Couldn't be helped I explained. Maybe next time if there was one. That seemed to satisfy her.

"I'll skim through the books again for any other clues," she promised and disconnected the line.

For the tenth time, I glanced at my watch. Nine o'clock had come and gone and still no word from Bradford. With each passing hour, the clue grew colder. Pacing the den, I reached for my phone on the coffee table and punched in his number. Damn, voicemail. Frustrated with the delay, I tucked the Pink Panther in my back waistline, grabbed my keys, and left the house. Firing up the Mustang, I backed out the drive and took off for the Maco mansion.

Chapter Nineteen
The Old Maco Mansion

The ivy-covered two-storied house hunkered back from the street behind a screen of overgrown pine trees and bushes. The once manicured lawn was now strewn with prickly weeds, pinecones, straw, and fallen branches. In the faint light of the moon, behind a rusty gate, I could detect the broken stone steps leading to the front sagging wooden porch and the door beyond. I killed the engine and headlights and peered from the safety of my car at the dark, creepy mansion, once again questioning the wisdom of my decision. Even with the Pink Panther within hands' reach, I realized I had wasted my time in coming here. No way would I risk my neck in the condemned house. Best to return home and wait for Bradford.

I reached for the ignition just as my cell phone rang. I fished it from my shoulder bag. Thank God, Bradford.

"Jolene? Where are you? I'm at your house and you're not."

"I'm at the Maco mansion," I answered with relief.

"What are you doing there?"

I told him, much to his displeasure.

"Don't leave the safety of your car, you hear. I'm on my way."

The line disconnected, and I rolled up the driver's

window for extra precaution, determined to stay put and out of trouble. The warning was still echoing in my thoughts when a woman's scream rent the night. Startled by the piercing shriek coming from the deserted house, I automatically swung open the driver's door and bolted up the stone steps leading to the front door. With the Pink Panther cradled confidently in my outstretched grasp, I eased open the unlocked front door and inched inside the inky darkness, my ears sonically zeroing in on every creek and groan of the old house. With practiced steps, I crept slowly through the foyer and into a large open room, which appeared to be a parlor or living room, I wasn't sure. Broken and deteriorated furniture dotted the space. A musty, mildewed odor permeated my nostrils bringing tears to my eyes.

I froze as whispers of sounds echoed from the back of the house. Unsure how to proceed, I allowed the atmosphere of the house to settle around me. My psychic radar filtered disturbing cosmic vibrations flowing statically from the farthest reaches of the mansion. With my heightening intuitive faculties on high, I swept the house for celestial visitors. None. The house was clean of ghosts.

A woman's whimper reached my ears, but I couldn't distinguish the direction in this cavernous room. I would have to explore the mansion to discover the origin. On silent feet, I moved from room to room in semidarkness, with only the light of a half-moon streaming through dirty, broken, floor-to-ceiling windows covered in filthy drapes.

Upstairs, I paused on the landing, imagining the slightest footfalls on the dusty hardwood floor. Spooked with the unfamiliar territory, and wishing I'd heeded Bradford's warning and stayed safe in the car, I took several hesitate steps forward where the inky darkness swallowed me. Relying on my instinct, I inched along the wall, feeling for doorknobs, and then pressing my ear against the panel for any sign of movement or female distress. Even though I despised the vampire goddess, I'd come too far to stop now. Damn, Bradford, what's keeping you? Carefully, I eased open the last door at the end of the hallway and stepped inside the room.

A faint rustling from the corner of the room froze me to the floor. My arms ached from gripping my .38, but I dared not lower them. Sweat beaded on my brow and upper lip, and my heartrate quickened as I tried to still my racing mind. What now? Someone or something was in the room with me as I could hear faint gasping breaths.

With the suddenness of an exploding bomb, a match flared, briefly creating a circle of light, highlighting a feminine hand as it struck the match to a candle. The light expanded, and I froze with horror as the shadowed person brought the candle closer to a figure tied to a wooden chair.

Great balls of fire—Michael Halsey.

Didn't see that coming.

Or the heavy object crashing down on my head.

****

My next conscious sensation was one of extreme pain. I groaned as I rolled over to my side and tried to lift my splitting head from the dusty floor. My stomach heaved and emptied itself. Wiping my hand across my mouth, I managed to push myself upright and lean against the wall. Everything began to swim, and I inhaled deep breaths to dispel the dizziness. The pounding in my skull deepened with every agonized breath.

Bradford's frantic voice penetrated the fog settling over me. How long had I'd been out, I hadn't a clue. Bradford's expected presence suggested not long, a couple of minutes at the most. Finally, the beam of a flashlight swung over me and Bradford knelt by my side.

"Be still," he ordered as he wiped my mouth with his handkerchief, then examined my head. "You have a gash on your scalp." I winced as he pressed the handkerchief against the bleeding wound. Bradford radioed for backup.

"I'm fine other than you pressing my brains into my sinuses," I protested, and reached to brush his hands from my sore head. "Take it easy, will ya? And I don't need the paramedics."

"I say you do. What happened?" His tone remained gentle, although, I knew he wanted to thrash me for disobeying his order to stay put.

I drew a shaky breath. "I heard a woman's scream and came to investigate."

"I told you to stay put."

"Um, I know, but I just reacted. I couldn't stand by and allow another killing." My hands trembled as I fought nausea. "I found Michael Halsey tied to a chair in the corner. Did you find him?"

"The house is empty. CSU is in route." He reached for my hands. "Do you think you can stand?"

A wave of dizziness seized me as I took his hands and climbed to my feet. "No, not yet." Bradford gently lowered me back to a sitting position, keeping my hands in his.

"Could you identify any others? Vanessa?"

"No, her face remained in the shadows when she lit the candle, but the hands were definitely female. Who else could've it been other than Vanessa? This is her last known position."

"And there's a third person involved," he said with certainty.

The distance echo of arriving sirens interrupted our conversation. Bradford climbed to his feet, and handed me his flashlight and my gun. "I'll show them in. You okay?"

I cradled my .38 in my hand. "Now I am, but hurry back. This place gives me the creeps."

"Any ghosts of the past hanging around?"

"No, it's the living I'm worried about."

Bradford chuckled. "At least you're in good spirits. Be right back."

I made a continual sweep of the room with the flashlight as Bradford's footsteps sounded down the hall. Although I had a splitting headache, my stomach had settled down, and the dizziness had abated. I had survived the attack with merely a cut scalp and accompanying headache.

My third escape from the Death Angel.

God, what a morbid thought.

Damn, Deena's right. This ghost thingy was out of hand and had to stop. Time for an intervention from the professional ghostbusters. Hopefully, Madame Mia had out-of-town connections. This required the best of the best in the business, and Madame Mia didn't quite make the cut.

I retrained the light beam on the empty corner chair, my thoughts racing to piece together Vanessa and her cohort's quick escape, as I hadn't seen a vehicle of any kind when I arrived. The dilapidated rear garage hardly seemed a likely place to stash a getaway car. I thought again of Careen observing Vanessa with Snellgrove in the graveyard. Could he be the third person? Or could she have misinterpreted the interaction? More questions without answers.

The approaching male voices and footfalls on the stairs announced Bradford's return with the paramedics, and I swung the flashlight beam to the door. One man and a woman EMT accompanied Bradford into the room.

"I'm fine, really," I whined as the paramedics squatted down beside me. "Just a small cut on my head."

The female paramedic slipped on medical gloves. "Let me be the judge of that." She probed the cut while Bradford trained a light over my head. The other paramedic slipped a blood pressure cuff over my arm.

The wound turned out to be minor and only required a butterfly bandage, but an egg-sized lump had formed under the cut. Even though Bradford and the EMTs insisted I go to the ER, I refused, and once standing steadily on my feet, they backed off. The paramedics packed up their first-aid boxes and left, leaving Bradford and I alone in the upstairs room, although reverberations drifted from downstairs announcing the arrival of backup.

I shook off Bradford's hand. "Any sign of Michael or Vanessa?"

He stepped over to the empty chair. "None, yet.

Are you sure of what you saw?"

"I'm sure. Michael Halsey was tied to that chair."

Bradford joined me at the door. "CSU will sweep the entire house for any evidence. In the meantime, let's get you home."

Since my headache hadn't abated, I didn't argue and allowed him to lead me downstairs and out to my car. He opened the passenger car door. "Get in."

"No, I can drive."

He ran a hand through his dark hair, looking weary. "Why must you be stubborn?"

"Because I can, that's why. I'm perfectly capable of driving myself. You have work to do." Shouts from the backyard halted our discussion.

"Stay here," Bradford ordered and dashed in the direction of the raised voices. I considered disobeying, but my head splitting in two argued for the passenger seat, so I chose that option. With my head back against the headrest, I closed my eyes and took deep, calming breaths, which eased the throbbing pain.

"Jolene, honey, open your eyes."

My eyelids popped open, and my head snapped up at Granny Tucker's voice, and the sweet scent of pipe tobacco drifted in front of me, filling me with a sense of well-being that my grandparents were close by.

"I'm listening, Granny. What are you trying to tell me? Scarlett promised your message would become clear in time, but it hasn't. Please tell me what you mean."

Silence. Only the fading scent of Grandpa's tobacco lingered. Frustrated with the continuing mystery, I climbed out of the car and stood on the sidewalk in complete confusion under the golden pool of light raining down from the streetlamp. The muted sounds of male voices reverberated from the back, bringing my attention to the commotion of the investigation. Without much thought, I followed the voices around to the rear of the house where I spotted Bradford and a circle of men casting tire tracks leading from the crumbling garage.

So my assumption had merit. A getaway car had been stashed out of sight. Bradford detached himself from the group and strode over to my side. For several seconds we stood in silence.

"Found something interesting?" I watched the officers with fascination.

"Car tracks leading from the garage if you can believe it."

"I can believe anything."

"You sound tired."

"I am, thought I'd go on home."

"I'd feel better if Officer Clark tagged along."

"He's going to anyway." I gave him a half-smile. "Right?"

"Just a precaution, mind you." Bradford pecked me on the cheek. "I'll check in with you tomorrow."

Officer Clark tagged my Mustang all the way home, and pulled into my driveway behind me. He waited until I'd gone inside and turned off the carport lights before leaving. In the kitchen, I downed a couple of aspirins, poured a bowl of milk for Tango, and made a cup of hot herbal tea. With tea in hand, I padded down to my bedroom and placed the steaming cup on the nightstand, shed my clothing, and took a quick shower.

When I emerged from the bathroom, Tango lay in the middle of the bed, cleaning himself, his loud purring a comforting sound to my tired ears. I joined him on the bed and sipped the hot herbal tea, my fuzzy mind trying to grasp the events of the night.

Finally, my eyelids fluttered closed, and I turned off the light and settled down to sleep. I must've dozed for several hours before I roused from my slumber disturbed by troubling dreams. Rolling over, I switched on the bedside lamp. 3:44 a.m.. Fully awake, I propped up my pillows to lean against, and allowed my mind to travel back to every harrowing moment. The frightened scream. The first step inside the creepy mansion. The fruitless search from room to room. Climbing the stairs to investigate the faint sounds from upstairs. Entering the last door at the end of the hallway. The faint rustling from the corner. The flash of a match strike. A woman's hand. Michael Halsey tied to the chair. Exploding pain. Unconsciousness.

Wait. Go back, Jolene. Think. You're missing something important.

"Jolene, honey, open your eyes." Grandma Tucker's voice echoed again in my mind. Excited now, I jumped up from bed and paced the bedroom floor, my thoughts racing. Back, I went, replaying every second of the night until suddenly, like the unexpected flare of a match in the inky darkness, I remembered what had awoken me.

The ring!

I froze in my tracks, my mind tumbling over the brief glimpse of a ruby ring on the hand of the shadowed figure towering over a gagged Michael.

Gagged! And beaten! Damn, how'd I miss that? What else had I forgotten? Needing a caffeine infusion to stimulate my energy level, and appease my addiction,

I headed into the kitchen and started a pot of strong, black coffee. Tango ambled in shortly thereafter and settled at my feet.

As I waited for the coffee to finish dripping, I grabbed colored pencils and a notebook from my office and sat at the kitchen table to draw a simple rendition of the ruby ring. As I continued to stare at the simple drawing, a sense of recognition came over me. I'd seen the ring before. Recently. But where?

Two cups of coffee later, I was still drawing a blank, but filled with the certainty that I'd seen the expensive ring before. Not on Vanessa. She only wore sapphires I'd learned from a quick Internet search. Someone at the Halloween party? I made a quick list of the women I remembered being there, but was unsuccessful in conjuring an image of their jewelry. Perhaps Bradford would know. I reached for my cell phone and noted the time. 4:30. I hesitated. Too early, I'd better wait for the sun to come up.

I poured another cup of coffee, and prowled restlessly around the kitchen, too keyed up to sleep. With two hours to burn, I dug through the pantry until I found a box of brownie mix and a can of chocolate frosting. From the freezer I pulled a bag of chopped pecans harvested from the farm. Ten minutes of prep, and into the oven they went, and I sat down at the table with another cup of coffee and waited for the sun to come up.

Chapter Twenty
Screw Christian Upbringing

Scarlett showed up on my doorstep just as the morning light breeched the kitchen window and struck me full in the face. She gave no warning of any kind. Just appeared sitting across from me at the kitchen table with a toothy smile on her foxy face. Keyed up on caffeine, I dropped my empty cup on the table with a clatter and colored the kitchen with a few choice words. Scarlett didn't bat an eye, just smiled wider. "Good morning, girlfriend, I'm here to collect my prisoner. Hey, brownies."

"Well, she's not here, dumbass," I countered, perturbed at her chirpy tone. Not only jittery and hyped up, tiredness skirted just below the nervous twitter brought on from an overload of caffeine.

Scarlett hiked a haughty brow. "What's got your ass tied in a knot? I thought you'd be glad to see me."

I heaved a nervous sigh, and pushed away from the table. "I am glad to see you, really. I'm a little out of sorts this morning, Scarlett." I poured another cup of black coffee.

"I believe you've had enough, don't you?"

I stared down at the steaming liquid and agreed, pouring it down the sink. "I am kinda overdosing."

"Why don't you tell me what's bothering you?" She patted the chair seat next to her.

I took my seat and gave her a detailed report of the last three days. "And this mystery just keeps getting weirder."

"A ruby ring, you say?"

I shoved the crude drawing across the table. "Do you recognize it?"

She shook her head. "Can't say that I do."

"I wonder if Careen—"

"Oh no," Scarlett cut me off. "My prisoner is heading to Purgatory, not on another wild goose chase. I'm telling you Vanessa van Allen is on the list."

"Have you seen her up there?"

"No."

"Then what's the harm in asking one question?"

"Claiborne, you really push my buttons."

I pushed back a tangle of kinky hair, and climbed to my feet. "Join the crowd, Scarlett. Give me a few minutes to dress and we'll head out."

"If I do this, you have to promise not to interfere again. Agreed?"

"Agreed."

I showered and dressed in record time and placed a quick call to Bradford. He didn't pick up the call. I left a message for him to stop by the house, grabbed my purse and bagged lunch, and headed off to the salon. Five minutes later, I pulled into the rear parking lot and entered the quiet shop. I deposited my lunch in the refrigerator before unlocking the facial room door and stepping inside to see Careen shackled to Scarlett's side with the golden handcuffs.

Careen's eyes burned with fire at my entrance. "You lied," she accused in a venomous voice. "Left me here with an empty promise. Now, I'm shackled to this bitch!"

Scarlett jerked hard on the handcuffs. "Settle down. What's done is done. Your time on earth is complete."

"I'm sorry, Careen, but I couldn't haul you around with me any longer. Really, we're not compatible. You make me sick."

"Just show her the picture, so we can get out of here," Scarlett ordered in a strong voice. "I've got another job lined up."

I quirked an eyebrow at her. "Far away, I hope."

"My presence has been requested out at Pineridge Plantation."

A mental picture formed in my mind of the magnificent antebellum plantation on the far reaches of the county. "I thought that issue had been resolved last year. What could possibly be wrong now?"

"This isn't about the living, Claiborne, so give it a rest. Show her the picture. I'm in a hurry."

A stubborn expression planted itself on Careen's face as I shoved the picture under her nose.

"Well? Do you recognize the ring?"

She was silent for a moment. "The bloodstone is remarkable."

"Is that a yes?"

She shrugged in a bored manner. "That's for me to know and for you to find out."

Scarlett gave another vicious yank on the handcuffs. Sparks flew. "Answer Jolene's question or I'll make your trip home a living hell."

Careen flashed a bright red. "Okay, okay. It caught my attention at the Halloween book launch."

I spoke up. "Do you remember the woman wearing it?"

"No, too many people in costume and my mind was elsewhere."

"Good enough." Scarlett turned to me. "Well, this is goodbye for now. You're on your own from here. Good luck." With those parting words, she and Careen faded away.

Satisfied with the progress I'd made, I relocked the facial room door and left the salon as it was too early to hang around, and drove home. Since I had a couple of hours to kill before work, I cleaned the house and fixed myself a small breakfast. The phone rang a summons a bit after seven. I groaned at the caller ID. Damn. Preston. Not the person I wanted to speak with right now, but I couldn't ignore him.

"Hello," I greeted in a neutral tone.

"Hey, cutie," his mellow voice came over the line. "I'm in the neighborhood and need some time with my girl."

Those loving words tore right through my heart and conscience. God, what on earth am I doing wanting two men? How do I get myself untangled from the quicksand of desire? My Christian upbringing commanded only one man per woman. Right now, as things stood, I was playing two fiddles, or better yet, letting two fiddles play me. However, I *wanted* Preston and Bradford in my bed. Both of them. Not at the same time, of course. I'm not that kinky.

My emotions whirled and swirled as the memories of Preston's love play planted themselves in my mind, and I grew warm with anticipation. Preston had great stamina. A man with a slow hand. Glancing down at my watch, I noted I had just enough time for some good ole fashioned stress relief.

185

Screw my Christian upbringing.

"I'll leave the kitchen door unlocked," I purred in my most seductive voice. "I believe you know the way to Satisfaction Lane." I chuckled with intent.

His quick intake of breath echoed over the line. "Just what the doctor ordered."

The line disconnected, and I hurried to the bedroom and pulled a condom out of the nightstand, then shucked off my clothes down to my voluptuous nakedness, and kicked Tango out of bed. Arranging myself over the tussled covers, I posed seductively facing the door. The instant he crossed the threshold, he would see my treats.

Several minutes later, the kitchen door opened and closed. I could hear footfalls coming down the hallway toward the bedroom. I licked my lips to moisten them and spread my legs a fraction for enticement. Anxious now, I kept my eyes glued to the bedroom door expecting Preston any second.

However, Mama walked in.

We screamed in unison. Mama threw up her hands to shield her eyes, while I scrambled from the bed in search of my clothes scattered about the carpeted floor.

"What are you doing here, Mama?" I howled, as I pulled on my panties and jerked my lace bra off the wardrobe tree. "Why can't you knock like other people, or better yet, ring the damn doorbell?"

Mama snatched up my jeans and threw them at me, her eyes afire. "Because I left you a message telling you I'd be right over, and I thought you'd be expecting me. Your father dropped me off. However, appears I'm not the person you expected."

I glanced over at the blinking message machine on

the nightstand. Why hadn't I noted that earlier? Geez. I had the brains of a warthog.

The kitchen door opened and closed. Oh, good Lord, Preston!

"Jolene." His voice rang down the hallway. "Get ready for your man because I'm hungry for some twinkie pie."

Heat suffused my face at Mama's thunderous expression. Feeling the wrath to come, I hastily drew on my blouse and scrambled for the door to head him off, but Mama blocked the doorway and turned to meet my lusty visitor.

He skidded to a halt just outside my bedroom, his face the color of Mr. Turner's new red barn, and his hands busily re-buttoning his shirt. "Uh, Mrs. Tucker, uh, I'm, uh, surprised to see you, uh, here."

Mama slanted a reproving look with hands on hips. "I just bet you are, *Dr. Neally.* Now, about this twinkie pie."

"It's not what you think, Mrs. Tucker," he stammered. "Honestly, Jolene is a fabulous baker."

"Uh, huh, I know all about Jolene's prowess in the kitchen, *Dr. Neally.*"

I gasped at her audacity, and walked over to the nightstand and pulled out a pair of scissors. "Here." I handed them to her.

Mama gave me a hard look. "What's this for?"

"So you can cut the damn umbilical cord." I snickered, furious and embarrassed with her intrusion and ready to pitch a classic Southern girl hissy fit.

The kitchen door opened and closed. "Jolene." Bradford's voice echoed down the hallway. "I hope you've recovered after our late-night excitement."

187

Two pairs of startled eyes bore into mine. I groaned. "It's not what you think." My voice sounded guilty even to my own ears.

Mama snipped the scissors for emphasis. "Then you'd better start explainin'."

****

Turns out I didn't have too. Bradford took one look at our ragtag group as we entered the kitchen and accessed the situation correctly. I believe my disheveled appearance along with my horrified expression, and Preston's awkwardly buttoned shirt provided a telling clue. If the situation bothered him, he didn't show it, because he gave me a wink, and said in a casual voice, "Jolene, make a fresh pot of coffee while I fill in the blanks for your visitors."

Mama and Preston took a seat at the table as I busied myself with the coffee and fixings.

"Now, let me start by saying that our late-night excitement was in the form of a police investigation. Jolene is helping me with a missing person's report only in an unofficial capacity." His tone reflected his authoritative position. "She has been helpful in the past, and I needed her special insight with this case."

Mama addressed me as I placed the cream and sugar on the table. "Is that special insight responsible for that gash on your head?"

"It helped," I shot back.

"Sam, I don't mean to pry, and I'm not questioning your story, but there's more to the story. Give it to me straight, or I'll make a special trip down to the station and have a nice quiet chat with your boss." Mama's tone was brittle. "I don't like my little girl being used by the police to root out criminals."

"And I'll join her," Preston added, his gaze locked on mine. "What's going on between you two? Is my girl keeping company with another?"

I thumped the plate of brownies on the table. "I'm not your little girl, Mama." I turned to stick my finger under Preston's nose. "And I'm not your girl, either, so both of you knock it off. I'm a willing participant and don't want or need your input."

"As you wish." Preston got up from the table and stomped out the kitchen door, slamming it behind him.

Damn, another one bites the dust. My strike out average had reached one hundred percent. Oh, well, perhaps I'd take a break from the dating scene for a while until I could enroll in a life management course out at the community college.

"Feel better now that you've run another man out of your life?" Mama asked in a sweet tone meant to aggravate me. "I'm mighty upset about this twinkie pie business."

Bradford choked on his coffee and set his cup down with a clink. Mama turned her full radar vision on him. "Um, so I guess you know all about this?"

His face burned red. "That is a question I'd rather not answer, Mrs. Tucker. This is between you and your daughter, and I'm wise enough to know when to keep my mouth shut."

Mama stirred sugar into her coffee cup, a wicked smile on her craggy face meant to rattle my cage. "Shameful. That's what it is. I can't imagine what your daddy would say if he knew how his daughter is carrying on." Her eyebrows arched mischievously. "And at her age, too!"

Bradford and I shared a knowing look, and I stifled

a giggle at his incredulous expression. Thankfully, Mama noticed my crude drawing on the table and picked it up.

"What's this about?" She stopped studying the drawing. "This looks like Betty's antique engagement ring."

"Betty van Allen?" Bradford's tone reflected his inner calm. My mouth opened and closed with surprise, and then speculation. Could Vanessa's mother be in on this scam? The third party? The lump on my head throbbed with remembrance.

"You say it's Betty van Allen's antique engagement ring?" I repeated for clarification.

Mama shook her head. "No, I said it looks like Betty's antique engagement ring."

Bradford picked up the drawing. "In all the time I dated her daughter, I never saw her wear the ring."

"That's because it was stolen long ago," Mama explained. "The ring belonged to Alfred van Allen's great-grandmother and had been passed down through the generations through the firstborn son. Vanessa was just a child when it went missing."

"So, you can't positively identify the ring?" Bradford asked.

Mama frowned. "I just said that. The ring in the drawing is similar to the ring I remember seeing on Betty's hand when she and Alfred wed. It's been ages, and my memory isn't what it used to be. I could be completely wrong in my assumption."

A truck horn sounded outside. "There's Harland now." She pushed away from the table. "I've got an eye appointment in fifteen minutes, so I don't have time to get to the bottom of this matter." She swung her gaze from me to Bradford. "I'm not done with this conversation, Sam. I don't like Jolene mixed up in police business. Find a way to work without her *special insight* or I will."

Mama placed a kiss on my cheek at the door. "I'm mighty ashamed of you, Jolene Tucker Claiborne. Twinkie pie indeed. Sleeping with two men. What would Becky think if she knew? "She didn't wait for my response, but launched ahead. "You need to get married and settle down with one man like your sisters."

I sighed with exasperation. "Give it a rest, Mama. Every dog should have a few fleas."

True to Mama's standards, she broke contact, gave Bradford a quick red-faced nod, and pinched me hard on the arm before bolting out the kitchen door.

When I turned back to Bradford, his face still held traces of embarrassment. "Lord, Jolene, I'll never be able to face her again now that she knows."

I shrugged. "Serves her right. Next time she'll ring the damn doorbell."

Chapter Twenty-One
No News Ain't Necessarily Good News

After Mama split the scene, we decided to divide and conquer. Bradford would pay a visit to Betty van Allen, and I would attend the Whiskey Creek Writers Guild meeting this afternoon at the library. Perhaps between the two of us we could fish out more information on the mysterious ruby ring, and we'd meet back up here at my house later in the evening to compare notes. Since Bradford had received a summons from Sheriff Snellgrove, he took off and I headed in to work.

The day passed without incident, and by four, I hung up my apron and drove over to the library on Main Street for the writers meeting. Uncertain what to expect, I'd brought along a notebook and an essay I'd written back in high school to pass off as a work-in-progress, or WIP, in writer's lingo.

The librarian at the main desk gave me directions to the upstairs room set aside for the meeting. When I entered, a dozen heads turned my way and I bobbed a greeting—not recognizing a soul from the Halloween party. I took a seat between two old biddies with their noses pointed toward the ceiling. Both ignored me but I kept my smile in place, not bothered by their snobbery.

"Welcome to the Whiskey Creek Writers Guild meeting." A young woman at the head of the table rose to her feet. "My name is Kathy Dickson, and I write poetry. Let's go around the table and everyone introduce themselves and tell what genre they write."

When my turn came, I pushed back my chair and stood. "My name is Jolene Claiborne, and I'm a wannabe novelist."

"You're Annie Mae's daughter," a man voiced. "I remember you from the book launch." He smiled, his greedy gaze roving suggestively over me. "The Lone Ranger if I'm not mistaken."

I returned the old goat's smile, silently wishing I could pluck his eyes off my boobs and slam them back into his wrinkly, ancient face. "Yes, I'm Annie Mae's daughter."

"What brings you here today?" Kathy questioned in a neutral voice.

"I heard Vanessa van Allen might be in attendance." My gaze registered their reaction and swiftly moved over their hands. No ruby ring. Plenty of diamonds though. "I believe she has a lot to offer a budding new author."

"As you can see, she's not here." Kathy's smile withered. "Vanessa's in isolation as she finishes her latest work, but I'm sure you can learn a lot from the rest of us."

A murmur of agreement sounded around the room, and the old biddies shot me a disapproving look. I resumed my seat. "Do you know where she is—in isolation, I mean?"

"We wouldn't tell if we knew." A male voice contained a strong suggestion of reproach. "You need to mind your own business, missy."

"That's right," another voice joined his. "Writers

respect the sanctity of privacy."

Other voices of discontent joined in and for a second I considered taking the path of least resistance to the door. Christ, I'd ignited a firestorm of fervor. Why such passion for Vanessa? Or could the passion be for Careen posing as Vanessa? Hmm. Seems like I'd have to test the waters of discontent to bring out the sharks if I wanted any usable information on the missing writer and the ruby ring.

Kathy Dickson held up her hand for silence. "Everyone quiet down, please. I'm sure our new member didn't mean to offend anyone. Let's get to work, okay?" She directed the last at me, and I gave her a nod of acknowledgment.

The group quieted down but the atmosphere had turned frosty. When I observed their faces, dislike stared back full force. Not deterred, I dropped my gaze down to my notebook and jotted down a few questions I'd ask when the opportunity presented. I didn't have long to wait.

"We'll start with reading our WIP," Kathy began. "And last week Nan Green was skipped. We'll start with her. Remember to keep your critique short and non-judgmental."

Nan Green read her sizzling WIP. As she finished, dead silence settled over the room. Most appeared embarrassed by the lusty erotica similar to what I'd read of Careen's work. The old biddies fluttered together like sparrows on a windy day. The men in the group had their mouths clamped shut, but for the old goat—his eyes had refastened on my boobs. I wanted to slug him, instead I seized the opportunity to steer the conversation back to Vanessa since she was the reason for me being there in the first place.

"Since I'm new and I don't know anything, I find the writing compelling. However, it reads a lot like Vanessa's work. Has she been mentoring you long?"

All eyes shifted from me to Nan Green. She flushed under the scrutiny. "I don't believe my work much reflects hers, but she has given me some pointers in the genre."

"Jolene's right," a woman said. "Your work does mimic Vanessa's. You would do better to develop your own voice."

"I disagree," another piped up. "Nan's voice is uniquely hers. Vanessa's shifts with each book she writes."

"Nan isn't plagiarizing Vanessa," an older woman added angrily.

"Vanessa's work is shameful," commented one of the biddies. "Makes me cringe."

"Are you disparaging Nan's work, Agnes?" an older gentleman with a beautiful mane of white hair questioned from the far end of the table.

"That is not what I'm saying," Agnes sputtered. "Nan is a fine writer, Robert."

Frustration crossed Kathy Dickson's face. "Enough," she shouted over the rising voices. "This is not how we conduct our meetings." Here she shot me a bleak, tight-lipped smile. "Jolene, you're disrupting the group with accusations of plagiarism. I understand you're new, but please keep your comments to the writing and not the writer."

The other group members gathered around Nan as tears pooled in her eyes. Agnes remained in her seat, but gave me the evil eye as if I'd killed her BFF. Damn, no wonder Mama didn't attend these meetings anymore. Panty-grippers. All of them.

Robert, with the beautiful mane of white hair, stood to his feet and pointed a long finger at me. "You, young lady, are no wannabe writer. What is your true motive for invading our group?"

Kathy Dickson shot to her feet. "I call this meeting to order. Sit down, Robert. There's enough drama without you adding to it."

Okay. Enough of the madness. My plan had failed. Time to confess up. I pushed from the table and stood. "Folks, Robert's right, I'm here on false pretenses." Gasps of indignation followed, but I lunged ahead. "I'm trying to locate Vanessa van Allen."

"But I told you that she's in isolation to finish her book," Kathy added scathingly. "We have no knowledge of her whereabouts."

"Vanessa is not in isolation as you believe," I said. "She's officially missing from the Baconton Writers' Retreat. I'm surprised you don't know as it's been on the local news."

"Most of us don't watch the news, my dear," one of the old biddies said. "Fake news, you know. Instead, we read books."

"Why the subterfuge?" Agnes accused. "We would've answered your questions if you'd approached us with the truth."

"Agnes is right." Robert's tone had chilled. "You could've been truthful from the start. We would've helped in any way we could."

I fished the crude drawing from my notebook. "I'm sorry for that." I held up the drawing. "You can help me now. Do you recognize this ring?"

When the drawing had been passed to each member of the group and none had recognized the ring, I tucked it back into my notebook.

"Are you finished?" Kathy's tone indicated she'd grown tired of the interruption to her meeting.

"Has any one of you seen Vanessa since Halloween night?" I questioned.

Again, no one had.

Kathy left her place at the head of the table and came to stand beside me, her face cold and disapproving. "Now that you're done with your interrogation, I must ask you to leave and never return."

The old biddies gave me the once-over and lifted their chins to the ceiling. I flushed under the heated looks thrown my way, and headed for the door with my Southern pride tucked between my legs.

****

"Not much luck with the local talent, I take it."

I glanced up from my plate of chow mien, and shrugged. "No luck at all, Bradford. For the life of me, I don't understand how you became entangled with that bunch of kooks. Panty-grippers. All of them."

"Vanessa was the only writer I was entangled with, as you put it."

"The Queen of the Vampires is the biggest drama queen of them all." I snickered. "I'm just glad Mama's shifted her interest to the new baby and away from bestseller-dom."

"Bestseller-dom? I don't believe I've ever heard that term before."

I scooped up an egg roll. "I just made it up, but it describes the mania I witnessed firsthand this afternoon. God, and you thought I was high maintenance."

We were sitting at my kitchen table eating Chinese take-out. Bradford had turned up several minutes after I arrived home and had thought to bring dinner, thus sparing me the chore of preparing a meal.

Bradford chuckled. "Jolene, you're higher maintenance than a convention of writers, and you're the biggest drama queen I know."

"Am not," I protested, without much conviction and changed the subject. "So, how's Snellgrove's investigation coming along?"

"Careen's body has finally been released for burial. Her family has made arrangements to have the body shipped to Hawkinsville. Not much progress has been made to identify her killer."

"Find Vanessa and you'll have your killer," I mumbled with a full mouth of egg roll.

Bradford set down his glass of iced tea. "We have no proof that Vanessa killed Careen."

"Careen fingered her."

"I'm sure we can't use the murder victim's word in court. We need concrete proof that Vanessa pulled the trigger."

"What about Mini Pearl? Any progress on how she came to be the murder weapon?"

"Stolen guns are hard to trace." Bradford popped a shrimp into his mouth. "I'm still working on it."

"I thought you weren't on the case."

"Officially, I'm not, but that won't stop me. I've got my sources working on it, and I hope to have word soon."

"What about Snellgrove's possible tie to Vanessa? Careen swore she saw them together in the graveyard just before we found her body."

"I can't tie them together. I even came right out and asked him. He denies knowing Vanessa at all."

"What about Betty? Did she have anything of value to say?"

Bradford scooped up a forkful of fried rice and popped it into his mouth and chewed vigorously. "She wasn't home."

"I think we've hit a roadblock with this case. Of course, we could pay another visit to Madame Mia's and see what the spirits have to say."

"No."

"They were helpful before." I pushed up from my chair, went to the cabinet and reached for the aspirin bottle. My killer headache had returned full force.

Bradford laid down his fork. "It'll snow in July before I step another foot in that woman's establishment."

"Okay, so where do we go from here?"

"We wait for the facts to come in regarding the cast of tire tracks from out at the Maco mansion. You keep plugging into the Great Divide, and I'll keep my feet firmly on the ground here. I have a couple of leads I'm going to check out, and I need you to concentrate on the ruby ring. Understood?"

I nodded my head, my mind plotting out a few leads of my own. Umm. Bradford wanted me to plug into the Great Divide? Okay, I could do that, although not certain how much the spirits wanted to play. Scarlett certainly didn't cotton up to the idea. Too busy tracking down... Ah, wait a minute. My favorite ghost was at this precise minute trippin' the light fantastic at Pineridge Plantation. I glanced at the clock above the stove. 10:00 p.m. Not too late for a quick drive out to the plantation, and luckily, with a slight detour, a speedy drive by Vanessa's house to see if Betty had returned home.

Chapter Twenty-Two
In the Midnight Hour

Bradford stayed longer than expected and it was close to midnight even before I could fire up my Mustang and head out of town in the direction of Pineridge Plantation. With the hour being later than I wanted, if at all possible, I'd swing by Vanessa's house on the way home and see if the lights were on signaling Betty's return.

At this late hour, traffic was light and twenty minutes later I pulled onto the dirt tree-lined driveway leading to the manor house and parked in the shadows off the road. I killed the engine and took in as much of the scene before me as possible in the weak moonlight. Not much had changed since my last visit here close to a year ago. That had been the night I shared with Bradford his true linage to the Reddings of Pineridge Plantation, but that's a long story and told elsewhere.

Through the shifting shadows I could see the manor house had received a fresh coat of paint, but the barn still needed some TLC, and the trees and shrubs could use a good cutting back. Since Pineridge had been handed over to the State for historical preservation, improvements had been painstakingly slow, but steady. Taking the Pink Panther from its holster, I tucked it in the waistband of my jeans and upon alighting from my car, I paused. Scarlett hadn't specified what problem brought her out here, so I had no clue where to begin my search.

Again, I tried paging her in the universal SOS, but the line remained dead. Frustrated, but not discouraged, my gaze swept the dark house seeking any sign that the Turnipseeds—the longtime caretakers—were still up and about. Nothing. No movement to indicate life. With cautious steps, I picked my way through the pasture overgrowth until I reached the lone restored slave cabin a short distance from the house. I'd start there.

Taking a small flashlight from my pocket, I scanned the porch for any signs of wildlife before climbing the creaking steps to the front door. The handle turned easily, and the door inched open. I took a bold step inside the small one room cabin and immediately encountered a family of spirits not happy at the intrusion.

An older man, apparently the patriarch, detached himself from the rest. "Please kindly leave our home, miss." He spoke in perfect English despite his tattered clothing and dark skin. "We've done our time and deserve rest from the Master's hand."

"I'm not here to disturb you, sir," I addressed the ghost. "Or your family. I'll leave you in peace. I'm looking for a friend and thought she might be here."

A female spirit joined him. "Grandfather, she must mean Miss Scarlett. She's here in response to Rosemond's plea."

The old man dissipated, leaving the young female spirit. "Please excuse my grandfather. He's old and tired and seeking his eternal rest. You'll find your friend in the big house."

Not wanting to spook her, I kept my voice neutral.

"Why do you linger in this cabin when you can collect your reward on the Other Side?"

"Because Grandfather isn't ready to leave his home. We wait for him."

I caught a hint of her tears and wished her well and took my leave, retracing my steps back outside to the porch where the darkness swallowed me. Snapping on the small flashlight, I made my way to the big house and stood in indecision at the back door. Rattling the doorknob to find it locked, I scrutinized my surroundings, hoping to locate a good hiding place to stash a key. I no longer had one. Looking high and low, I came up with zip, and sighed in frustration and relief. Frustration that Scarlett wouldn't answer my repeated SOSs, and relieved that I couldn't enter the big house to search for her.

"Well, so much for wasted time," I told myself and spun on my heel intending to head for the car. That's when I noticed the tiny slit in the bricks along the boxwood hedge. With one finger I withdrew the key, surprised and aghast at how simple it would be for thieves to empty the house of historical treasures under the blanket of darkness.

As I stood in the shadows with key in hand, I rethought my plan to enter the house uninvited. I was the intruder here and should turn around and go home. Forget investigating. Let the law unravel the mystery of the two women. Yawning with fatigue, I replaced the key in its hiding place and skirted around to the front of the house all the while sending out the universal Morse code for help in hopes that Scarlett might deem it worthwhile to answer.

Not a peep. Okay, time to make rubber on the road.

Either that or use the key. Giving up isn't in my DNA, but my intuition warned me away from entering without an official invitation. With my mind settled, I made my way back down the dirt driveway staying in the shadows of the tree line for extra protection from prying eyes.

Back at the Mustang, I discovered two problems. One, a flat tire, and two, a dead cell phone battery. Great, I'd forgotten the car charger again. Now what? No means of communication and no knowledge of changing tires. Stranded by stupidity in the midnight hour. Story of my life. And then I lifted my eyes to the big house looming in the semi-darkness. There I could use the key and find help in the form of a landline, or I could wake the caretakers and request help the normal way. Sure, there'd be hard questions to answer. Like, what are you doing parked halfway down the driveway in the tree line at this time of night? But at least, I could avoid a trip to jail and another strike on my arrest record.

With the decision made, I climbed out of the Mustang and trudged back up the middle of the driveway, no longer caring about prying eyes. I intended to wake the household anyway.

At the back door, I knocked loudly several times. When no lights flicked on after a couple of minutes waiting, I repeated the action with more gusto with the same results. Apparently, the Turnipseeds weren't in residence. And since they weren't home, they wouldn't mind if I utilized the phone, I reasoned, it being an emergency after all. I would be in and out in a flash with no one the wiser. Drawing in a deep, frustrating breath, I retrieved the key out of its hiding place, unlocked the door, and slipped inside. Pausing to orient myself, and slow my pounding heart, I waited for my eyes to adjust to the inky darkness before moving into the connecting kitchen.

Mentally, I pictured the layout of the house and the location of the downstairs phone in the library at the back of the house. Way back. Okay, Claiborne, this is it, get a move on. With the tiny flashlight beam cutting through the murkiness, I headed for the library on silent feet, pausing only to listen for any sign of life. Hearing only the ticking grandfather clock in the entrance hall, I surmised that I was indeed alone in the creepy mansion. Since I had an unpleasant history with the place, and knew it was crawling with the spirits of the past, an uneasiness settled over me, and I found myself eager to use the phone and get out ASAP.

"Scarlett, are you here?" I whispered, hoping for a response as needing her help was the reason for my being here anyway. Down the hall, the misty shape of an old black woman garbed in a long, striped cotton dress with the traditional African head-wrap slave women favored materialized.

Tempy. The faithful house slave. Brave and beautiful in the face of hardship. The precursor of today's strong, modern black woman.

"The spirit you seek is here." The words planted themselves in my mind.

"Thank you, Tempy. You may seek your eternal rest now." I hoped to help this lost soul find her way heavenward.

Her eyes filled with pain. "No rest until all come home." She faded with the last word.

Tears stung my eyes as I thought about her

wandering about the house waiting for the last solider to return from the bloodied battlefield. How many souls had been brutally sacrificed to King Cotton? Over six hundred thousand men, women, and children had paid the ultimate price for freedom. Black or white, it didn't matter. Death doesn't recognize boundaries or skin color. It strikes when least expected.

Shaking off the morbid thoughts, I continued my silent way to the library, pausing only to whisper Scarlett's name, hoping she'd pop in for a chat. At the double doors to the library, I hesitated as an unknown jingle resonated from the front of the house. Hmm. Sounded like multiple keys clanging together as a person walked in my general direction. I threw a quick glance over my shoulder, then slipped inside the library, and pressed my ear against the panel. Nothing. Good. Just my overactive imagination working non-stop.

I directed the flashlight beam on my watch. 1:30. Would I be able to find help at this late hour? I found the phone on the antique desk and fished around for a phonebook. With my cell phone dead, I couldn't access Bluetooth, so it was up to my fingers to do the walking. After several attempts, I finally found a twenty-four hour garage service and gave the man directions to my location. Unfortunately, he was on another call and wouldn't be able to get to me for several hours. I'd have to sit tight until he showed up.

Hanging up the phone, I stashed the phonebook back to its assigned space and turned to leave, anxious to return to my car and lessen the chance of being caught in the mansion without permission. In the kitchen, Scarlett's misty form materialized out of the semi-darkness.

I stopped dead in my tracks, and gasped with surprise. "Must you do that? My heart almost jumped out of my chest."

"I'm here at your request, Claiborne. Get on with it, I'm busy." Her misty form wavered with energy. "What do you want?"

"Help with the van Allen case."

"That case is closed as far as Heaven is concerned."

"How can you say that when Vanessa hasn't been located?" I blew out an exasperated breath. "She killed Careen, and we have to find the proof. Bradford and I are still suspects in her death. I need your help."

"That's your problem, Jolene. I've been warned to stay away from you and do my job, and I intend to obey."

"You obey?" I challenged.

"Yes, obey," she squawked, her eyes burning with rebellious fire. "It's that or vacate my mansion on the south side for an upper berth in Hell. That's not happening, girlfriend, so drop it. You're on your own."

I had hit a dead end and felt a wave of tiredness and defeat wash over me. "You're right, Scarlett, it's my problem and I'll find a way." I heaved a mournful sigh and reached for the doorknob. "I won't bother you again."

"Wait."

My hand dropped to my side, but I didn't turn around. "I'm listening."

"Sheriff Snellgrove."

"What about him?" Silence met my question. I turned around. Scarlett had disappeared. Not wasting any time to think about Scarlett's clue, I skedaddled out of the mansion, stopping only to return the key to its hiding place, and hightailed it back to the safety of my car to wait for the man.

He woke me at dawn. Groggy with sleep, I exited my car while he changed the tire. Thankfully, the man was quick and efficient, and after ten minutes I was back on the road to Whiskey Creek. As I drew close to town, the Westgate neighborhood entrance came into sight. Although dead on my feet, I decided to swing by Vanessa's house anyway and see if Betty had returned home.

The sun crested the horizon as I pulled onto Dartmouth Drive, its golden tentacles reaching out to touch the shimmering white bricks of the towering house at the end of the street. I watched in amazement as the full force of the sun's rays bathed Vanessa's mansion in its sparkling light, and I knew with an inner certainty I had found the House of the Rising Sun.

Chapter Twenty-Three
Dig Up the Stink

Uncertain how to proceed, I parked several houses down from Vanessa's and allowed the morning silence to refresh me in hopes of forming a workable plan. The logical side of my brain argued that I should go home, down a pot of coffee, and call Bradford. The creative side screamed for action.

I chose somewhere in between. Consumed with the need for answers and caffeine, I drove the remaining distance to Vanessa's house and parked in the driveway. The garage door was closed, so I couldn't tell if anyone was home. Undeterred, I continued to the front door and rang the doorbell.

The instant the door swung open, the addicting aroma of coffee put a smile on my face, and I said a cheery good morning to the uniformed maid.

"Good morning to you, miss." Her smile didn't quite make it to her eyes.

I inhaled another whiff of coffee. "Is Mrs. van Allen home?"

"She's having breakfast."

"And it smells delightful. Would you mind seeing if she's receiving visitors?"

The maid stepped back and swung open the door. "Please follow me, miss?"

"Claiborne," I supplied with another smile. "Jolene

Claiborne."

She led me to a sitting room just off the kitchen, and I seated myself on a lovely blue print chair to wait for her return. A rumble in the lower regions of my stomach alerted me to the hour and the immediate need for nourishment. Especially coffee. I could feel the twittering of withdrawal as I waited. Clenching my trembling hands in my lap, I again inhaled the rich scent of roasted beans and sent out a silent plea for the gods to grant my wish for a strong cup of black coffee.

The maid appeared in the doorway. "Please follow me."

When we entered the breakfast room, I was delighted to see another place setting at the table. The chair had been pulled out, and I sat down across from Vanessa's mother, who smiled at me. "I'm surprised to see one of Annie Mae's daughters at my door at this early hour, Jolene. I hope there's no problem with your mother?"

I literally drooled as the maid poured coffee into the cup at my elbow. "Oh, no, Mrs. van Allen, Mama is fine." I lifted my eyes from the steaming cup to her. "I was in the neighborhood and wanted to check up on you. I know you must be frantic with worry about Vanessa."

"How sweet, my dear, I'm fine. Vanessa will return home soon." She waved a bejeweled hand, minus the ruby ring, at the maid. "Please prepare a plate for our guest, Sophia. I'm sure she's famished."

Her strange answer disturbed me, but I played it cool with a nod, and reached for my cup, taking several sips, almost dying on the spot as the strong, rich flavor exploded in my mouth. Definitely not my usual grocery store brand. One of the expensive brands. Probably packaged in gold leaf, for the rich and famous.

Sophia sat down a plate in front of me piled high with scrambled eggs, bacon, fruit and a buttery, flaky croissant before refilling my cup with the elixir of the gods. She then disappeared back into the kitchen without a word.

For several minutes, I concentrated on filling my belly with the deliciously prepared food, giving me some time to figure out how to proceed as I had launched into this visit without much thought. Really, I had to stop being as impetuous with my decisions as they kept landing me in difficult positions. I sighed inwardly with the knowledge that I would go to my grave with this wacky characteristic.

As I continued to eat, I kept a diligent eye out for the slightest activity within hearing range. Sophia's movements in the kitchen signaled morning cleanup. I ignored her and zeroed in on Betty van Allen sitting across from me with an interesting expression on her lined face.

Her shuttered gaze and furrowed brow suggested Vanessa's mother wasn't buying my cockamamie story of neighborly concern. No, those snake eyes, so like her daughter's, had a bull's-eye on me. For the first time, I realized that something about her bothered me. I couldn't put my finger on it, but the woman bugged me in a negative way. I shifted in my chair and set the empty coffee cup down. Time to get some answers.

"I can't remember when I've had a more delicious breakfast, Mrs. van Allen," I boasted in a sincere tone meant to put her at ease. "Thank you for inviting me to join you."

"I could do no other."

My face flushed hot at her tone. Although the South is known for its hospitality, there is an unspoken agreement that one calls before dropping in on a whim as every female deserves a chance to put on their "Sunday go to meetin' face" and present themselves in the best possible light. I had broken the golden rule of proper belle-dom—a serious offense—and Betty van Allen didn't appreciate being seen in her morning robe and makeup-free aging face. No, siree, those snake eyes accused. Mama would hear about this for sure. Well, too late to worry about it now, and since I was in hot water anyway time to swim with the sharks.

"I apologize for not calling, but my cell phone died, and I was worried about you all alone out here," I ventured. "Have there been any updates on Vanessa's whereabouts?" I watched her closely for any clue to her true feelings, and wondered if she knew about my run-in at the Maco mansion. And what about Careen? Had Betty known about the switch all along? Living in close quarters, how could she not know the difference between her daughter and a stranger? Unless mother and daughter's closeness is just a ruse. Possible. Mother and daughter could've conspired the fraud and hid the truth from Careen for some unknown reason. A scapegoat? For what? And why?

She peered at me over her coffee cup. "No updates, but I'm not worried. I told the police she can be particularly evasive when confronted with writer's block. She has disappeared many times before—only to show up when least expected. So you see, my dear, it's only a waiting game I've played many times before."

Since I knew these disappearances corresponded to

Careen assuming Vanessa's identity, I believed her, and had already begun to formulate my response. "So you're not concerned about the blood they found in her trashed cabin?"

"More likely she had a temper tantrum and accidently cut herself." Her tone remained relaxed at my raised brow. "Vanessa is high spirited and used to getting her way. She can be difficult at times."

"But you filed a missing person's report," I shot back, confused by the woman's attitude. If Mama had treated me and my sisters with such indifference, we might've turned out warped like Vanessa—a steroidal bitch on a witch stick! Poor thing.

She looked so exasperated that for a moment I thought she might slam down her cup and leave the table. "Vanessa's financial empire is vast and must be protected at all times, my dear. I filed the missing person's report at the advice of my attorney. I have all the legal documents necessary to protect Vanessa and myself." Her frosty smile set my physic frequencies tingling—a sure sign of a cosmic misalignment.

Jackpot. Now to dig up the stink. "You have durable Power of Attorney and control over her assets?" My mind tumbled over itself with pressing questions. With Careen dead, could her family have a financial claim to Vanessa's vast wealth? Could they prove Careen's authorship of the Dark Enchantment Vampire Series? What about the missing manuscript Vanessa claimed would be another bestseller? It was worth a fortune. And what about Michael Halsey and his role in this entanglement? Whatever it was, something had gone terribly wrong for Careen's brother.

The breakfast room grew quiet. Not even a peep

from the kitchen broke the silence as I sipped my coffee. Goose bumps peppered my skin as a subtle shift in the vibrational frequency penetrated my concentration, and the sweet aroma of pipe tobacco embraced me. My cup froze midway to my lips as my danger preceptors kicked into high gear.

Then, from the far reaches of the house, a shuffling noise and soft voices reached my hearing. A movement from my peripheral vision caught my attention, and I turned to see Sophia standing in the doorway leading from the kitchen. My eyes zeroed in on the butcher knife in her hand. Another beep-beep of the danger meter. Time to skedaddle. With a certainty, I knew the Queen of the Vampires had returned to her roost, and was right now, watching with evil intent.

I swung my gaze back to my hostess. Quick awareness flickered in the woman's golden eyes. Calculating and dangerous. A look I'd encountered before. My quest for information had now turned into a mission to get my sweet ass out of here before the Death Angel had another crack at me.

Fear poked me into action. With a light smile, I forced my hand to set down the cup and dab my mouth with the linen napkin resting in my lap. "Thank you for a delicious repast, Mrs. van Allen, but I must rush off. I have a full book of appointments at the salon." I hugged my shoulder bag close to my side and pushed back the chair. If either woman made a move in my direction, the Pink Panther would even the odds. I'd shoot first and ask questions later.

Betty mimicked my actions and climbed to her feet. "Please stay a while longer, my dear. I get lonely out here and would enjoy a longer visit with you." She moved to the block the entrance. "I can't let you leave without giving you a tour of the house."

I unsnapped my shoulder bag and slipped my hand inside to grasp my gun. "Some other time." The tension in the house built to a breaking point. "I told my sister, Deena, I would be stopping by your house for a short visit. If I don't arrive at the salon shortly, she'll be parked on your doorstep."

My hostess bought the lie and escorted me to the front door. "Please give my regards to your mother, Jolene," she said as I stepped outside onto the front porch. "I'll give her a call later today and thank her for having such a considerate daughter."

Not wasting any more pleasantries on her, I scurried back to my car and watched her disappear inside the house. Adrenaline coursed through my veins as I realized the implications of my discovery. Vanessa, and possibly, Michael Halsey, if they hadn't murdered him too, hid just within reach.

My luck held and I arrived home without a speeding ticket, burst through the kitchen door in a frenzy, and snatched up the receiver from the wall phone. Ignoring Tango's wail, I punched in Bradford's number.

"I found Vanessa," I gushed in a squeaky voice when he answered the call.

"Where?"

"In the House of the Rising Sun."

"Stop with the riddles, Jolene, just tell me."

"Her house."

"What were you doing there?"

"Long story, but I believe Betty could possibly have motive for wanting her daughter temporarily out of the way. And what if she was aware of Careen's presence all along? What if she's the mastermind behind all this?"

His sigh echoed over the line. "The details?"

I gave him a quick lowdown of my nighttime venture, including Scarlett's cryptic message about Snellgrove, my morning chat with Betty in which she admitted she had durable Power of Attorney over Vanessa's assets.

"You have to admit that's a powerful motive for kidnapping and murder."

"I doubt it, however, your information is helpful, Jolene, but promise me you'll stay out of harm's way. Remember your mother's warning to go to the Chief? I'll take it from here."

I frowned, ready to protest, but rethought my position. I had no further compulsion to return to Vanessa's house and face the old dragon and her fire-breathing brat. No, I needed to concentrate on Deena's wedding and Billie Jo's upcoming family addition. Plus, multiple issues needed ironing out at the salon. And then there was Preston, and how to mend that fence. Bradford leaving Whiskey Creek I would not think about at all.

"Don't give me another thought, Bradford. I have other fish to fry."

"Good girl. I'll keep you in the loop."

Satisfied, I disconnected the line, showered and dressed for work in a comfortable pair of dress slacks and heels, and headed out the door. With Vanessa's impending arrest, my mood had improved considerably, and I drove to work without a care in the world.

Deena greeted me at the rear entrance. Not good.

Her brown eyes gleamed fanatical with tension, and she held on to the doorknob as if it had plans to skip town.

"Jolene, you promised me." Her arms waved with every high-pitched word. "You promised."

Holy crap. There goes my carefree day. "Okay, Deena, calm down. I've neglected my duties as Maid of Honor, but today that ends. You have my full, undivided attention. I promise."

Deena's arms dropped to her side. "Well, I'm glad you finally recognized your neglect. I'm out of my head with this wedding and running the salon. Billie Jo is out of commission, and I haven't found a barber to take her place. Lizzie and Gail are at each other's throats over some man, and the nail tech gave her two-week notice this morning."

"We just hired her," I lamented. "What's Marisol's problem?"

"It's her man Lizzie and Gail are drooling over."

"Damn, there's enough single men in this town to go around, Deena."

"You and I know this, but those two dingbats don't." She flung out her hands in despair. "I've tried talking to them, but every time he walks through the door, they flutter around him like he's the only man on earth, which sets off Marisol, and bang, fireworks. The clientele is complaining about the noise. Atlanta is looking better and better."

I patted her cheek. "I'll call a staff meeting for this afternoon and put an end to this nonsense. At lunch, I'll swing by the beauty school and have a looksee at the barber students. This evening, you and I'll spend quality time tying up loose ends with your wedding. Sound like a plan?"

217

"It's a start, sis, but it's not the reason why I'm angry with you."

My restraint suffered a setback and anger crept into my voice. "Well, then what's the problem?"

"You'll see." She grabbed me by the arm and practically dragged me through the door to stop in front of the locked facial room. "Your invisible friends are back."

Chapter Twenty-Four
Steaks and Blackberry Wine

I pressed my ear against the panel, and from within the room I could hear the faintest rustlings like the furtive darts of a furry pest. "Maybe it's a mouse," I suggested.

"A mouse? Don't be silly," she scolded in a loud whisper. "The shop is sprayed regularly by an exterminator. And be quiet. We don't want to alert the staff."

"A rat then," I added in a whisper, and stepped away from the door, now certain we had a four-legged varmint residing in the salon. "I don't suppose you checked it out?"

Deena shook her head. "Open the gates of Hell? That's your specialty."

"Then it may not be what you think, sister, dear."

"Then what do you suggest we do, sister, dear?"

"Nothing. Let the rat have the room for the day. In the meantime, keep the door bolted shut. Whatever's in there, we don't want a client letting it out."

With the situation handled, we parted ways. Deena to her office and I to my first appointment, which happened to be a talkative Mrs. Eisenberg.

"How's my favorite client this fine morning?" I gave her a quick hug, then began laying out my tools on the counter.

She beamed a smile in the mirror. "Just fine. The Mister and I are taking an Alaskan cruise in the spring."

With Mrs. Eisenberg chatting my ear off, I worked fast, and before she could launch into another story, I had shampooed and rolled her hair and set her under the dryer. My next client also went quickly as did the rest of the morning. Just before noon, an unexpected visitor waltzed through the front door and made a beeline for my station. His massive presence created a stir of speculation among the patrons and sparked an undercurrent of electricity in the invisible realm, which had me uneasy and ready to hide. I laid down my scissors and comb on the counter as Sheriff Snellgrove approached me.

"May I have a private word with you, Miz Claiborne?" His hand rested on the butt of his sidearm, and his eyes had a sheen of purpose that gave me the willies.

Oh hell. This can't be good.

"Give me a minute to finish my client, and I'll be right with you." My voice quivered almost as much as my hand. I hated to admit it, but this man scared the living hell out of me. If he arrested me, I might disappear into some murky pond between here and Greenwood County never to be heard from again.

"Make it quick, Miz Claiborne. I ain't got all day." He tipped his hat and spun on his heels to stalk to the nearest chair in the reception area.

"More trouble?" My client's eyes reflected wild curiosity in the mirror. I could almost hear the telephone lines buzzing with flapping lips.

I finished with her hair, and watched her parade to the reception desk to pay her bill, a wide smile plastered on her face. Yep, headed straight for the nearest landline. This I knew because she refused to carry a cell phone. She bragged often that she got along fine without it this long and didn't plan to change.

Not bothering with cleaning up, I stopped by the reception desk to speak with Holly before leading Snellgrove into Deena's empty office, silently thanking my lucky stars she had left for an early lunch date with Ryder. After closing the door behind me, I motioned for him to have a seat in one of the chairs across from the desk.

"What can I help you with, Sheriff?" I sank down into Deena's plush desk chair and reached for a pencil to keep my hands from visibly trembling.

"It's about the Careen Halsey case." He removed his cowboy hat and perched it on his knees. "The cause of death has been officially ruled as a suicide. The case is closed." The corner of his mouth lifted in a sly smile. "I'm here to bring you a little peace seeing how you and Detective Bradford were implicated."

Since I knew this to be untrue, the news startled and disturbed me, but I kept my silence, not wishing to give away information that could land me in harm's way as Bradford had warned. Best to play dumb and let the sheriff have his say and get him out of here fast. If my suspicions about the man proved true, I needed to watch my step. One slip of the tongue could have dire consequences. My breathing quickened, and I leaned back in the chair and clasp my sweating hands together. "I appreciate you going out of your way to bring me good news."

"Well, there is another matter I need to bring up." His mean eyes flickered over me.

"Yes?"

He lifted a small clothbound bundle from his blazer pocket and placed it on the desk. "Your gun. We're finished with it, and I thought you might like to have it returned. It's a sweet piece."

My stomach bottomed out as I stared at Mini Pearl resting in her cloth shroud. Once my prize possession, it had now been used to take a young woman's life. I abhorred it and wanted nothing to do with it. My mouth opened to speak, to tell him to take it away, but no sound passed between my lips. As I sat frozen in horror, the sweet scent of pipe tobacco tickled my nostrils.

"Jolene, honey, open your eyes." Grandma Tucker's voice echoed again in my mind. My head snapped up bringing my startled gaze to Snellgrove's smirky visage.

"I can see I was wrong about you, Miz Claiborne," he boasted. "I'll dispose of it for you." He reached for the gun.

For a second, I considered agreeing, my revulsion overwhelming, but my ghostly grandparents' intercession stopped me. They showed up only when something was amiss. And here was evidence to a murder being placed in my hands by the man possibly responsible for the grisly crime. Why? If he disposed of the gun, Bradford would never be able to prove murder and find justice for the young writer.

"You're mistaken, Sheriff Snellgrove." The words burst from my mouth just as his hand closed over the gun. "I'm glad you're returning Mini Pearl." Here I gave a shaky smile. "You just caught me off guard. I never expected to see her again."

"Her? Just like a woman." His brow quirked with

ridicule as he released the gun and sat back in the chair.

With enormous effort, I reached across the desk and curled my fingers around Mini Pearl, ignoring the stinging jolt of electricity upon contact, and drew the offensive weapon toward me. With the other hand, I opened the top drawer and placed the cursed thing inside, knowing I would never handle it again. Exhausted by my mental turmoil, I focused all my energy on getting rid of my unwelcome visitor.

Ignoring his snide remark, I climbed to my feet. "Once again, thank you for stopping by. I can honestly say I hope I never see you again." I laughed as if joking.

Snellgrove followed me to the door. "Right back at ya, ma'am." He tipped his hat and sailed out of the salon. Seeing him climb into his sheriff cruiser, I bolted back into the office, locked the top desk drawer, and reached for the phone receiver and dialed Bradford's number.

****

Mini Pearl emerged from her shroud with pearl grips gleaming like shark's teeth. I shuddered as Bradford turned the gun over in his hands. "Strange business, this. Not a normal police procedure. Snellgrove crossed a line by returning this gun to you, but I'm glad you had the foresight to accept it and turn it over to me."

"I'm just glad you could take it off my hands." A fog blanketed my brain, making it hard for me to converse calmly. "I was afraid you'd be out on another case, and I can't stand the thought of it being here. Why would he believe I'd want it back with its gruesome history?"

Bradford rewrapped Mini Pearl and stuck it in a plastic bag. "I can't answer that question, honey, but I intend to put my ear to the ground. Someone's talking somewhere."

I slipped off my heels and sank down on the sofa. "Deena will be back soon, so we have to hurry. I don't want her knowing anything about this."

"Why don't you drive out to the ranch after work? We'll have dinner on the veranda and relax. If the mood strikes, we'll crack open the files." Bradford strode over to the sofa, sat beside me, and drew me into his embrace.

Feeling his strong arms tighten, I let out a long breath and closed my eyes savoring the sensation. Tears pooled in my eyes as I pictured Mini Pearl resting in Careen's still hands in the abandoned graveyard. Someone had brutally murdered her and left her corpse to be picked off by the wildlife. With the mental image implanted in my mind, I opened the floodgates and cried like a baby, and continued crying as I thought about all the unexpected changes wrecking my life. Especially his looming departure for Wyoming.

After my sobs turned quiet, Bradford dried my cheeks with his handkerchief, gave me a quick kiss, and took his leave. I put on a new face and went back to work, relieved with Mini Pearl's removal and worked the rest of the day in a serious mood, keeping my distance from Deena as her sparkling smile indicated her return to sanity.

The salon closed without any further incidents leaving me and Deena to finish up the cleaning chores. Seeing my sister glance repeatedly at her watch, I suggested she head out for her date with Ryder.

She gave me a stern look. "I don't want to leave you with all of this work. There's still an hour of hard cleaning."

We were unloading cleaning supplies from the dispensary into the hallway close to the facial room. I motioned to the locked door. "I prefer to handle our rat problem on my own, Deena. We're not sure who's in there, and I prefer you stay in the clear."

"Can you handle it on your own?"

"You ever deal with a rat?"

Her brows drew down in thought. "Not lately, and especially not a dead one."

"Okay then, you head out, and I'll take care of the rodent problem."

Deena wasted no time arguing, gathered her things, and exited out the rear entrance. Left alone, I first did a quick cleaning job on the salon before heading back to the locked facial room and the pest inside.

Not sure I wanted to open the door at all, I hesitated, then pressed my ear against the panel hoping to gauge the movement and determine whether my guest was dead or alive. No sound. Nothing. I eased open the door and snaked my arm around to the light switch. White fluorescent light flooded the room, lighting the corners. Nothing scurried beneath my feet. Apparently, my guest hailed from the Other Side. Hmm. Strange that I couldn't discern its presence.

"I know you're in here, so please do me the curiosity of showing yourself," I announced in my sternest voice. "If you plan to stay I need advance notice. No acceptations or I'll be forced to call in the Georgia Giant and believe me, you don't want that. Scarlett doesn't share well."

My guest failed to materialize. Whoever or whatever shared the space with me wasn't playing ball. A quick inspection of the room turned up no visible results, so I turned out the light, bolted shut the door, and also left by the rear entrance.

At home, I showered and changed into comfortable jeans and a shirt and drove out to Bradford's ranch on the outskirts of town. The sun had set when I parked behind his pickup truck and rang the doorbell.

The door swung open with gusto. "Come in, my sweet." He handed me a glass of blackberry wine as I stepped inside. "I have the steaks ready to go on the grill. I hope you're hungry."

"Always," I responded and followed him out to the comfy screened-in patio adjoining the house. Taking my favorite rocking chair, I sank down and nursed the wine, my mind tumbling over the fast-moving events of the past week.

"You're quiet. What's going on?" Bradford sat down in the chair beside me with a cold beer in hand.

"Lately, a lot." I gulped down the wine and held out the glass for a refill. "Billie Jo is out of commission for the foreseeable future, Deena is relocating to Atlanta after her wedding, I'm bleeding employees, and I need an assistant to handle my overflow. Any chance Diamond might be persuaded to change careers? Mrs. Eisenberg was just asking about her today, and I'm seriously considering making her an offer she can't pass up. I need her more than you do."

Officer Diamond Presley had come to my rescue when the mob put a bull's-eye target on my back. Lucky for me, my undercover bodyguard had worked in a beauty shop before becoming a cop. Once she joined our team, her sense of humor and sharp street smarts captured the respect of the staff and patrons alike. Now that I thought about it, she'd be the perfect solution to my employment woes.

Bradford chuckled. "Diamond is irreplaceable, Jolene, and she's up for detective with me leaving the force. I doubt you'll make any headway with her, but you can try."

"I'll give her a call next week and make a lunch date." I changed the subject. "About Mini Pearl."

Bradford filled my glass to the brim with the dark berry wine. "Put away for safekeeping," was his answer, which suited me just fine. As long as the cursed thing was out of sight, it would remain out of mind.

He took a long pull from his beer. "I swung by Vanessa's house unannounced this afternoon."

"And?"

"I found nothing out of the ordinary. Betty seemed genuinely surprised to see me and even suggested I search the house. Which I did and found nothing suspicious."

"She had ample warning, Bradford. Betty knew I'd run straight to you, giving her time to hide the evidence. Someone other than her and the maid are living in that house. And somehow Sheriff Snellgrove figures into this."

He climbed to his feet and disappeared into the house, emerging several minutes later with the steaks. "I have the same suspicion as you, honey, but I have to prove it." He laid the steaks on the hot grill. "Snellgrove is as wily as a fox, and I've run into a dead end. I am at a loss what to do next."

"We're no closer to the truth?" I inhaled the

delicious aroma of grilling beef and felt the slight stirrings of hunger.

"I didn't say that."

"So, what do we know?"

Bradford flipped the steaks, releasing a burst of aromatic delight, making my mouth water. He turned to face me with tongs in hand. "Well, for one thing, we know that Careen did not commit suicide. How Snellgrove fixed that, I'll find out. Second, we know that Vanessa is alive according to several witnesses. And third—the clue of the ruby ring. We know its owner is an accomplice."

My earlier visit with the vampire queen's mother flashed to mind. "Betty van Allen is the accomplice, and Snellgrove her sidekick. And I'd bet that ruby ring is in her possession. I suggest you get a search warrant."

"The judge needs more than your ringing endorsement, Jolene," he reminded me. "He won't issue a warrant without sufficient cause."

I downed the last sip of wine. "Well, at least you're free of Snow White."

He lifted his bottle in a mock toast. "Here's to the good things in life, my dear." With that done, he removed the steaks from the grill and opened another bottle of wine. Under the sparkling, star-studded sky, we stuffed ourselves on food and laughter. Oh, and yeah, more wine.

Chapter Twenty-Five
You Are My Sunshine

I awoke the next morning in Bradford's bed satiated, but with a whooper of a hangover. Rolling over and seeing his side of the bed empty, I groaned with self-disgust and loathing for giving in to my primal needs, and covered my face with a pillow. Christ, I needed psychotherapy in the worse way. Sleeping with two men in less than a week and loving every second of it? What does that say about my moral standards? Mama was right in saying that I've got to get control of my panties.

"Good morning, sunshine." Bradford's cheery voice filtered through the pillow. "I have coffee and donuts, unless you'd like something else to get your motor running?" His suggestive tone had me flailing from under the covers, and I emerged to witness his rugged face wreathed in laughter.

He handed me a cup of steaming coffee. "Umm," I said after the first sip. "You remembered how I like it."

"I remember everything about you, Jolene." He propped himself against the pillows. "You are my sunshine in every way, and I love you."

Most women lived to hear those timeless words spoken in a loving manner, but not me. For me, time ceased with those three dreaded words. I froze with the cup against my trembling lips. I dared not raise my gaze

229

to meet his as I knew he'd only see pain and confusion reflected there. You see, I'm terrified of love and the "until death we do part" and all that marriage stuff. One divorce is enough. Never again, had become my motto over the years. I enjoyed the benefits of a serious relationship, but only in separate residences and plenty of space between us—the more the better. This gal wasn't looking for a wedding ring to seal the deal.

His fingers brushed my cheeks and forced my chin upward. His eyes glowed gentle and calm. "It's okay, Jolene. You don't have to say the words. I understand your fear."

I felt a pang of sadness for us both. Not long from now we would be saying goodbye forever, and, over time, he would forget all about the girl he left behind in Whiskey Creek, Georgia.

Coffee forgotten, I set the cup down on the nightstand and placed my hand in his. "The time isn't right for us, Bradford. If you were staying, maybe we could work out our issues, but your life is changing for the better. My life is here."

"I'm not leaving the planet, Jolene. Wyoming is only two thousand miles away."

"And that's forever, Bradford. Face it. When you leave, it's over."

At his look of heartbreak, a part of me wanted to give in, to give him what he wanted—a promise of a new life in Wyoming. But I balked. Whiskey Creek held too many memories. The sweeping cotton fields dressed like winter snow bunnies, all white and gleaming. The intoxicating scent of freshly tilled red dirt ready for spring planting. The cobblestone streets on Main Street, and the Saturday downtown Farmers

Market with homemade goods for sale, and lastly the peanut farm where I grew up with my family. I loved the South. It was home.

His phone chimed, giving me the opportunity to grab my clothes and disappear into the master bath. Twenty minutes later, showered and dressed, I found Bradford in the kitchen loading the dishwasher. With his back to me, he hadn't heard my approach, I paused, studying the smooth movement of his muscled physique. My heart constricted as I continued to stare, implanting his memory to be brought out and replayed after his departure. Why the sweet torture? Damn those three cursed words.

I must've made a sound because he glanced over his shoulder and saw me frozen to the floor. His Mona Lisa smile ripped into my heart like an eagle's talons snagging a baby bunny for an early morning snack.

"The chief has requested a meeting with me first thing this morning. I need to head out," he said in a low, composed voice. "You're welcome to stay longer."

Hang around his cozy kitchen? The place where we shared love and laughter? No, I was ready to ride my Mustang at breakneck speed back to town, leaving "I love you" in the dust. The sooner we put last night and this morning behind us, the better.

I kept my tears in check as he handed me into my car and closed the driver's door. "Drive careful on your way home." He leaned into the opened window and pecked my cheek. "I'll call you this evening."

As I drove off an overwhelming rush of sadness filled me. Pressing hard on the gas, I let the Mustang loose and arrived home without a speeding ticket and devoid of any lasting regrets. I wasted no time, but fed

Tango, changed into a cute, form-fitting jean skirt and blouse, and drove to the salon. And straight into another cocked and loaded entanglement as Preston's white Lexus SUV came into view.

My brain blew a gasket. "Geez, not again," I screamed over the jazz music booming from the car speakers. "I can't take another relationship confrontation this morning." Bradford's tender "I love you" continued to clang in my mind like Sunday morning church bells. In my distress, I failed to perceive a subtle change in the car's atmosphere.

"I take it your two-timing ways have finally caught up with you," Scarlett said from the passenger seat.

"Look who's calling the kettle black." I gave her my evilest eye possible while zipping into my parking space. "I can't talk now, Scarlett."

"Find the time, Cruella. You've got a tiger on your tail."

"What's that supposed to mean?" I watched Preston climb out of his SUV.

"Trouble is stalking you. Keep your eyes and ears open. Watch your step. Carry a big stick. Look over your shoulder. Duck and ask questions later. Got it?"

"Dead or alive?"

"Both."

"Who's in the facial room?"

"The dead one."

"Ha, ha. A name?"

Silence answered. Preston drew nearer.

"Give me a name, Scarlett."

"Don't have one. Your other boy toy is here. See ya."

No further questions were possible as Preston had

opened my door. "Jolene, I want to apologize for walking out of your house the other day. I know you didn't mean what you said."

I climbed out of the car and slammed the door. "Wrong. I did mean it. I won't allow a man to make my choices, or question the ones I make. And while we're at it, I'll not be joined at the hip, understood?"

His hand rested lightly on my shoulder. "Of course, darling. I wouldn't think of crowding you." That same hand dropped to his side. "Let's talk tonight over dinner. There's a new restaurant in Valdosta with rave reviews. We could take the long way home."

I was in no mood to be generous. "Not tonight, Preston. I have a full day of appointments, and an evening with Deena and her wedding plans. Some other time."

"Soon?"

His expectant face left me with no other option but to agree. I took my leave of him and unlocked the rear entrance door, stepping inside to the morning quiet and headed straight for the facial room, now more curious than ever about my mysterious invisible guest. All thoughts of Bradford vanished as Scarlett's unexplained warning circled in my head. I withdrew my key ring, selected the appropriate key, and inserted it into the lock.

The door swung open with a gentle push. All lay still and quiet as an odd waiting silence settled over the room. Goose bumps peppered my skin as I switched on the overhead lights from the doorway. My danger meter beeped an urgent alert. I backed away and inhaled a deep breath to keep fear at bay. Unbidden, something sinister had taken over my facial room. The vibrational

233

field felt wrong, and I never dismissed intuition. I shivered as cold, stale air began to filter in from an unknown source.

"Okay, I know you're in here," I told the *thing* in a shaky voice. "This is my salon, and I want you to leave now." I hesitated, then added as an afterthought, "In Jesus's name."

The door slammed shut in my face forcing me to jump back and collide with the opposite wall.

Okay. Enough said. Shaken, I relocked the door and bolted into the kitchen to make a pot of ultra-strong coffee. I glanced down at my watch. 7:53. Excellent. Deena is always here by eight. Plenty of time for a powwow before the staff and clients arrive.

Dreading the coming confrontation with Bridezilla, I plopped down on a chair and sent out a Universal SOS to Scarlett. With coffee in hand, I then waited for either the live or dead one to show up first. Several minutes later the back door opened and closed. Footsteps sounded in the hallway.

The live one. Good. Best to get the bad over with first. Climbing to my feet, I stuck my head out the door. "Coffee's ready. Got a minute?"

"Yeah, I need to talk with you anyhow." Deena's tone reflected more bridal woes. Just what I needed.

I handed her a cup of black coffee and sat across from her at the table. "You go first."

Deena gulped down a swallow of hot coffee, not evening flinching. "No, you first. Your news can't compare to mine."

My stomach clenched at her stricken face. Damn. Now what had the Universe dumped in my lap? Wasn't a murder, a kidnapping, and an evil entity haunting my salon enough? "The good news is we don't have a rodent problem, and my invisible friends aren't back."

"And the bad?" Deena peered over her coffee cup.

"One of Hell's angels dropped in for a visit."

"We have an uninvited ghost?"

"Yes and no." I pushed back from the table to fetch the coffee pot. "Our guest is definitely uninvited and looking for trouble, but it's not a human spirit or ghost as they're called."

"So what are you saying?"

"I'm saying we need an exorcism."

"How do you exorcise a beauty shop?"

"With a Catholic priest."

"And where do we get one of those?"

I refilled our coffee cups to the brim. "In the yellow pages, where else?"

"Mama's not going to like this," she pointed out. "We're Baptist."

"Mama's not going to know," I grumbled. "And I'm confident the demon in the facial room doesn't care which denomination we hail from."

"Do you suppose the priest would exorcise the family while he's at it? You know, throw in a two-for-one kind of a deal?"

I laughed. "I could ask if he'd give a family discount."

She fell silent, her eyes locked on mine. "I guess it's my turn to share."

I stilled under her intense stare. "Only if you want to."

"I do." She let out a burst of hysterical laughter. "I do. Ironic, I should use that phrase when I'll never say it to Ryder. The wedding is off. His ex-wife is back in town, and I saw them together. They were kissing."

Shocked, I paused to gather my wits. "Maybe you misunderstood? Where did this happen?"

"At Barron's."

"Oh, Deena, the lighting in that restaurant is deplorable. You probably mistook another man for Ryder. That can happen, you know."

Her face brightened. "I didn't see them but a minute before the waiter seated them in another section, and I didn't dare confront them in public."

"I suggest you share your fears with Ryder concerning his ex-wife before calling off your wedding."

"Thanks, sis." She rose from the table. "I believe I'll go call him now." She made it to the door before turning back to look at me. "The bad lighting explains why I imagined Vanessa and her agent having dinner in a corner booth."

I scampered from my seat. "Vanessa van Allen? In Barron's? With Cash Hitchcock? Are you sure, Deena?"

"Not after talking to you, I'm not. Probably another mistaken identity."

"Tell me everything."

"I saw a woman who bore a striking resemblance to Vanessa van Allen having dinner with Vanessa's agent from Atlanta."

"You didn't think to call the police? She's a missing person."

"I had other things on my mind, Jolene. Like my fiancé kissing another woman!"

Seeing her heightened distress, I backed off. "I'll pass the information along to Bradford. You go call

Ryder."

Deena pushed out the kitchen door, and I reached inside my shoulder bag for my phone. Punching in Bradford's number, I waited for him to pick up, excited with the confirmation that Vanessa van Allen was indeed alive and well and we were close on her trail.

****

"You're jumping to conclusions, Jolene, based solely on secondhand information." Bradford raised his hand as I opened my mouth in protest. "I'll investigate Deena's claim and get back with you." His tone had a definite bite.

We stared at one another over the insurmountable "I-love-you" wall, and I knew the time had come for me to clear the air. "About this morning—"

"I'm here on a case, not personal business, so pay attention. I don't have time for your excuses."

Well, shut my mouth. Rebellion flared like a supernova, and I clenched my teeth together to keep my toxic tongue in its cage. Once unleashed, I'd set fire to him and everyone in my path, and since we were sitting at one of the outside tables at Shake-N-Shack during a packed lunch crowd, that wouldn't be a wise choice. Several of my longtime clients lunched nearby, and every once in a while, one of the feline bitches threw covert glances our way.

"Bad idea to meet here," Bradford commented at the female surveillance. "We need to continue this discussion in private."

Perturbed, I bit into my hotdog. "Not until I'm finished," I muttered with a full mouth.

"Is Deena available for a quick chat?"

"Not at the moment. She's working out a

237

problem."

"I'll track down Cash Hitchcock as soon as we're finished and swing by Barron's and talk with the staff."

"What about Vanessa?" I shoved the last bite into my mouth.

"There's still an APB out for her. Don't worry, we'll find her."

"Damn right, we'll find her."

"I meant the police, Jolene."

"I did too."

Bradford looked at me. "Swear to it."

I raised my right hand. "I swear to leave the Queen of the Vampires to the police. I also swear to mind my own business, unless provoked."

"You provoke easily."

"True," I conceded. "But I'm done with Vanessa and her band of bloodsuckers. I have a bigger problem at the salon."

"Anything I can help with?"

"Not unless you personally know a Catholic priest."

Bradford's face twisted. "Ah, leave me out of it."

I smiled. "Yeah, that's what I thought."

We finished lunch and parted ways, me to find a priest and him to track down Careen's killer.

Chapter Twenty-Six
Where Have All the Good Priests Gone?

I came up empty handed with my search for a Catholic priest willing to exorcise my facial room of the uninvited guest. The only Catholic Church in Whiskey Creek didn't believe my story and showed me the door with instructions to never return. I blew through the two Methodist's guys, and the ever-faithful Baptists used colorful language to describe my expanded imagination. Even my pastor turned me down and recommended I come in for counseling. When I exited his office, I was sure Mama would be receiving a phone call as soon as I disappeared around the corner.

With Madame Mia on vacation, I turned to the Universalist and Mormons. They couldn't help but recommended the Jehovah's Witnesses. Nope. I lost them in the translation. They pointed to the Presbyterian Church down the road. They rejected me, too.

However, I did receive help in the most unlikely place. The Pentecostal Church of the Holy Rollers. They welcomed me with open arms and promised to rid my salon of the devil's messenger as soon as they could find a replacement for their spiritual leader. Seems he ran off with the secretary's husband. But in the meantime, if I was willing, they would stand in the gap by laying hands on me and praying in tongues until the

Holy Spirit baptized me in tongues of fire. Although Mama had warned me against such a practice, I figured it wouldn't hurt, so I agreed. I came out of there with a limited dictionary of mumbo-jumbo and a parcel of new friends.

With my bones vibrating with spiritual energy, I returned to the salon and finished the day in a happy frame of mind. Even though I was tempted to exorcise the facial room myself, I decided to hold off until the weekend and do research on the subject. Since Deena never returned from lunch, I tackled the cleaning chores solo, closed the salon, and headed for the house and a hot shower.

Clothed in lounging pajamas, I warmed leftovers and watched a recorded episode of my favorite soap opera. Afterward, I cleaned the kitchen and then sat down with my notebook to record my recent discoveries on the Halsey/van Allen case. I jotted these down and did a quick scan of the information to reacquaint myself with the twists and turns of the entwined cases.

Thoughts:

Vanessa had a falling-out with her agent, Cash Hitchcock, over a suspected false royalty statement. Was the agent skimming money off the top? Cash knew Vanessa's secret. Possibly about Careen? What were they doing together at Barron's? Why is Cash still in town?

Purvis Dupree of Firebrand Publications and Vanessa had once shared a bed. Check and see who published Vanessa's earlier work. Blackmail?

The mysterious caller in the study had been Vanessa demanding Careen to switch places. Careen feared for her work and hoped to stop the charade. Careen had not only met Vanessa but her death Halloween night. Careen identified Vanessa as her killer. I have doubts.

Where's the missing manuscript?

What happened in the cabin? Where is Vanessa?

What's Michael Halsey's part in this? Where is he?

Sheriff Snellgrove was arguing with Vanessa in the graveyard. What's his part in this? What's the connection? Scarlett confirmed he's involved.

Careen was wearing the Snow White costume when we discovered her. She didn't commit suicide. Who doctored the autopsy? What about Mini Pearl?

Who has the ruby ring? Whose car made the tire impressions at the Maco mansion?

Is Betty van Allen an accomplice? What about the financial repercussions in the event of Vanessa's death? Betty has a secret.

Was Careen killed by accident? Could the killer have mistaken her for Vanessa?

Vanessa is hiding at home. Why the pretense? What's really going on behind the scenes?

What about Peaches Noble and Maylene Lovett? Where are they? Both hated Vanessa and wanted to stop the publication of her exposé. Check their whereabouts.

With the manuscript missing, the book deal is dead. Who has it?

Vanessa is the key to both cases.

Still feeling as if I were overlooking an important clue, I reread my notes three times before my tired and itching eyes forced me to stop. Yawning, I glanced at the kitchen clock. 10:57. I pushed back from the table and started to make a pot of coffee to keep me awake, but changed my mind. This could wait. Dead on my feet and feeling the burn of frustration, I turned out the lights, and with Tango on my heels, I made our way to the bedroom. Within minutes of laying down, I fell asleep and dreamed of planting a wooden stake in Vanessa's cold, dead heart.

****

The phone call came early the next morning. I'd just climbed out of bed when the landline peeled a summons. Caller ID showed Bradford's office number. I snatched up the receiver. "Hello."

"Deena was right. Cash Hitchcock was at Barron's the other night with a woman."

Bradford's words riveted my attention. "He stayed in town to meet with a local romance author he was interested in signing. His story checks out. I met with the woman, and I can see how Deena was mistaken in the dim lighting. Same height and dark hair."

"So Vanessa is still at large?"

"Yes, no sign of her."

I thought of my notes. "Hang on, let me get my notes." I padded down the hall and into my office, retrieved my notebook and went back into the bedroom. "Still there?"

"Yes, I'm listening. Go ahead."

"Do you know if Peaches Noble and Maylene Lovett are still in town? Or what about Purvis Dupree?"

"They're registered in one of the hotels out on I-75. They've been questioned and profess to have no knowledge of her whereabouts. They're leaving this afternoon."

I read down the page. "Umm. What about the tire

impressions taken at the Maco mansion? Any results?"

"I'll check with forensics. Anything else?"

"The missing manuscript."

"I don't follow."

"No manuscript, no book deal. Peaches Noble and Maylene Lovett both had reasons for killing the project. Vanessa had it at the writers' retreat. She's missing, along with the manuscript. So that means their secrets are safe."

"I think you're barking up the wrong tree with those two, Jolene."

"A reasonable assumption," I conceded. "Have you checked out Betty's Durable Power of Attorney?"

"Yes. Legit."

"You sound tired."

"I am. Ready to make a change."

"Wyoming?"

"Yeah, had an offer on the ranch this morning."

"Gonna accept it?"

"Yeah, might head out sooner than expected. Can't leave until I tie up some loose ends though."

"Hang in there," I said with a sad note. "You'll figure this out. You're a good cop."

"Thanks for the vote of confidence, Jolene. Listen, gotta go. Keep your nose clean."

With that the line disconnected. I hung up the receiver, started the coffee, and went to take a hot shower—keeping my feelings under tight control. I would not think about Bradford leaving. I would not think about his declaration of love. I would not think about my life without him. I would not.

Dressed in a cute new number from Chico's, I downed a quick breakfast of cereal and coffee and headed out the door for work.

Deena met me at the rear door. "Ryder and I are back on track."

"I thought as much when you didn't return from lunch yesterday."

"Did you talk with Sam about Vanessa and her agent at Barron's?"

"Yeah, turns out the woman was another writer he wanted to sign. Vanessa still hasn't been accounted for."

"Now what?"

"I have no idea, Deena. I made a promise to Bradford to stay out of it, and for once, I'm going to keep the promise."

She cut me a slanted look. "I've heard that before."

I held up my right hand. "I swear to mind my own business."

We cut our conversation short as the staff and my first client were scheduled to arrive in a few minutes. I worked through the morning and through lunch pausing only for a quick snack of cheese crackers and chocolate milk. The afternoon was pretty much the same as the morning rush, and I was finishing my four o'clock perm when my cell phone jangled. Caller ID displayed the farm landline.

Excusing myself, I hit the talk button. "Hello."

"Jolene, is your mother there with you?"

"I haven't seen her all day, Daddy."

"Well, she's been gone for hours, and I thought maybe she stopped by to visit with you girls about Deena's wedding. She said there's not enough time to complete the preparations."

"That's nonsense, Daddy. Everything's done but

the small details."

"That's what I told her, honey, but you know how your mother is. She was driving out to Betty's to drop off a bowl of her homemade chicken and dumplings. But now I'm getting worried about her. She should've been home by now."

My danger meter sent out a beep, and my stomach clenched at the thought of Mama behind closed doors with a possible kidnapper, or worse, killer. Calm down. Keep a cool head. Don't jump to conclusions. And for God sakes, don't upset Daddy any further. Think girl, think. Breathe. Breathe. Good. Now, get more information. "What time did she leave?" I kept my voice relaxed. "Was it in the morning or afternoon?"

"Around ten this morning, I believe. I was in the barn when she left."

I expelled a long breath. "Have you tried her phone?"

A pause. "Of course, Jolene. I've left several messages. Not like her to ignore my calls."

"I'm sure she's been busy and doesn't recognize the time." I slowed down my speech. "Don't worry, Daddy. I'll track her down and send her home."

"Call me when you reach her, honey."

"Sure thing, Daddy."

I disconnected the line and hit Mama's contact button. The call went straight to voicemail. I left a message for her to call me or Daddy. Not wanting to alarm Deena unnecessarily, I finished the roller set on my client, put her under the dryer, and made a beeline for Deena's office.

She was on the phone when I entered her office. I sank down into a chair across her desk to wait for her to finish her call. My face must've shown my concern for two minutes later she placed the receiver on its cradle. "What's wrong? Not another client in the facial room I hope."

"Daddy called. Mama's not answering her phone."

"What's unusual about that? She can't hear the ringtone most of the time."

Relief washed over me, and I released a tired sigh. "That would explain it. We're worrying over nothing. I bet she's on her way home now."

"You seem overly concerned, why?"

"Because she visited Betty van Allen."

Deena's nose scrunched up. "In layman's terms, please."

I filled in the details of my visit with Vanessa's mother, and my suspicions of her involvement with Careen's murder and Vanessa's disappearance.

"I didn't think it was possible for me to be surprised by anything you say and do, Jolene, but I am. And now Mama's in the middle." Her face showed disapproval.

"I thought you said we had nothing to worry about?"

She lifted the receiver from its cradle and punched in a number. "That was before. This is now."

"Who are you calling?"

"Mama." No answer. She left a message, then redialed.

"Who are you calling now?"

"Daddy, to see if Mama's home."

That call turned up the same result. Deena punched in another number.

"Who now?"

"Ryder." Her voice was tense.

"What for? He doesn't know where she is."

"I'm aware of that, Jolene. To cancel dinner. You and I are going to find her."

I waved my hands in protest. "That's not necessary, Deena. And besides, I have a roller set under the dryer."

"For once we're going to do it my way. Lizzie can finish your appointments. Mama may be in danger."

After she hung up with Ryder, there was no talking her out of driving to Betty's, so we grabbed our purses, made arrangements with Holly to cover my last appointment, and dashed out the rear entrance to see Mama and Billie Jo pull up in Billie Jo's old Dodge Charger.

Relieved, Deena and I rushed over to see the Charger's backseat covered with shopping bags.

Mama's eyes sparkled as I drew near her opened window. "Jolene, we hit the jackpot at the mall. Got everything on sale. This will be the best dressed baby in Whiskey Creek."

I leaned in the open window. "We've been worried sick about you. Daddy called and said you've been gone all day and not answering your phone."

"That's my fault, Jolene," Billie Jo spoke up. "When Mama stopped by the house I mentioned a sale at Augusta's Baby Shop. We lost track of time."

"Well, no harm done." The tension drained out of Deena's voice. "Mama, promise you'll check your phone once in a while from now on."

Mama snapped open her phone and scrolled down the missed calls screen. "I guess I should call your father. He's called five times."

"He said you were dropping off chicken and dumplings at Betty's," I said, curious if Betty had mentioned my earlier visit.

"Strange thing that." Mama glanced up at me. "Sophia claimed Betty wasn't home, but I swear I heard voices. Sophia put me off, so I handed over the dish of dumplings and left. Odd. I swear I heard voices. Oh well, just an old woman's imagination."

Wrong. For some unknown reason, Mama's friend was embroiled in Vanessa's disappearance. Publicity stunt? Could be, but unlikely. My thinking tended to be on the dark side. Money? Without a doubt. But how to prove it? Call Bradford with this new information? I shook my head. No, he'd warn me to stay out of it, or worse, discount Mama's observations. And what about my vow to stay out of it? I wobbled for a second. Oh, what the hell. One look wouldn't hurt and might even set my mind at ease. With my brain cells smoking, I kissed Mama and Billie Jo goodbye, told Deena to have a nice evening with her honey, and hopped in my Mustang. I had one destination in mind and burned rubber all the way there.

Chapter Twenty-Seven
The Stakeout

I parked down the street from Vanessa's House of the Rising Sun and waited. For what I hadn't decided, but if the Vampire Queen made an appearance, I'd document the activity with my phone and hand over the evidence to Bradford for further investigation. My main purpose for being here continued to be collecting evidence of Vanessa's continued deceit. This farce had gone on long enough. She was alive. I knew it deep down in my psychic knowing. Funny how that works.

My gaze roamed the front of the house. From all indications, Betty hadn't returned home. The house was dark, no lights shone from the windows. The dashboard clock read 5:45. As twilight settled in, the streetlights switched on, but still no movement from the house. An hour crept by and still I waited. By 8:00 I grew impatient. A cop I'm not and sitting alone in the dark wasn't my idea of a fun evening.

When the dashboard clock rolled around to 9:00, I decided to stretch my cramping legs and quiet my screaming bladder. Peeing outside wasn't my first choice, but neither could I knock on the neighbor's door and request the use of the facilities. No, I had to find a concealed area or go home. The smart move would be to head for the house, but I'm not smart or a quitter, so I decided to find a nice bushy bush and squat.

I left my vehicle and skirted around the glowing streetlights until I drew abreast of Vanessa's house. Still no movement from within, but my progress set off the neighborhood canine patrol. Ducking behind the neighbor's dark house, I found what I was searching for and took care of business.

Once cleaned, and the wet wipe disposed, I froze as a faint light flared in one of the back windows of Vanessa's house. I knew it! Someone was moving about. Sophia? Betty? Or the illusive Vampire Queen? At this point, it didn't matter. Like a coon dog on the scent, I hustled across the yard and wormed along the fence until I spotted a huge, towering pine tree which offered concealment.

From my position behind the tree I observed another flare of light in the kitchen. Strange behavior for the homeowners. Apparently, the person or persons were slowly making their way to the front of the house. Why the subterfuge? Itching with curiosity, I dashed from tree to bush until I crouched close to the garage. On silent feet, I peeked over the windowsill. With the muted streetlight streaming into the window, I could just make out three figures. Sheriff Snellgrove. Damn, the lying sneak. In on it all along. Betty and Sophia, too.

Betty ducked into the car and popped the truck. Then the three disappeared back inside the mudroom door. With the muted streetlight and weak light from the trunk, I had a good view of the entire garage. Several seconds passed before Snellgrove and Sophia emerged from the house struggling with what could only be a cloth-wrapped body.

Hell's bells. I gasped several breaths to stay quiet,

images of my cold, dead body flashed through my mind at the thought of discovery. Trembling, I fell to the ground, clutching my shaking hands to my chest. Sweat beaded on my brow and lip in the cool night air as my legs muscles tightened—ready for flight as my danger meter screamed at me to run like hell.

Now on automatic, I withdrew the Pink Panther from my shoulder bag and snapped off the safety. A sense of unreality settled over me as I crouched under the window and heard voices over the roaring in my ears. Self-preservation kept me still and quiet. Reason had fled at the sight of the shrouded body. As my breathing slowed, a sense of judgement returned. As long as I remained hidden from the occupants of the house, I was safe. But only if I escaped detection. One peep could sound the alarm.

My swirling thoughts settled on Michael Halsey's cloth-wrapped body. It had to be him since he, too, was missing. Although I hadn't physically seen Vanessa that night in the Maco mansion, I had seen Michael gagged and beaten. Powers of deduction pointed at him. Careen's brother had stumbled onto the truth and had paid the ultimate price.

Loud whispers snapped me back to the situation, and placing my shoulder bag on the ground, I again peered over the edge of the window to see Snellgrove and Sophia shove Michael's body into the truck. From the house, another figure emerged and slipped into the driver's seat. The other two quickly followed, and the rumble of the garage door opening signaled their departure.

I dropped to the ground and fumbled for my purse, dumping out the contents in my haste. Fearing discovery, I halted my search, and waited for the taillights to indicate their departure. As the garage door rumbled downward, I snatched up my shoulder bag and made my way back to my car.

As I climbed in, I could just make out the disappearing taillights down the street. Firing up the engine, I trailed behind them at a safe distance. Once I knew for certain their destination, I would alert Bradford of my discovery. I dogged them all the way to the Maco mansion.

Another surprise. What's up with this crumbling house? Returning to the scene of the crime made no sense at all. Surely, they didn't intend to bury the body in the backyard. Confused with the implications, I killed the engine and waited for their next move.

From my parallel parking spot down the road, I observed the car pull around to the dilapidated garage in the back of the house. From the shadows, Sophia got out and opened the double doors and the car pulled inside. Moments later, four figures emerged with the shrouded body sandwiched between them.

Four! I'd only seen three at the house. The fourth figure had to be Vanessa van Allen. Victory surged through me. I'd found her. My shoulder bag lay in the passenger seat. Snatching it up, I dug around for my phone, but came up empty-handed. Christ. I'd lost my phone back at Vanessa's. What to do?

Get the hell outta here.

Get the evidence.

Hell no.

My hand reached for the ignition. The engine fired up and I circled the block, all the while my indecision beating the crap out of me. Finally, just to shut up the screaming voices in my head, I circled back to the house and parked in the shadows. Just one look in the windows. That's all. Promise. Slipping out of the car, I skirted around the neighboring houses until I reached the Maco house. Front or back?

Front. More light and closer to my V8 300 horsepower get-away car. Armed with the Pink Panther, I eased behind a line of overgrown bushes flanking the front windows, and peered inside. Nothing. Not a sound, no movement in the semi-dark house. Ducking down, I repeated the action with the entire downstairs windows, and found nothing. If I hadn't seen them with my own eyes, I would've swear they had disappeared into thin air. Impossible. There was only one sensible thing left to do—go home and call Bradford on the landline.

You could check out the inside.

Hell no.

Coward. You have a gun.

True, but only one life to live, so can it.

I retraced my steps, stopping only to peek inside the garage. Car still there. Faint voices echoed from the house. Fearful of being discovered, I ducked down behind a tall azalea bush beside the garage and held my breath. The voices drew near, and the garage door creaked open. Seconds later the car fired up and backed out with its lights out. I peeked through the bush to see the car disappear around the corner.

As the stillness of the night settled around me, I emerged from my hiding place, and glanced around in the semi-darkness. I was alone at the back of the Maco mansion. The cloudless November sky had a million stars overhead. The half-moon face gave a shimmery, silver glow highlighting the small backyard. Should I explore the creepy, abandoned mansion, or hightail it back to safety?

I decided to let the house answer the question. If the back French doors were unlocked, I'd try my luck. If not, I'd head to the house and call Bradford. Crossing my fingers that the doors were locked, I crossed the yard and jangled the doors. Locked. Whew. Homeward bound in one piece for a change.

I spun on my heels, took several steps, and heard a soft click. I froze in my tracks, and slowly glanced over my shoulder at the opened French door. Crap. A wave of cold moved through me, and immediately I cranked up my psychic radar for any unseen visitors from the netherworld. On the edge of my vision, a white mist twisted into the shape of a young woman in a long, pale blue, flowing, turn of the century gown. Not Scarlett. Too young and blonde.

Our eyes locked. She pointed to the house, and slowly dissipated. Okay, I was going in. Scared, but determined, I tiptoed through the French door, and sent out an urgent SOS to Scarlett, hoping she'd join me, anxious to share my recent exploits with my BFF.

The silence of the house closed around me as I crept through each downstairs room searching for the hidden corpse because I knew it had to be here. Why else would Vanessa and her band of cohorts return to this particular house? Who and where was the owner? There had to be a connection. I knew it. One of the first things I'd look into in the morning.

At the foot of the staircase, I paused, frustrated with the lack of sufficient light. So far I'd turned up nothing because I couldn't see in the dark. This was a waste of time, and I needed to get out of here before they returned. Bradford and his team could comb the area better than I. As before, a wave of cold hit me between the shoulders, and my ears buzzed with cosmic electricity. That followed with faint notes similar to my front doorbell.

"I came as soon as I received your message." Scarlett's voice echoed softly in the carnivorous room. "I just returned from Scotland where a mulish lord refused to leave his crumbling castle for the delights of Heaven. But I outsmarted him with a tasteful display of twin treats. After that, he followed me like a lovesick puppy dog. You know, Jolene, I believe I'll request a transfer, too. All this work and no play is unfair. I deserve a vacation."

She materialized in front of me garbed in her biker threads, minus the leather vest. I understood at once. The wet T-shirt left nothing to the imagination. No wonder the Scottish lord almost swallowed his tongue. Scarlett didn't own a bra, and her nipples stood out like twin headlight beams. I pulled my gaze from her not-so-tasteful display, which I left unsaid because I needed her help, and pointed at the stairs. "Be a dear and have a looksee for a shrouded corpse up there for me."

Scarlett cocked a questioning brow. "I believe some background information would be helpful."

"Listen up." I cast a darting glance about me. "I witnessed the Vampire Queen and her minions carry Michael Halsey's dead body in here not more than thirty minutes ago."

"Impossible. I told you Vanessa's name is on the list."

"F the list. It's wrong. I saw her."

"I saw the list. She's there."

"The damn list is wrong, Scarlett, and so are you. Michael Halsey is dead. Now go find him."

"I don't take kindly to your tone of voice, Jolene." A white light surrounded her, pulsating wildly. "Or taking orders from a ditzy broad."

I relaxed my stance, and softened my voice. "I'm sorry, Scarlett. I'm petrified and ready to mind my own business."

"Then why don't you?"

"Because I'm a ditzy broad with emotional issues." I dragged my hand through my hair, ruffling the braid. "And Bradford is moving to Wyoming."

"Is that code for something?"

I blew out an exasperated breath. "Never mind. Are you going to help me?"

"I'm still here, aren't I?"

With Scarlett lit up like a flashlight, I followed her up the staircase and down the hall, my footsteps clattering on the hardwood. Every room was searched thoroughly, but turned up no bodies. Nothing. Not even disturbed dust on the empty room floors.

Downstairs, another search was repeated. Nothing. Ready to call it a night, I stashed the Pink Panther in my shoulder bag when the mysterious lady in blue materialized by the French doors.

"I heard Annabelle Maco was on her yearly sabbatical down here," Scarlett said.

I eyed the beautiful ghost. "She knows something. See if you can get her to talk."

"I think not. She doesn't like me or my wardrobe. Thinks it's tacky."

"It is, Scarlett, but so what? Give it a try."

Scarlett shrugged her ghostly shoulders and joined Annabelle by the French doors. After a short chat, the Lady in Blue dissipated and Scarlett joined me.

"The rumor is true. She doesn't like me but she does you. Said you have the heart of a lion. Go figure. Anyway, the body's in the cellar."

I swallowed back the lump in my throat. "Okay, lead the way."

The cellar turned out to be a spider's paradise. Cobwebs hung from the ceiling and draped every surface. Following in Scarlett's wake, I dodged one after another, and bit my lip to keep from screaming when the tarantula-sized creatures scurried underfoot. Several minutes passed before I spotted the shrouded body stashed under a worktable in the far corner of the spooky room.

"I assume you'll want to check the identity of the body?" Scarlett voiced.

"That's why we're here." My feet remained glued to the cement floor, the odor of death nearly choking me.

"Well, I'm not going to do it. This is your party."

Reluctantly, I crouched down on the dusty floor and tugged the cloth until it loosened and fell away from the body. I let out a scream and stumbled back in surprise. "Oh, my god, Scarlett. It's not Michael Halsey. It's Vanessa, and she's wearing the ruby ring!"

Chapter Twenty-Eight
Guess Who's Coming to Dinner?

"Calm down, Jolene, and tell me everything." Bradford's tense voice echoed over the landline. "I can't understand your hysterical ramblings. Now, start at the beginning."

I inhaled several deep breaths and sank down on the kitchen chair, my hands trembling. The clock over the stove read 1:00 a.m. "I found Vanessa, Bradford. She's at the Maco mansion. In the cellar." I popped up from the chair and paced the floor from the stove to the pantry. Back and forth, back and forth. "She's wearing the ruby ring I told you about. God, the look on her face."

"Where are you now?"

"In the kitchen."

"Get out of there now."

"My kitchen, Bradford. As soon as I found Vanessa, I got the hell outta there."

"Good. Listen, I'm going to get dressed and ride over there…wait, there's a call coming through on my cell"—there was a clunk of the receiver being laid on the counter, the sound of murmured voices, and finally—"That was the chief. The Maco mansion is on fire. I've gotta run, Jolene. I'll call you when I know something."

The line disconnected, and I sank down onto the

chair with despair. Two steps forward and one step back. Why did this keep happening? Just when I think the case is cracked, another stick is thrust in the fan, throwing everything out of kilter. Tango tangled himself under my feet, purring loudly, bringing my attention to the coziness of my warm kitchen. Gazing around, I drank in the familiar orange-and-white checkered curtains above the sink, the white oak cabinets with oiled bronze knobs, the stainless steel appliances, and autumn-colored braided country rug under my Granny Tucker's antique scratched oval wooden table and chairs. The bright orange seat cushions Mama had made in her sewing room out at the farm. Clean and shining wood floors, and lastly, the farm painting Becky had painted her last year of high school—hanging in its place of honor near the door. My favorite room in the house. Always warm and inviting like my Granny Tucker. Even now, I could imagine the sweet aroma of Grandpa Tucker's pipe tobacco filling the room and my heart with the peace of his comforting presence.

I yawned sleepily, but knew the instant my eyes closed, the image of Vanessa's still, white face would haunt me. To stay awake, I made a pot of coffee and defrosted a batch of cinnamon rolls from the bakery. My stomach rumbled, and I realized I hadn't eaten since lunch. With a steaming cup of coffee I sat down at the table, munched on a roll and waited for Bradford's call, which I suspected wouldn't come for several hours yet. With a full stomach, I dozed off at the table. The shrilling telephone woke me at five.

"Hey, it's me," Bradford said when I answered. "The house is a total loss. Went up like dry tinder the fire chief said. They'll conduct a search as soon as the fire is completely out and environmental services allows a search."

"How long will that take?"

"Can't answer that question."

"What now?"

"I'm going to head over to Vanessa's house and talk with Betty."

"My phone is somewhere in the backyard Bradford, if you wouldn't mind finding it for me."

"I'll see what I can do. Anything else?"

"Yeah, who owns the Maco property?"

"A Greenwood county resident. Mrs. Hazel Jessup is listed with the tax office. I'm going to pay her a visit as soon as I'm finished with Betty."

"Do you know the cause of the fire?"

"You know I can't give you an answer. It's under investigation."

"There's a connection with that house, Bradford. I know it. Let me know when you find Vanessa, okay?"

"Will do. Now, you're out of this investigation. Get on with your normal life and forget about this whole sorry mess. I never should've drawn you into it in the first place." His tired sigh sounded over the line.

"I've done all I can anyway." I disconnected the line. Wide awake, I took a hot shower and sat down with my notebook to jot down my conversation with Bradford. Then I fed the cat, cleaned the kitchen, and caught up on household chores before leaving for work.

I spent a busy morning behind the chair, and at lunch made a quick run to the Second Street Maternity Boutique to pick up a gift certificate for Billie Jo. I overspent, but felt better for neglecting her this past week, and the certificate should put a significant dent in her wardrobe needs. After that, I swung by several cell phone outlets to comparison shop the newest models in case my phone was gone for good.

The afternoon sped by much the same as the morning. I cut, colored, and permed my way to exhaustion, and by five, I was ready for the cocktail hour. Holly flagged me down as I was carrying an armload of dirty towels to the laundry room. "Dr. Preston is on the phone."

I handed over the towels and picked up the receiver. "Hello."

"You're a hard lady to track down. I've been calling your cell phone all day."

"I lost my phone and haven't replaced it yet. What's up?"

"You owe me a dinner date, remember. Let's drive down to Valdosta and have a nice steak dinner."

Steak sounded heavenly, and a quiet night with no murders or ghosts sounded even better. "I'd love to spend the evening with you, Preston."

"Great. I'll pick you up at seven." His voice deepened. "Be prepared to be swept off your feet, woman. I have an important question to ask you."

My stomach clenched at the unspoken words underneath his seductive tone. Christ. My uncomplicated dinner date had just turned complicated. Twisting the phone cord around my finger, I said a polite goodbye and placed the receiver on its cradle.

Deena came out of her office and made a beeline for the reception desk. "Ryder and I have an appointment with the caterer at six. I'd like you there if you have no other plans. The wedding is closing in and

I need to tie up loose ends."

"Preston and I are driving down to Valdosta," I said.

"You don't sound enthusiastic."

"He has an important question to ask me."

Deena laid her hand on my arm. "What's going on, Jolene, besides the ghost in the facial room? I know you're helping Sam with a case, but you haven't been yourself lately."

"Bradford loves me."

"What?" Deena's high-pitched screech brought several employees on the run, their expressions one of concern. One of the lingering clients glanced up from Lizzie's chair, her face beaming with curiosity.

"It's all right. Nothing to worry about," I assured them, then propelled Deena into her office, and shut the door.

She plopped down in her desk chair and shot me a huge grin. "When did this happen, and why haven't you said anything?"

I sank down in a chair across her. "It just happened, and I don't want to deal with it. Can we drop it, please?"

She nodded. "I'm here when you want to talk."

"Thank, sis. I may take you up on that but not today. I need to get home. Preston's picking me up at seven."

"This isn't going away, Jolene. You've got to choose between Sam and Preston," she said as she walked me to my car.

I slid behind the wheel. "No, I don't. Bradford is leaving Whiskey Creek as soon as he closes on his ranch."

"He has a buyer?"

"Yes, he delivered the news yesterday morning."

"So you've decided not to relocate to Wyoming?"

"I'm not leaving Whiskey Creek." I shut the door and fired up the engine. In the rearview mirror, I could see Deena wave as I pulled out of the rear parking lot and headed for the house.

****

Thirty minutes before Preston's expected arrival the doorbell rang. I opened the door to see Bradford leaning on the doorjamb. My gaze froze on his long, lean form, and I swallowed back the sudden lump in my throat. Butterflies assaulted my stomach as a rush of warmth poured over me, and I realized that I loved him. Jolene Claiborne had done the unthinkable and fallen madly, passionately, head-over-heels in love with Samuel Bradford. Christ. Shoot me now.

"Hey, sunshine." He removed his Stetson. "Got a minute?"

My tongue stuck to the roof of my mouth while the earth rocked beneath my feet. Sheer terror filled my veins with ice, but I stepped back and opened the door wider.

He crossed the threshold, and removed his hat. "Nice shoes. They match the red in your dress." His eyes met mine. I struggled to breathe. Say something. Do something. Yet, I stood there speechless, locked in my own nightmare. This couldn't be happening. Not now. Pull it together, Claiborne. Love doesn't last. Fight it.

"I have a date." My voice was strangely calm, all emotion held in check by iron will. I wouldn't crumble. I wouldn't touch him. I wouldn't give in to the love choking me.

"With the doctor?" His voice held a spark of sadness.

I steeled myself against its appeal. "Yes, with Preston."

The blue in his eyes faded. "Well, I won't stay. I wanted to go over the details of your encounter last night at the Maco mansion. Officially."

I moved into the den like a frozen zombie and eased down on one of the wingback chairs flanking the fireplace. Bradford sank onto its twin. He pulled out a small notepad from his front shirt pocket. "You reported finding a woman's body in the basement at 1288 Sixth Street, correct?"

"Vanessa van Allen, yes."

"The body hasn't been identified." His voice was wooden. "The fire consumed the house and garage. Are you sure it was Vanessa van Allen?"

The image of Vanessa's still face rose in my mind. "It was her. She was wearing the ruby ring."

"A ring wasn't recovered."

"No ring? I saw it. Vanessa had the ring." My voice rose with disbelief.

"The medical examiner didn't find any jewelry on the body, Jolene."

"Betty came back for her ring," I declared, certain of my conclusions. "She's guilty as sin. I presume she has an alibi."

"You are correct. Betty denies any involvement in the Maco fire or Vanessa's whereabouts. Sophia swears they hadn't left the residence since yesterday morning. The neighbors collaborated the story. The physical evidence was destroyed by the fire. And since the body hasn't been identified, Betty wasn't informed of Vanessa's death."

"Did you find a connection between Hazel Jessup and Betty van Allen?"

"Not yet. Still checking. These things take time." He tucked the notepad back into his front shirt pocket and rose. "That's all I need for now, but I will have more questions as the investigation continues. The State's Fire Marshal's arson investigator has been called in along with the GBI. Can you give me a description of the car?"

"I'm not sure, but I believe it was a blue four door late model Cadillac."

He jotted the description down on his notepad. "Any specific features you can remember about the car that would help to identify it?"

I shook my head. "No. What about Snellgrove?"

"Solid alibi."

"So, it's my word against theirs?"

"For now, yes. I'll be in touch." He strode to the door, then turned to face me and brushed a light kiss upon my lips.

I shut the door with a soft click, and leaned against the panel with a heavy heart. Seconds later, I heard the roar of his diesel engine and crunching tires as he backed out of the driveway and drove away. Peeling myself from the door, I went into the hall bathroom and dabbed my watery eyes with a tissue. From the master bedroom Tango's purring sounded, and I tracked back to the bedroom to gather a light sweater against the chill. In the bedroom, I plucked a white cashmere wrap from the closet and draped it over my shoulders. Gathering my purse, I left Tango curled in a ball in the middle of the bed, and made my way to the kitchen to wait for Preston.

As I pulled out a chair, a dense fog boiled out of the opened pantry door and twisted into the wavering form of a woman I never wanted to see again.

Queen of the Vampires. Vanessa van Allen.

Before I could utter a sound, another fog bank rolled out of the pantry.

Geez, enough already. Careen Halsey still costumed as Snow White with golden handcuffs dangling from her skinny wrist.

And last—but certainly not least—the storm clouds spit out one pissed-off heavenly bounty hunter in black jeans and leather. Scarlett leveled a gleaming silver handgun at the twins, then cocked a wry smile over her shoulder at me. "Guess who's coming to dinner?"

Chapter Twenty-Nine
The Three Witches of Whiskey Creek

"Get them outta here, Scarlett," I shouted, my face hot and frowning. "I'm not dealing with this ordeal any longer. All of you get outta my kitchen."

"Not until my manuscript is in my agent's hands," Vanessa van Allen haughtily proclaimed. "Heaven can wait. The next bestseller can't."

"Bestseller? How dare you pass off my work as yours," Careen screeched, her ghostly figure bobbing in the air like a child pulling a balloon string. "Peaches Noble had you pegged correctly. You can't write squat. I'm the true talent in the room. You're nothing but a murderer."

"Killer? I didn't kill anyone."

"Ha. You murdered me."

"I did not."

"You did."

I placed my hands over my ears as the two began squabbling between them. Finally, when I couldn't stand it any longer, I stalked out of the kitchen and back to my bedroom. Tango wasn't in sight. Probably cowering under the bed with the house invaded by the three witches of Whiskey Creek. The clock on the nightstand read 6:57. Great. Preston should be here any minute. The doorbell rang. Scarlett materialized beside me. "Your date is here, and you look like hell."

I glanced in the dresser mirror, grimacing back at the frazzled woman. I did look like hell. My flushed face and angry expression added a decade to my forty years. Forty. Christ. I was too old for all this drama. "Scarlett, please go away and take them with you. I'm finished with the evil twins. They can go to Hell where they belong."

"Boy, you are in a funk. It won't be easy, but we'll be gone by the time you get back from your date. I promise."

I left the three witches of Whiskey Creek battling it out in the kitchen and made my way to the front door.

Preston whistled when I opened the door. "Wow, you look scrumptious tonight, darling."

Darling. Crap. I forced a weak smile and took his offered arm. "Thank you, Preston. You look nice yourself."

Dressed in a dark, casual suit, he made a dashing figure. Not ruggedly handsome like Bradford, but clean cut and nice. Husband material Mama would say. However, I wasn't Mama and wanted no husband. Depending on how the evening progressed, this might be our last date. If he pulled out the "I love you" card, he'd be history.

With my feelings riding on my shoulder, I allowed him to hand me into his white Lexus SUV. I snapped my seatbelt and struggled to keep a smile on my bland face. Disaster surrounded me like the cashmere sweater draped on my shoulders as the urge to dump him mounted. Better to do it in the driveway where I could make a quick escape. My stomach clenched and unclenched as butterflies again assaulted my belly. Anxiety nipped at my heels. God, why hadn't I downed

A Dead Pig in the Sunshine

a Zanny before leaving?

Preston jumped into the driver's seat, buckled his belt, and started the engine. "Is everything okay with you, Jolene? You're quiet."

I gazed out the window at the streetlights casting a merry glow on Pinecone Lane. Most houses lining the streets had warm, yellow light spilling from the windows, and I could imagine happy families sitting down together for the evening meal. Turning away from the window, I threw a wary eye at him. "Deena's wedding is almost here, and as Maid of Honor, I've been the go-to guy. Billie Jo is out for the remainder of her pregnancy, and we're short staffed at the salon." I left out my part in Bradford's investigation. The atmosphere was tense enough. "Mama and Daddy might put the farm up for sale and move to Florida, and Tango discovered a nest of mice in my laundry room. My superpowers have abandoned me."

"Is there anything I can do to ease the strain?"

Yeah, take me home and find a nice girl to settle down with. I shook my head. "No, but thanks for asking. A glass of wine will brighten my mood." Or two or three, I left unsaid.

We hopped on I-75 and drove south to Valdosta, spending most of the trip in casual conversation. Each time Preston deftly steered the dialogue back to us, I redirected it to safer ground. My goal for the evening remained steadfast—return to Whiskey Creek unscathed by relationship drama that occurs when one party, being me, wasn't all that into the other, being him.

An hour later, we were seated at Freddie's Steak and Seafood in downtown Valdosta. The waiter poured two glasses of Cabernet Sauvignon to accompany our prime rib steaks and hurried away to bring our salads.

"My coworkers at the hospital rave about the prime rib here, Jolene." Preston swirled his wine in the crystal glass, brought it to his nose, whiffed, and then took a sip. "Excellent." He set down his drink.

I gulped two mouthfuls. "I prefer a cheap brand of blackberry wine, but okay, just as long as my glass stays full."

A frown furrowed his brow. "Perhaps you should slow down, my dear. I don't want you too relaxed. I have an important question to ask you."

I set down my glass and reached for the basket of rolls the waiter placed on the table. "No questions tonight, Preston. My mind is crammed with other issues. For both of our sakes, don't push. I really shouldn't have come tonight seeing how I'm so outta sorts."

My words had the necessary effect. Preston turned his attention to the salad placed in front of him, and for five minutes, we consumed the food in front of us in awkward silence. My mood continued to deteriorate as the meal progressed.

As the waiter cleared away the dirty dishes from the table, Preston reached inside his jacket and brought out a small, black box. He placed it in front of me. My wineglass froze mid-air.

"I know it's only been three months since we started dating," he said with a hopeful smile. "But I've grown extremely fond of you, and hope to take our relationship to the next level. Open the box."

With shaking hands, I set the wineglass down on the pristine linen tablecloth. In the background couples were chatting, glasses clinking, laughter and gaiety blended with soft music. The perfect backdrop for a marriage proposal. I balked, my arms cast in cement at my side.

"Go ahead, open it," Preston said, his eyes shining like a young boy with a new toy to share with a friend. "It won't bite." He reached for the box and began to open it. My hand snaked out and covered his.

"I see dead people," I announced over the background noise. "Not only do I see them, I talk to them."

The chatter around us ground to a halt. The waiter paused, cast me a horrified look, and scampered away with a tray of deserts. Several pairs of eyes watched me with disbelief before turning their heads to avoid my hostile stare.

Preston cleared his throat. "I'm not sure how to respond to that, my dear. If you don't want to live with me, then say so, but please don't make up lies to hide your true feelings."

I blinked at him, my anger building. "No one calls me a liar but my mama, and that's only because she can. I'm trying to be nice here but you're making it hard. Whatever gave you the ridiculous notion that I'd be interested in marrying you?"

He opened his mouth to speak, but I cut him off. "The only thing I wanted from you was sex. Sex and only sex. Not I-love-yous or any other nonsense. Especially after three months of casual dating."

He laughed loudly, drawing more curious looks our way. "Casual dating? God, what a fool I am. You're in love with that detective you're playing around with." He opened the box to display a pair of exquisite

271

diamond dangle earrings. "These were a gift to show you my affection and dedication to our relationship. Marriage? Yes, I want that someday. But not now. We're not ready."

My temper took a dive at his crestfallen features. Remorse rushed in. "I'm sorry, Preston, but you said you had an important question to ask me. I assumed you were going to propose with that ring box in your hand."

"Never assume, Jolene. I wanted to ask you to be my one and only. That's all, but it seems I've made a horrible fool out of myself."

****

The three witches of Whiskey Creek were waiting for me when Preston dropped me off around eleven. The ride back home had been uncomfortable, and my predication of a last date came true. Preston walked me to the front door, told me goodbye, and then turned on his heel and drove away.

Exhausted with the emotional rollercoaster, I ignored the bickering coming from the kitchen and made a beeline for my bedroom to see Scarlett lounging on my bed like a sleeping tiger.

"You promised you'd be gone." I launched my purse at her, only to see it pass through her wavering figure to land in the middle of the bed. "You lied."

"I do that on occasion," she answered with a yawn. "How's your latest boy toy? Not good?"

"You could say that. Now please leave."

"I can't without them, and the pair are proving to be a handful."

I kicked off my heels and peeled out of the dress and hose. "Then shut them up so I can go to bed."

"Can't do that either."

"Where's Tango?" I peered under the bed in my bra and panties.

"How should I know? Your pussy doesn't like me."

"He and I share that sentiment." I went into the bathroom to take a shower. When I emerged ten minutes later, my mood had improved, and I felt better equipped to help my unwanted guests cross over to the Other Side.

Scarlett still lounged on my bed. "He'll call you after his anger cools, Jolene. I know men. They always cave when the sex is good."

"Preston isn't my concern at the moment, Scarlett. The house needs cleaning of three unwanted guests." Dressed in a short, flannel nightie, I padded into the kitchen, and stood next to the stove watching the evil twins circling one another like two roosters in a henhouse. Geez. What did I ever do to the Universe to deserve this?

Scarlett appeared next to me. "Writers make the worst ghosts, wouldn't you agree?"

I cocked a snide smile. "Not just writers, Scarlett. Now help me put an end to this confrontation so I can get some sleep."

"Have any suggestions?"

"You're the bounty hunter."

A loud whistle blasted my eardrums, and I clamped my hands over my ears. The evil twins stopped bickering to turn and look our way. I dropped my hands to my sides and opened my mouth wide to stop the ringing in my ears.

"Okay, hear this," Scarlett began, "The long, black

train leaves the station in five minutes, got it? Any last words you have to say, now's the time." The golden handcuffs shackled Vanessa to Careen. Both screeched a loud protest, then both said in union, "Me first."

"I want to question Vanessa." I plopped down on a seat at the table. "Careen, you keep quiet for now."

Careen settled down. "Only if I get justice."

"Agreed. Here's the rules: I question, you answer. No interruptions, no arguing."

The evil twins cast mean looks at the other, but finally nodded their heads. Scarlett supervised from the stovetop.

"First question, Vanessa. Did you murder Careen?"

"No. She's my paycheck."

"Who did?"

"Her brother, Michael."

"That's a lie," Careen burst out, pulling against the handcuffs.

"No, it's the truth," Vanessa declared. "I saw him from my hiding place in the garage. Remember our phone call? We agreed to meet there and switch places. You were to disappear, and I would assume my rightful place as Vanessa van Allen as we'd done many times before."

"Mistaken identity. Go on," I urged.

"As soon as Careen shut the garage door behind her, I heard a muffled gunshot, and saw Careen crumple to the floor. Michael stood over her with a small handgun with a silencer. They must've planned to kill me from the beginning. Believing he'd shot me, he hid the gun on the top shelf behind some boxes, then returned to the party. In one minute, he'd destroyed my well-laid plans."

"So you covered up the crime by moving the body?"

"Yes. I dragged Careen to the back of the garage, covered her with an old blanket before slipping into the house. As planned, my Snow White costume perfectly matched Careen's, and no one knew the difference. Not even Michael. He thought I was Careen when he cornered me in the butler's pantry to tell me the deed was done. I convinced him it would be best for me to get rid of the body, and he left when the party broke up. At my first chance, I told Mother everything. We planned the fight with Sam to get rid of him. I retrieved the gun, then we moved the body."

"You and your mother?"

"Yes, and Sophia. She had a trusted friend who proved extremely helpful. He placed the gun in Careen's hand and fired a second shot to make it appear as a suicide if the body was ever discovered which we didn't anticipate with the site being abandoned for so long. We tossed the body behind a large headstone at the back of the cemetery."

"She was in on it all the time?"

"Had to be. Sophia and Mother made it possible for me to carry out the pretense. Without them, none of this would've been possible."

"And the friend?"

"Snellgrove."

"I knew he was tangled up in this mess. Tell me why you concocted this whole charade, Vanessa?"

She jangled the golden handcuffs. "Jealousy. I recognized Careen's talent with the first sentence of her Dark Enchantment series. She was young and naïve, and bore a striking resemblance to me, so I seized the opportunity to live the life I've always dreamed. We both profited from the exchange."

"Until it backfired."

"Until she double-crossed me is what you mean."

"You lie!" Careen glowed a bright white. "Liar. I'm innocent."

My body peppered with goose bumps at Vanessa's ghostly chuckle.

"Michael showed up at the Baconton Writers' Retreat the next day full of himself. He and Careen planned the whole ugly scheme. With me gone, she could easily step into my life without the complications of a pretense."

"I'm confused," I confessed. "With the discovery of Vanessa's body in the garage, wouldn't the body double come to light? I mean, damn, this is confusing. I don't know what I mean."

"I was never to be found," Vanessa said. "Careen, posing as me, would tell my mother she'd accidently killed Careen. Betty would then help her daughter dispose of the body. When Careen needed to make an appearance in Hawkinsville, she would appear as herself. Really a brilliant plan when you think about it. One person, two identities—only she and Michael would know the truth."

I whistled in amazement at the deceit of both parties. "So all this time, you've been playing along with Michael? What happened at the cabin?"

"Michael discovered my true identity when he asked me a family question I couldn't answer. We tussled, and he slashed my arm with a knife. He forced me to go along with him."

"To the Maco mansion? What's the connection?"

"He and Careen met there often when he was in town," Vanessa said. "The property belongs to their great aunt."

"If he forced you, then how did he come to be beaten and tied to a chair?" I asked her. "Your story doesn't mesh, Vanessa."

Careen snickered. "She's a liar."

Vanessa ignored her. "I managed to knock him out with an old chair. I tied him up and then used his cell phone to call my mother. Sophia called her friend for more help."

"Sheriff Snellgrove." I spat the name with disgust. "Careen saw you arguing with him at the cemetery where they found her body."

"We were arguing over the price of his silence."

"This would make a great book," Scarlett said from her perch on the stovetop. "Completely unbelievable but entertaining."

I made a dismissive wave. "Let her finish, Scarlett. I want to know who tried to bash my brain in."

Vanessa picked up where she left off. "Well, after they arrived, we decided Michael knew too much."

"You killed him?"

"No, just gave him a good thrashing. We hadn't figured out what to do with him when you showed up and scared us plenty. Sophia didn't mean to hit you so hard."

I rubbed the still sore area. "Who was wearing the ruby ring?"

She seemed surprised with the question. "What ruby ring?"

"The same one I saw on your corpse."

Vanessa's shoulders drew in, her face pinched and

strained. "That's all I know." She blinked in and out several times, becoming almost transparent.

That was the end of my questions. With her burdens in tow, Scarlett bid me farewell. The clock above the stove read 3:00. The witching hour. In my bedroom, I picked up the receiver to call Bradford, and changed my mind. Too much information for the phone. Tomorrow would be soon enough for him to arrest Vanessa's mother and the other co-conspirators.

Chapter Thirty
Just When You Believe You Have It All Figured
Out

The doorbell rang early the next morning. I opened
the door to a local florist deliveryman holding a
stunning autumn bouquet of peach spray roses,
burgundy mini carnations, butterscotch
chrysanthemums, and dusty miller. I gasped with
delight when the man handed over the orange vase of
flowers. I closed the door behind him and placed the
arrangement on the foyer table and reached for the card.
It read:

I'm sorry for last night. Please give me another
chance to win your heart as you are the woman of my
dreams. Look inside the bouquet for the special gift I
picked out just for you.

Preston

I pressed the card to my chest as my resistance
melted, and a rush of warm, fuzzy affection washed
over me at his thoughtfulness. From within the bouquet,
I pulled out a white box with gold script I recognized
from the jeweler down the block from Dixieland Salon.
I paused with indecision, then opened the box.

The kitchen phone shrilled but I ignored it, and
continued to gaze in wonder at the simple, inexpensive
Casper the Friendly Ghost bracelet charm resting on a
blue velvet background. Several bricks crumbled from

the wall encasing my heart. I tried to shore up the crack, but something gave as I stroked the smooth, white enamel.

My attention wavered as the phone shrilled again. Tears pooled in my eyes as I made my way to the kitchen. Bradford. I let it ring several times more before I picked it up, needing the time to corral my conflicting emotions.

"We need to talk," he said in a neutral tone when I answered. "I'm in the neighborhood. Can I stop by?"

"I'll make coffee." My tone matched his, although my heart rate sped up at the prospect of seeing him. The white mother-of-pearl charm mocked me from its velvet bed. My mind drifted to Preston and his thoughtful apology.

"See you in five." The line disconnected. I set the opened box and card on the table and went to the counter to make coffee. As the coffee dripped, I pulled a roll of orange Danish rolls from the refrigerator and popped them in to bake. To give the kitchen a cheery burst of color and scent, I placed the bouquet of flowers in the center of the table. A car pulled into the driveway.

A knock sounded at the kitchen door, and Bradford stepped in and took a seat. "Good morning."

I poured a mug of coffee and placed it in front of him. "Good morning. Let me check these rolls and then we'll talk."

"I see your date went well. You finally shared your secret."

So he noticed the flowers and the Casper charm. "Yes, and no. I overreacted and made an ass of myself." I joined him at the table with a mug of coffee. "What's up?"

"You were right. The body has been positively identified as Vanessa van Allen."

"I had unexpected visitors last night."

"Of the earthly kind?"

"Once upon a time."

He picked up his mug and sipped. "A new mystery?"

"God forbid. The evil twins and Scarlett."

His cup landed with a clunk on the wooden surface. "Vanessa and Careen? Together? What brought this about?"

"I haven't a clue, but Vanessa was in a chatty mood with an interesting story to share. Hold onto your chair because you're not going to believe this tale of double-crossing doubles." I repeated last night's conversation. In the background, Tango purred under the table, and the tangy aroma of baking orange rolls filled the kitchen.

He whistled when I stopped talking. "This is the wildest tale I've ever encountered. If it's true."

I left the table to pull the hot rolls from the oven. "Careen swears Vanessa's lying, but I believe her. It explains Michael's continued presence here in Whiskey Creek. He didn't realize he'd killed the wrong woman until that last night at the writers' retreat."

"There are still several loose ends that need explaining, and evidence to collect. That's one reason I wanted to talk with you. We haven't been able to find any trace of the car you described."

I spread icing on the hot rolls and transferred them onto a plate. "You should check to see if Sophia owns a car. And Snellgrove."

"He drives a Ford truck." Bradford pushed back from the table and crossed to the counter where he poured coffee into his mug. "I'll also check Michael Halsey's mode of transportation."

"What about Hazel Jessup? She's a relative so she could've been involved." I set the plate of rolls on the table. "Her house is the crime scene."

Bradford took his seat and reached for a plate and fork. "Impossible. Hazel Jessup is ninety-five and housebound." He scooped up a couple of rolls. "Hazel's attorney takes care of her property."

"He's doing a piss-poor job. That old house should've been razed to the ground years ago. I'm surprised it's lasted this long. It's a magnet for bored teenagers and the homeless." I took a bite of warm roll, the combination of cinnamon and sweet orange icing had me licking my lips. "Umm."

"The cause of the fire is still under investigation, but it smells like arson." He upended his coffee mug and placed it back down on the table. "I've got to run up to Hawkinsville this morning, but should return by the afternoon." He pushed back from the table and reached for his Stetson. "Diamond can get a message to me if needed." He shoved his hat on his head, reached down, and kissed my upturned nose. "When this is over, sunshine, you and I have some serious talking to do about our relationship. I'm staking my claim, and it'll take more than Casper the Friendly Ghost to chase this ole cowboy away."

****

When I arrived at the salon, Deena shared a quick word with me and then off she went to the First Baptist Church for a meeting with the organist and the wedding singer for hire. Mama was in on it, I believe, and Billie Jo too, which left me holding down the fort. And that was perfectly fine with me since I needed the alone time to work out relationship issues smothering my brain cells. I do my best thinking at work. The swishing of running water, whirling blow-dryers, and chatting clients were the perfect foil for this stressed-out hairdresser to zone out. I could wrap a perm, roll hair, wax lips, and just about any other job associated with hairdressing in my sleep, which was why I spent many hours ironing out problems in my favorite think tank—Dixieland Salon.

This morning's problems were different in two ways. Preston Neally and Samuel Bradford. Both were vying for my attention. Two highly respected, sought-after Whiskey Creek bachelors, and I had my choice. The detective or the doctor? The detective had a big gun, but the doctor knew how to manipulate body parts in ways that left one blasting through the stars in search of the Almighty. I fingered the ghost charm on my bracelet.

"Something's cooking in your pot and it's tickling your nose," a voice broke into my steamy thoughts. I glanced in the mirror to see Mrs. Eisenberg's inquisitive green gaze mirrored back. "Must be a man," she twittered.

"Or two." I flashed a coy smile and touched the ghost charm.

Her grin grew wider. "No wonder you're lollygagging in fantasyland." She clicked her tongue. "I had two beaus once upon a time before wrinkles came to live on my face."

I wrapped another roller into her silvery hair.

"Beauty never fades, Mrs. Eisenberg."

She reached up and patted my hand. "Sweet girl, tell this old woman about your two beaus."

A sudden shyness came over me at the prospect of sharing my complex situation with a client. Even one as long-standing as Mrs. Eisenberg. Deena's my usual go-to person, but with her overloaded with last minute wedding details, this seemed ideal. And I really did want some advice from this gentle old soul.

"Casper must be a special gift," Mrs. Eisenberg said. "From one of your men, I'm guessing by the way you keep touching it. Tell me about him."

I dropped my hand from caressing the charm. "You guessed right. The charm has a special meaning."

"Tell me about them, Jolene." Her encouraging motherly smile gazed back at me from the mirror.

"The charm was a gift from Dr. Preston Neally."

"Ah, a doctor. I'm impressed. Go on, tell me all about your handsome doctor."

"Well, Preston is a nice man. Successful, financially secure, owns his own home, and dependable and stable. Has a bright future here in Whiskey Creek. Oh, and thoughtful."

"He sounds delightful, my dear. And the other?"

"Detective Samuel Bradford."

Mrs. Eisenberg's eyes grew wide. "Oh dear. Him again? Are you sure that's wise, honey? I mean, he's a looker for sure, but you've been bucked off that horse a time or two. Stick with the doctor. He's a sure bet."

I grimaced in good humor. "Sam's a good guy, Mrs. Eisenberg. He's stuck his neck out several times for my family. He deserves another chance."

"I heard he's leaving town. How does that fit into

your plans? Your family and business are here."

Good question. I'd asked myself the same thing numerous times since that ill-fated night of lovemaking. Mrs. Eisenberg's hand closed over mine. "I can see you're in for a hard time, honey. Choosing between two men ain't easy, but neither is following your heart. Love is never what the movies make it out to be, Jolene. Just when you think you have it all figured out, they stab you in the heart. Hard work, love."

I nodded my head but remained quiet, ready to move onto a safer subject. Luckily, she too clammed up, her eyes glazed over as in deep thought. Probably rehashing marital difficulties of her own.

The morning passed quickly, without incident, and when I next noted the time, it was after lunch. With my next client running late, I ran back to the kitchen for a quick bite to eat. When I drew abreast of the facial room door, a weird sensation of pinpricks showered my body. I stopped and touched the doorknob to find it hot. I jerked my hand away and stood frozen, staring at the closed panel, uncertain how to handle the growing crisis. Just this morning I heard an offhand remark from Lizzie's client about the creepy hallway and not wanting to use the restroom. And not just her, our nail tech had complained several times of spooked and lost customers. She had even threatened to shorten her two-week notice by one week if we didn't fix the "creepy hallway."

The rear entrance door opened, and I glanced up to see Deena stroll through with a pleased expression, which quickly faded when she spotted me. "Please tell me there's not another problem in the facial room? One Hell's angel is enough."

I shook my head. "Not yet, but our visitor is getting frisky."

"You said you'd take care of it."

"I haven't found anyone willing to perform an exorcism."

"Don't say another word." She glanced down the hall, then stepped over to the kitchen door, opened it, and peered inside. "It's empty. Can't take the chance and have our conversation being broadcast."

"Let's continue this discussion in the kitchen, Deena. I'm starving and don't have much time before my client arrives." She followed me into the kitchen and took a seat at the table, while I dug around in the refrigerator for the brown paper bag lunch I brought from home. With the bag and a bottled water, I sat across from her at the table.

"Clients are complaining again." I took a bite of my peanut butter and jelly sandwich. "They don't like our creepy hallway."

"What happened with the Catholic priest?"

"They showed me the door."

"Why? Did you say something off-putting?" She pinched off a bite of my sandwich and popped it into her mouth.

"Ah, other than I have a demon in my facial room?" I drank down several gulps of cold water. "He then asked me if I'd been to confession lately, and I responded with a laugh."

"That was off-putting, Jolene."

"We're Baptist, Deena. We don't confess our sins in a closet."

"Do you suppose Pastor Inman could help?"

"I tried. He suggested counseling and threatened to

call Mama."

"Oh, good heavens, not that. Can you imagine if she knew? Any suggestions?"

"All out of holy men, Deena. Although the Pentecostals were the most help." I polished off my sandwich.

"What about Scarlett? Can she help?"

I downed the last drink of water. "She's our last hope, but it'll have to wait for a better time. She's shackled to the evil twins at the moment."

Deena gave a twisted smile. "On a better note, my wedding is less than two weeks away and everything is in order. Smooth sailing ahead. How's things between you and Sam?"

I told her the latest, including the visit from the evil twins.

"I wish I hadn't asked." She rose and pushed away from the table. "I'm worried, Jolene. You've placed yourself in danger too many times. One day you're going to get seriously hurt or worse."

I agreed with her but couldn't voice my feelings lest I upset her further, yet neither could I treat her worries lightly. As I'd done in the past, I pasted on my big sister smile, and dropped an arm over her shoulder. "From this day forward, let's concentrate on getting you married to the greatest man on the planet, okay? I promise there'll be no more drama from your Maid of Honor."

Deena lifted her face to mine and planted a kiss on my cheek. "You promise?"

I made an X sign over my heart. "Cross my heart and hope to die."

Chapter Thirty-One
Cross my Heart and Hope to Die?

All my good intentions came crashing down around 3:30. I'd just finished a color job when Bradford strolled through the door like a red-caped bullfighter facing an enraged bull after a long and gruesome fight. My stomach tightened when his steeled visage focused on me. Reading his urgent vibrations, I hurried my client to the reception desk where Holly waited to take payment. "Reschedule my next appointment, Holly. If she raises a fuss, see if Lizzie can squeeze her in. I have an emergency."

Meeting Bradford at the desk, I linked my arm in his, and steered him to Deena's office. When we pushed through the closed door, Deena glanced up from a pile of papers on her desk. "I was just going over the supplies list." A worried looked creased her face. "What's wrong?"

Bradford removed his hat. "The GBI wants to interview Jolene pertaining to the murder of Vanessa van Allen." He rumpled his hair nervously with one hand. "I'm here to bring her in."

Deena shot out of her chair and raced around the desk. "Oh my God, is she being arrested? Questioned for what? Should I call Mama and Daddy? T.J. Pickens?"

I grabbed her arm and brought her quaking body

close. "Calm down, sis. Everything will work out. We have a wedding, you know. I'll not let anything get in the way of your happiness." We stood nose to nose. "Let Bradford explain." I released her, and she sank down onto a chair.

Bradford set his hat down on the desktop and took Deena's hands in his. "Jolene's right, Deena. The GBI need more information for the investigation into Vanessa's death. She's only a witness." He turned to me, and I instantly knew. For all his assuring words, he was worried. The emotion lined the crinkles around his eyes and mouth. And there, just a flicker of doubt reflected in the sapphire eyes.

I stilled myself and tried not to cry as fear's icy fingers squeezed the breath from my lungs and the strength from my limbs. I dropped onto the chair next to my sister. "I need a minute, Bradford, and then we'll head out for the station."

He released Deena's hands. "We need to talk, Jolene. About you know what."

"Like how I'm going to explain my presence in the Maco mansion on the night Vanessa van Allen was murdered?"

He nodded. "Yeah, you can't waltz in there and tell them the truth."

"Why not?" Deena asked. "Jolene's known for engaging in dangerous pursuits. She was only trying to help you."

"That's the cincher, Deena," I spoke up. "I'm not supposed to be involved with this investigation. Bradford could end up losing his job."

"I'm sorry, Sam, but you quit your job," Deena pointed out. "What difference does it make if it gets

Jolene out of trouble?"

"I'm not in trouble," I countered. "I'm a witness." I paused, then lifted my eyes to Bradford's. "However, she's right. I acted on my own. You had nothing to do with my decision to stake out Vanessa's house. Or my decision to follow them to the Maco mansion. I thought I was helping you build a case."

"But I'm the one who broke the rules when I sought your help." He pushed away from the desk and paced the floor. "I'm responsible for you being in the position you're in."

"And what position is that?" I questioned with a spike of anxiety.

Bradford stopped his pacing to face me. "Honestly, I don't know. The GBI has access to all your previous arrest records and Snellgrove's report on Careen's suicide with your gun."

"My stolen gun, you mean," I corrected him. "And Careen was accidently killed by her brother when he mistook her for Vanessa. I told you the story."

"And I have no proof," he stated, sounding exasperated. "You can't tell the GBI ghost stories, Jolene. They depend on physical evidence to make their cases."

"Then find the evidence to clear her." Deena squeezed my hand.

"I'm working on it. In the meantime, we need to get down to the station before the GBI gets restless." Bradford strode over to the desk to retrieve his hat. "I'll have her back before the shop closes, Deena. Try not to worry."

"And don't call Mama," I warned her. "She'll make things worse for me."

"I doubt that, Jolene, but I'll keep quiet for now." Deena squeezed my hand. "One phone call is all it takes, Jolene. I have T.J. Pickens on speed dial."

I paused at the door. "I don't need an attorney, yet. And again whatever you do, please don't call Mama and Daddy. Or Billie Jo. They deserve a rest from my troubles. Besides, there's nothing to worry about."

Deena's eyes watered. "Promise?"

I nodded my head and then laughed. "I'm beginning to sound like a politician with all these promises I'm making."

Bradford cupped my elbow. "We need to get going before they come looking for us."

I kissed my sister on the cheek and tasted her salty tears. "Call Ryder, if you need to talk. My soon to be brother-in-law knows how to keep a secret. Deena, I can't leave my gun in my workstation. Lock it in the office safe box."

We left the office, and I hurried over to my workstation to retrieve my shoulder bag with my gun stashed inside while Bradford went out to his unmarked police car. Back in Deena's office, I handed over the gun, and ducked out of the salon without any fuss and climbed into his unmarked police car. He fired up the engine and backed out of the parking space, made a quick turn, and headed toward the station.

"I'm frightened, Bradford. I've never been questioned by the GBI," I confessed as we wound around a quiet neighborhood street lined with tall pine and oak trees shedding their summer foliage. Leaves of red, orange, and muted yellow floated on the cool breeze to carpet the lawns and street in patches of color and pine needles. Ghosts and pumpkins, witches, and scarecrows still dotted the occasional lawn of a procrastinating homeowner.

Bradford's hand gripped the steering wheel before he glanced over at me. "Just give them the details as you did me. However, leave Scarlett out of it. They wouldn't understand. There's an official report on the incident, so don't worry."

"But what if they suspect I had something to do with her murder? That could happen, you know. Daddy says the innocent end up in jail just like the guilty. I was at the scene of the crime. And Careen was killed with my stolen gun. Bad mojo is written all over this. I'm going down."

He reached over the seat for my hand. "I won't let anything happen to you, sweetie. You wouldn't be in this situation if it weren't for me."

"There's no blame, Bradford." I squeezed his hand. "Dealing with the dead has repercussions. You needed my help. What else could I do?"

I felt a bit unnerved at the prospect of the coming interview as the redbrick police station came into view, and we swung around to the rear of the building to Bradford's parking space. Now that we were here, my hands grew clammy with my sinking mood.

Bradford unbuckled his seatbelt. "Okay, let's do this."

I forced my feet to move as my mind buzzed with thoughts of catastrophe. Not knowing what to expect, I sent a silent appeal heavenward for help. This could go either way—good or bad. My fate rested in the hands of the two GBI agents waiting beyond the steel, gray door.

****

The dreary, colorless waiting room hadn't changed

since my last visit. A dank, stale odor blanketed the room that never saw nature's glowing sunlight or the fresh open country air streaming through an open window. I took the seat in the corner and waved off Bradford saying I needed a few minutes to steady myself. In reality, I didn't want him to witness the full measure of anxiety making its way through my limbs. Taking several deep breaths, I crossed my fingers and sent another SOS heavenward that I wouldn't barf at the GBI's feet. Peanut butter and jelly doesn't taste the same the second time around.

Five minutes passed before a uniformed policeman—Officer Brown, his nametag read—stepped into the room. "If you'll follow me, ma'am. Agents Farmer and Stillwell are ready for you."

My footsteps faltered. Farmer and Stillwell. Christ. My stomach heaved, and I swallowed hard. Bradford could've warned me I would be facing the same two agents that had arrested Daddy for the murder of Theodore Herrington. I'd pissed them off big time that Sunday morning when they accosted Daddy in the church parking lot with half the members staring on. God, I'd practically challenged them both to a duel. Now, to face them again when my ass is the one in the frying pan? Damn. I was going down for sure.

Officer Brown stopped in front of a closed door, tapped twice, and then ushered me into a bright, sunny office complete with coffee and pastries and cookies of every sort laid out on a paper cloth draped table against the far wall. My mouth dropped open in surprise.

Agent Andy Stillwell stood to his towering six-foot-four inches and pointed to the chair opposite him across the desk. "Have a seat, Miz Claiborne. Coffee?"

His bass tone chirped.

I darted a glance at the other man perched sidesaddle on the edge of a large desk. Agent Ian Farmer. Younger. Bald. Overweight. Shifty eyes. No smile. Taking the seat indicated, I placed my shoulder bag in my lap. "Coffee sounds wonderful."

Ian Farmer slipped off the desk and sauntered over to the table. "Cream and sugar?"

I nodded. "A touch of both, please."

He added a dollop of cream and a teaspoon of sugar, grabbed a plate and loaded it down with sweets, then placed them in front of me on the desktop. He resumed his perch, his eyes never leaving me. I reached for the hot coffee and sipped. At least the coffee was good.

"We brought you here, Miz Claiborne." Agent Stillwell rested his forearms on the desk and leaned toward me, "because we believe you killed Miss van Allen and set fire to the old Maco house to cover your crime."

His words slammed into me stealing my breath. My hands were shaking, and as casually as I could, I set the disposable cup down next to the plate of sweets to keep from dumping the hot liquid in my lap. Bradford got it wrong. I'm not a witness, but a suspect. "Have you figured out my motive?"

"Jealousy," Ian Farmer said. "She was dating your ex, Detective Samuel Bradford."

The back of my neck tingled. "Sam Bradford and I broke up months ago. I'm dating Preston Neally. A doctor. Well-respected doctor I might add."

Stillwell opened a file. "Let's review your file, shall we?" He held up a forefinger. "One. Your arrest

294

record shows the pattern of a habitual violator."

"Misunderstandings," I huffed. "Read further and you'll see all the charges were dropped."

"Detective Bradford stated there was a scuffle between you and Miss van Allen on the evening of the thirty-first."

I took a quick breath of utter astonishment at Agent Stillwell's words. The sting of accusation nipped my skin, and I flushed with antagonism and humiliation. "Detective Bradford implicated me?" I grabbed the sides of the chair, my heartrate kicked into high gear. "He told you I picked a fight with Vanessa on Halloween?" I gave an anxious little cough. "I did no such thing. I might've spied on her, but fight? That's ridiculous."

"Tell us about the incident, Miz Claiborne." Ian Farmer growled. "Detective Bradford gave the impression you upset the victim. Made her cry. He said, and I quote 'Something clearly happened between them. Jolene has a quick temper. I was worried for Vanessa.' "

A whisper of terror shot through me at Bradford's betrayal. The overhead fluorescent lights blinked several times mirroring my pounding heart. Adrenaline rushed through my veins like frozen needles. I gasped in several breaths in hopes of restoring oxygen to my panicked brain and slumped down in the hard chair. The seed of trust that had taken root shriveled in the dry dust of my shocked heart, and I felt the walls of self-protection close in. All the progress I'd made since opening my heart to love evaporated in the blink of my watery eyes. Anger burned so hot inside I thought I would melt the cold, hard steel chair. I shoved a hand across my wet cheeks. From the corner of the room I spied the familiar misty shape of a woman. Scarlett! Strength poured into my frame, and I straightened in my chair determined to thwart the GBI's plans to pin Vanessa's murder on me.

"I deny Detective Bradford's statement," I shot back. "I never had any bad words with Vanessa van Allen on Halloween. I never confronted her in any way. I overheard her conversation with another party which upset her. You have no proof I wanted to harm Vanessa."

Agent Stillwell held up another finger. "Two. Do you deny the scene between you and the victim at the Baconton Writers' Retreat last week?" His eyes narrowed. "You purposely vomited down the front of her dress in which she retaliated with a hard slap, knocking you to the floor."

Another misty shape joined Scarlett. Vanessa. I shook my head. "I don't deny it. She assaulted me, not the other way around. Again, you have no proof I wanted to harm Vanessa. If you persist on this line of questioning, I'll answer no further questions without my attorney present."

Farmer and Stillwell exchanged a look. Stillwell leafed through the file to bring out a single sheet of paper. "Tell us about the night you discovered the victim's body at the Maco mansion."

I gave the same skeletal account I'd given to the Whiskey Creek Police Department. I kept it short and sweet. My sense of civic duty had been sufficiently tested, and the authorities could go to hell as far as I was concerned. Bradford's betrayal had sealed my lips, and I gave no consideration to the fact that they could be purposely leading me astray.

"Why didn't you call 9-1-1 immediately upon discovering the body?"

I kept my face impassive. "Because I lost my phone while on stakeout, Agent Stillwell. Read my statement." From the corner of my eye, I spied another white mist twist into the shape of a woman. Careen. Ah, the three musketeers had arrived.

The battering continued. The next question came from Agent Farmer. "Let's go back to the stakeout, Miz Claiborne. Why were you spying on the van Allen's? What's your interest in this case?"

I gave it some thought, reaching for the coffee cup. Agent Farmer had dumped the perfect opportunity in my lap to rat out Bradford, but a rat I'm not. Taking a sip, I let them stew in their own impatient juices. "My mother is my interest, sir. I didn't trust Vanessa or her agent with my mother's financial stake in the published cookbook. Thieves crawl out of the woodwork when they smell a quick buck."

Stillwell made a note. "So you suspected Vanessa and her agent"—he glanced down at the file—"Cash Hitchcock of swindling your mother?" He looked dubious.

I met his gaze equably. "Everyone has a price." In my peripheral vision, I detected movement, and rested my gaze on Scarlett making her way to my side. She whispered in my ear. Now it was my turn to smile. "Let's wrap this up, boys. I know you don't seriously suspect me of killing Vanessa van Allen, otherwise you would've read me my rights. Remember, I've been down this road a couple of times and know the drill." I could've kissed Scarlett for reminding me of this small detail.

Scarlett and the evil twins surrounded the two unsuspecting agents. Both men frowned as ghostly hands pinched and pulled at their flesh, and shouted horrible tidings with rotting breath. They flinched. Stillwell cursed. Farmer bolted up from the desk and dashed out of the room without as much as a goodbye. Agent Stillwell slapped the file closed. "We're done for now, Miz Claiborne, but don't leave town," he snarled, and then followed his partner out of the office with the hounds of hell nipping at his heels.

Chapter Thirty-Two
Neutering the Hounds of Hell

Officer Diamond Presley was waiting for me in the hallway when I came out of the office. She pushed up from the wall she was leaning against and shot me a huge grin. "Damn girl, what-d-ya do to those two hell hounds? They almost mowed me down gettin' outta there. What a bunch of asses."

I shrugged. "Must've been something I said." I laughed with her. "But thankfully, I don't have to spend the night in your luxurious accommodations, although, I'm glad to run into you. Let's have a girl's night out after the dust settles." I glanced at my watch. 5:00. The salon was probably closed by now. I hoped Deena wasn't waiting on me.

"Sure thing, girlfriend, but I have a message for you from Sam."

"I don't want to hear it, Diamond." I pivoted on my heel with the intention of finding the nearest exit. Diamond caught my arm and swung me around to face her.

"What's got your ass in a sling?"

I jerked my arm free. "That low-down, sniveling dog, Detective Samuel Bradford, that's who. Don't ever mention his name to me again, understand?"

A fierce scowl crossed her face. "Now you listen up real good because I'm only going to say this one time." She pointed her finger under my nose. "No one says a bad word about Samuel Bradford to my face. Not even you. He's a good man, and I don't know what he's done to tangle your panties in a wad, and that's between y'all, but you need to stop spitting shit at me."

A door opened, and an officer stepped out into the hall. "What's the trouble, Presley?"

Diamond relaxed her stance. "No trouble, Sergeant. Just boyfriend trouble."

"Take your girl chat elsewhere," he ordered, then ducked back inside the door.

"We'll continue this discussion in my patrol car," Diamond growled in a tone of voice that let me know I was in for a stern putdown. "Sam's been called away and asked me to get you back to the salon." She shot me another cold look. "I'm more of a mind to take you out back and whoop your stupid ass."

I let that zinger slide and trailed shamefully behind her to her patrol car parked in the back alley. She unlocked the driver's door and slid behind the wheel. I reached for the passenger door handle when her snide voice hollered out, "Oh, hell no. You ride in back where you belong."

"Come on, Diamond, enough is enough. I know you're mad at me, but don't make me ride in back like a criminal."

"You are one."

"I'm also your friend. Or was." I forced a weak smile. "There is my side of the story, you know. Give me a chance to explain."

"Okay, get in, but leave the trash talk out there on the sidewalk."

I slid in the passenger seat and buckled my

seatbelt. "I'm not the bitch you're making me out to be, Diamond. Your precious Sam ratted me out to the GBI."

She fired up the engine and backed out of the parking space. "You got it wrong, Jolene. Sam's not the type."

"That's what I thought too, but they had information that only he and I knew, and I sure as hell didn't share."

Her brow furrowed. "Are you sure he's the one?"

"What do you mean, am I sure? Of course, I'm sure. It was a private conversation." I thought back to our heated confrontation outside Vanessa's study on Halloween night and our audience of costumed partygoers. I smacked my forehead with the palm of my hand. "The big yellow bird and his sidekick heard every word."

"Seems to me you've been doing a whole lot of speculating without the facts." Diamond shot me a look as she pulled into traffic. "I know for a fact that the GBI has been parading guests from your momma's Halloween book launch party in for interviews for the past two days. They messed with your mind, girl."

"That would explain it."

"And you so hot to jump on the blame Sam wagon."

"I'm bad." I flushed at her tone.

"Not bad—stupid."

"I've been called worse."

She turned onto Love Avenue, and around to the rear parking lot behind Dixieland Salon and killed the engine. I reached for the door handle. "Thanks fo—"

"Shut up and listen because I'm doing you a

favor." She gently pushed me back against the seat. "I like you, Jolene. Have from the start. But you're dumb as shit when it comes to men. Especially Sam. He's one of the good ones, and you're doin' him wrong."

"But—" She held up her hand when I started to interrupt. I slumped back against the seat, shamefaced and mildly angry with her interference into my private affairs. She was, after all, a new addition to my short friend list, which didn't include unwanted advice.

"Let me finish." Her brown eyes softened. "Being a police officer ain't easy, especially for a black female. Sam's had my back from the get-go. He helped me get through my granny's death, and encouraged me to widen my ambitions. Because of him, I have a shot at becoming the first female detective with the force. Now, he's leaving Whiskey Creek for a better job in Wyoming, and I know he wants you along."

I lifted my hand in appeal. "My life is here. My family and business."

"Sam told me about the doctor you've taken up with."

"He never shares."

"Yes, he does." Her eyes challenged me. "You don't listen." She continued in my silence. "Sam's afraid he's going to lose you, Jolene."

"Sam broke up with me, Diamond. Not the other way around. And Sam's afraid of nothing."

"He's a cop. We live in fear."

"What are you saying, Diamond?"

"You've got to choose. The cop or the doctor. Wyoming or Whiskey Creek."

"It's not that easy. I'm prone to relationship failure."

"Failure is just a stepping stone to success."

I reached for the door handle. She didn't stop me. "Thanks for the ride, Diamond."

"Make a choice, Jolene. And soon."

I shut the door, stepped back, and watched her patrol car disappear around the corner. For a moment I stood in the empty parking lot, her chastisement pricking my conscience. Shaking off the depressive mood, I withdrew the back door key and let myself into the semi-dark salon. Silence, but for the gentle hum of the refrigerator, wrapped around me and I made my way to Deena's office to retrieve my gun.

In the office, I switched on the overhead light and made my way over to the desk and settled down in Deena's plush chair. On the desktop, a white sheet of paper caught my eye. A note from Deena. She'd left me a pre-paid temporary cell phone in the top drawer. I opened the drawer and pulled out the phone, and slipped it into my shoulder bag. From the third drawer, I pulled out the heavy, silver box, and retrieved the Pink Panther.

With my gun tucked away in my purse along with my new phone, I locked the salon and drove home. There I quickly changed into my sleuthing ensemble, fed the cat and myself, reset the alarm and scooted out the door into the growing twilight.

****

The streetlights lining Dartmouth Drive cast its golden light upon the pavement, making my candy-apple red Mustang stick out like a sore thumb. An empty house down the street with a FOR SALE sign in the front yard made for the perfect hiding place, so I parked in its driveway and made my way back down to

Vanessa's house. As I got near, I spotted a familiar car parked close to the house and out of the light.

Mama's Ford Fusion—great balls of fire what's she doing here? I dashed for the hedges and squatted down out of sight. Although I was dressed entirely in black, the night hadn't settled in, and I was still visible. Faced with this new situation, I threw out my previous plan. Somehow, I had to get Mama out of the house without raising Betty's suspicion.

With a new plan taking shape in my mind, I backtracked to the Mustang, and drove directly into Betty's driveway behind Mama's car. Then I took out the cell phone and dialed Mama's number. Static crackled over the line. Mama picked up on the fifth ring. "Hello."

"Mama, don't say a word," I said over static. "And don't let on it's me."

"Harland, darling? I can hardly hear you. What? Yes, I know I'm running late, but I'm having tea with Betty."

Crackle. "Good. Get out of there, Mama." Loud static. "Now."

"I can't hear you, but I'll be home soon." The line disconnected. Did she get my message?

Five minutes passed and still no Mama. Five more to say her goodbyes and then I was going in. I watched the digital dashboard clock count down. Four. Three. Two. One. Okay, plan B. Easing out of the car, I skirted the house, cautiously peering into each window until I located Mama in the living room sipping tea from a delicate china cup. From my position I could see her lips moving rapidly. Betty, with a matching teacup, sat opposite her on a blue wing-back chair. I scanned the room and spotted Sophia standing close to the teacart. No Snellgrove or Michael Halsey.

This required some thought. Ducking down under the windowsill, I weighed my options. I could call her back and hope Betty's suspicions weren't raised. Or I could take the direct approach and knock on the front door. I bit down on my lower lip. Think ole girl. Okay, decision made. Again, I skirted around the house and eased into the Mustang's driver's seat. Taking the cell phone out of my back pocket, I redialed Mama's number. The static had worsened. She picked up on the second ring.

"I said I'd be home, Harland."

I could barely hear her tense voice over the popping line. "You're in danger. Get out."

Fizzle. Pop. "Oh, Deena, it's you. I'm trying to honey, but Betty insisted we have tea and ruby red cupcakes." A loud buzz. "How could I refuse such a dear friend in her hour of need?"

Before I could respond, the line disconnected. Ruby red cupcakes. Code for ruby ring? And had I imagined it, or had she slurred her words at the end? A jolt of adrenaline shot through me, and I punched in Diamond's number. The snow-clogged line crackled and popped. Hold on, please, just a bit longer.

"Hello." Sputter.

"I'm at the van Allen house," I shouted over the hissing line. "They drugged her, Diamond. I'm going in."

"What?" she screamed. "I can't hear you." Hiss. "Who is this?"

The line died. I snapped shut the phone and threw it onto the passenger seat—not sure if Diamond had heard and understood my plea for help. That meant I was on my own. I was going in. Hyped up on adrenaline, I hid the Pink Panther in my shoulder bag, exited the car, and walked up the front steps as if it were the most natural thing in the world. At the front door, I took a deep calming breath and rang the doorbell.

A couple of minutes passed before the door swung open spilling light onto the front porch. Outlined in the doorway stood Sophia, a neutral expression on her lined face.

"My father sent me here to fetch my mother." I tried to sound casual in spite of the blood roaring in my ears, and gripped the leather strap over my shoulder tighter.

"Your mother is finishing tea with Miss Betty." The maid opened the door wider. "This way."

I followed Sophia toward the murmur of voices. As we drew close to the living room, I recognized Betty's voice and then Mama's reply. They were talking about funeral homes in a straight, reasonable fashion. Mama's voice sounded perfectly steady, no slurring as I had imagined. Clearly, I had miscalculated the situation. Damn phone. However, now that I had gained entrance to the house, I needed to get Mama and myself safely out of here ASAP.

When we stepped into the living room, Mama glanced up from her teacup with questioning eyes. "Jolene, honey, what brings you all the way out here?" She set the cup down on the coffee table. Betty followed suit.

"Daddy sent me to fetch you, Mama." I tried to keep my voice light. "He's worried about you driving after dark with your failing eyesight. Gather your purse and let's go." When I went over to stand beside Mama, she raised her eyes in silent question. I gave her an almost imperceptible shake of my head.

She seemed to understand and climbed to her feet. "Betty, thank you so much for your gracious hospitality in the midst of your tragic loss. If there is anything I can do, please call me." She picked up her purse from the couch and clutched it to her side. "Again, I'm sorry about Vanessa. She made my cookbook dreams come true."

Betty stood. "Annie Mae, Vanessa loved working with you. She told me many times how lucky I was to have a friend in you." She walked over and hugged Mama. Arm and arm, they made for the front door. I trailed behind them, and Sophia behind me.

We had reached the butler's pantry when a loud crash echoed from another part of the house. My heart pounded hard. I pretended not to notice but the others drew to a halt.

Betty gave a snort. "The cat," she explained. "Sophia, I believe the cat needs to go outside."

Nothing seemed right about this explanation. Vanessa hated cats. Everyone knew that. She'd posted it all over the Internet. No, someone else was in the house, and I didn't care to find out who. I tapped Mama on the arm. "We really do need to get on the road. Daddy's expecting us." My hand tightened on Mama's arm as Sophia's eyes darted to me, then back at Betty. A door slammed.

Mama jumped closer to me. "Betty, we won't keep you any longer. Jolene?" She grabbed my hand.

Sophia stepped in front of us, blocking the exit.

Betty behind us. "We can't allow you to leave." The maid's eyes hardened. "Do as we say, and no one will get hurt."

"I called the police." My hand eased toward my shoulder bag and my gun. Mama squeezed my hand tight, her fear transferring through her sweating palm.

"Don't be foolish," a voice behind me admonished. "You and your mother won't be hurt if you hand over your purse to Sophia and join me in the living room."

Chapter Thirty-Three
Today is Not a Good Day to Die

Sheriff Snellgrove's demands were reasonable if you wanted to hand over your only chance of survival. Since I'd been in this position a couple of times I knew mine and Mama's life depended on the Pink Panther snuggled at the bottom of my shoulder bag. Handing it over was just plain stupid. And then again, my .38 special handgun was no match for the sheriff's sawed-off shotgun most likely pointed at my back.

Mama's hand slid out of mine. "Best to listen to him, Jolene. We have to trust he means what he says."

Trust a criminally insane sheriff to keep his word? One look at Mama's flushed and sweating face and I knew I had to do something fast. She tottered and I instantly reacted. Stepping away from her teetering form, I went for my gun only to have Sophia's arm snake out and pull Mama's collapsing form to hers in a stranglehold.

"Hand the gun over, Miz Claiborne," she demanded, "or I'll squeeze the life out of your precious momma." Her arm squeezed hard. Mama coughed as she fought for air.

My hand closed around the grip. Still, I hesitated. My eyes darted to Betty. No help there. The Ice Queen's smile gave me frostbite.

"You're trying my patience, Miz Claiborne." The

sheriff's voice hardened. "Sophia will kill your mother, trust me."

I believed him, and yet I still hesitated. One thing for certain, Mama and I both were going to die if I handed over my gun. All moisture evaporated in my mouth as I stood there in defiance—my brain cells smoking as I explored every avenue of escape. There had to be a way out of here. From my peripheral vision, I scoped out my surroundings. Nothing. Boxed in by walls and killers. My gaze settled on Mama's slumping form. Even if I were able to get my gun out of my purse without Sophia strangling Mama, Snellgrove would plant buckshot in my back, and today wasn't a good day to die.

As one last act of desperation, I sent up a hasty prayer for deliverance, or at least another chance to get away. That done, I withdrew my gun and placed it in Betty's outstretched hand.

"Good girl." Sophia released her stranglehold. Mama staggered against me, her heavier weight causing me to stumble. A strong hand from behind steadied me and helped me to gain control of Mama's flailing form.

"That was uncalled for, Sophia."

Although I'd only heard him speak at the Baconton Writers' Retreat, the baritone voice struck a chord, and I turned to see Michael Halsey's boyishly handsome face smiling down on me.

"I told you to stay out of sight," Snellgrove snarled. "I had everything under control."

Michael tugged down his bunched shirtsleeves. "Yes, I can see that, Sheriff. You've bungled this from the start." He tucked Mama's arm in the crook of his arm. "Mrs. Tucker, allow me to escort you to the living room where you'll be more comfortable."

I stood in speechless amazement and confusion as he steered my bewildered mother away from the others. Sophia poked me with her long, skinny finger. "Hand over the purse."

With my mind in a whirl, I did as instructed and hustled after Mama anxious to keep her in my protective sights. Michael Halsey may be presenting himself as a white knight in shining armor, but rattlesnakes only shed their skin, not their poisonous fangs. In the living room, Michael was pouring Mama a cup of steaming liquid from the silver tea service. She lifted her frightened eyes to me in silent appeal from the sofa.

"Tea, Miz Claiborne?" His smooth cultured voice was conciliatory, mesmeric. He handed the cup to Mama and turned to pour another. Betty and the others came back into the room. Sophia resumed her position by the teacart. Betty plopped down next to Mama on the sofa, and Snellgrove stood like a towering pine over by the fireplace, his face a mask of rage.

Surrounded on all sides, I had no choice but to accept the invitation. Mama and I exchanged several comforting glances before Michael handed me a cup and saucer. That's when I noticed the ruby ring on his pinky finger.

By now I was so shell-shocked I didn't even flinch at this latest surprise. The hot tea rose like bile in my parched throat, but I continued to sip the bitter brew, stalling for time, anything that would buy me another chance to even the score.

"Snellgrove, ready the car," Michael barked. "Sophia, get the bags, and Betty, you get the duct tape.

Can't have our songbirds chirping, can we?"

Mama, who'd been quiet till now, spoke up. "Tell me why, Betty. We've been friends since high school."

Those softly spoken words stopped Betty cold. Her face held a trace of pity. "I'm sorry you got mixed up in this, Annie Mae. I always liked you." Offering no more, she spun on her heels and left the room to do Michael's bidding.

Now that the others were off in the far reaches of the house, I offered him an easy smile. "You know, I had you pegged as a victim."

"Yes, that was my intention all along." He got up from the sofa and poured himself another cup of tea from the service. "More tea, ladies?"

"I need to use the bathroom," Mama said instead.

"As soon as one of the women return," he answered, then turned his attention back to me. "Tea, Miz Claiborne?"

"No thanks. But I would like to know why you killed two women."

The smirk slid off his face. "Mistaken identity killed Careen. Vanessa?" He shrugged his shoulders. "She thought she could outsmart me, but I came out on top." He resumed his seat on the sofa beside Mama. "I killed her before she could kill me which she tried numerous times."

"You removed the ring just before you torched the place."

"The ring would tie the body back to Betty."

"Not so. It was stolen years ago," I reasoned.

"And bought in a pawn shop by my mother." He admired the glowing ring in the lamplight. "She gave the ring to Careen upon her high school graduation. It rightfully belongs to me."

"Vanessa said—"

His cup clattered on the saucer. "Said nothing to you, Miz Claiborne. She was with me up until her last breath."

"The dead speak, Mr. Halsey."

Mama shot off the sofa. "I have to go now." She wrung her hands. "Now, please. I can't hold it." Her gaze darted around the room before settling on me. She winked. I got her message loud and clear.

Bolting out of my chair, I launched my cup and saucer at him. It clattered harmlessly on the carpeted floor but it gave me enough time to grab the silver teapot from the cart. Surprised by the attack, Michael dropped his hot teacup in his lap. His screech died as I whacked him upside the head with the teapot, splattering the hot liquid on the pristine decor. Mama scrambled over to my side, her purse clutched to her side. "Quick, the others must've heard the commotion."

The thud of heavy footsteps drew close. Had to be Snellgrove in those ugly alligator cowboy boots. "Hide behind the sofa, Mama." I plastered myself against the wall and raised the teapot. When his massive form burst into the room, I aimed for his head, but only grazed his shoulder. He staggered, then straightened, knocking the pot from my hand. We stood face to face. With all of my strength, I jerked my knee upward. He dropped to the floor in a fetal position, his hands cupping his smashed balls. His screams raised the roof, bringing Sophia and Betty on the run.

Sophia arrived first, but Mama was waiting for her with a vase of flowers. I creamed Betty with a hardcopy of Vanessa's latest book lying on the coffee table.

Exhausted, but alive, Mama and I made for the front door. We threw it open and launched ourselves out into the cool, autumn night, the distant wail of a siren heralding the end of our dangerous ordeal.

The rest of the night passed painfully slow. Diamond arrived first, then the paramedics, Bradford, and last, the GBI. Mama and I were checked out for any possible injuries, and then gave a short statement before being released to go home. The commotion brought out the neighbors, and they gawked from the sidewalks as uniformed officers taped off the area with yellow crime scene tape. Daddy arrived amid the whirling lights and first responders carting out the injured. He rushed to Mama's arms.

"I'm fine, Harland," she said when he calmed down enough for her to get a word in. "Jolene and I bagged the whole bunch." She turned a bright face in my direction. "Clobbered 'em good, we did."

After making arrangements to pick up her car in the morning, Mama and Daddy took off for the farm, promising to stop by the salon tomorrow while they were in town. I kissed them both goodnight, and headed for my car. Diamond waylaid me between the front lawn and the driveway.

"I heard you want to hire me away from the department." She laid a reassuring hand on my shoulder.

"The rumor is true. I need the help."

"What's the pay?"

"Minimum wage and tips."

"Not much less than I'm making risking my life."

"I'll throw in a lifetime supply of manis and pedis."

314

"I'll get back with you." She opened the Mustang's driver's door, then looked over her shoulder at Bradford making his way to us. "Give him a chance, Jolene. You gave him a real scare with this stunt, but I suspect he'll get over it soon enough." She turned and walked away.

I slid behind the wheel and shut the door. Bradford stuck his head in the opened window. "I have a lot to say to you, but I'm too damn mad right now, so I know I'll screw it up. Go home and I'll swing by in the morning."

"I'll want details," I told him as the engine roared to life. "This case is so twisted, I can't figure it out."

"I know." He slapped the car door. "I'll have all the answers in the morning."

I backed the Mustang out of the drive and as I drove away, I glanced in the rearview mirror. Bradford stood like a statue, watching me. Tomorrow promised answers to lingering questions. The case would be closed, and Bradford would be free to leave Whiskey Creek. And that would bring up one last important question.

Chapter Thirty-Four
Two Men and a Hairdresser

The next morning dawned bright and clear. A cold front had pushed through bringing cloudless skies and bitter artic air. To keep out the chill, I bundled up in a corduroy jumper over a turtleneck pullover and lace-up boots. I tucked my hair into a chignon and added a cashmere beret and my Casper bracelet to complete the winter ensemble.

Since I'd scheduled only late appointments, I had a long, silent breakfast with just the gentle hum of the kitchen appliances and Tango's insistent purring for background noise. The temporary pre-paid cell phone had been chunked into the garbage can, and I'd unplugged my landline. The constant ringing drove me buggy.

I did, however, read about the arrests on the front page of the *Whiskey Creek Gazette*. The story was short, limited in details, and Mama and I weren't mentioned—thank God. Today I would keep my head down and avoid all drama. No ghosts, no murder mysteries, no writers of any kind. Especially reporters.

The staff had arrived by the time I pulled into my usual parking space and pushed through the back door. At the click of the door closing behind me, I smiled as the murmur of female chatting, whirling hair dryers, and whishing of running water combined in a symphony of harmonious music. I sighed with perfect contentment. Dixieland Salon was home. This collection of eclectic people were my family and friends. I paused as Deena stepped out of her office and scurried in the direction of the reception desk. The front doorbell jangled, and an excited eruption of oohs and aahs piqued my curiosity. My close brush with death had heightened my appreciation for the little things, like this moment in the safety of my beauty shop.

My boot heels click-clacked on the hardwood floor as I made my way to the reception area. At the locked facial room door, I rested a hand on the panel. The wood moved beneath my hand. Odd. Our unwanted guest still lingered. A problem to be dealt with later. Today, no drama. No ghosts. No trouble-making denizens of Hell.

When I rounded the corner, my mouth dropped open. The reception area overflowed with flowers of every color and shape. Baskets, vases, and buckets of floral arrangements. Roses. Daisies. Carnations. Asters.

Deena spotted me. "Jolene, you've got to stop him. Good Lord, if it continues there won't be a flower left in town. Look at them!"

"I am," I managed to croak out. "What's going on?" A dozen pairs of eyes rested on me.

"There's more in my office. They've been arriving all morning."

I walked over to the reception desk. "Who are they from?" I fingered the velvet petal of a Gerber daisy.

She giggled. "Sam."

"Impossible. He's pissed at me."

"Jolene, you ninny. This is what love looks like."

I plucked a card from the arrangement of daisies. It

read: *Come away with me.*

From the white roses: *Wake up with me on snowcapped mountains.*

The Asters: *Walk with me in wide open spaces.*

The Carnations: *With me, every day will be a new adventure.*

When I looked up from the card, I was surrounded by a dozen patrons with smiling faces and unopened cards in their outstretched hands. Even my staff had stopped their work to look on. Their clients perched on the edge of the stylist chairs in anticipation of my reaction.

Feelings and sensations bombarded me from every side. With a shaky smile, I received the cards from each lady, thanked her, and moved on to the next. I shoved the dozen unopened cards with a personal message from Bradford in my shoulder bag to read in private.

The front door bell jangled. Every eye turned expectantly. Aahs of disappointment rose at Preston's arrival. All eyes went back to me as I went forward to greet him.

"Good morning, pretty lady." He dropped a kiss on my cheek. "I'm afraid to ask about the flowers. Never seen so many outside of a florist shop." He chuckled. "Why is everyone staring?"

I fingered the Casper charm. "They were hoping you were someone else."

His gaze took in the flowers. "Detective Samuel Bradford. My competition. So? What's it going to be? Me or him?"

"This isn't the time or place." I felt the heated gaze of a dozen curious eyes.

"You have to make a choice."

"I have."

"And?"

Again, the front door bell jangled. All sound ground to a halt as every eye swung to the man entering the shop. Detective Samuel Bradford with Stetson in hand.

Wonderful. Two men and a hairdresser. And an audience. Better and better.

He smiled. I smiled in return and excusing myself, went to greet him. "You bought me a flower shop."

"I have half a mind to take them back after that dumb stunt you pulled last night." He cast a glance at our audience. "Your doctor is here. Is there somewhere we can talk in private?"

"Deena's office," I suggested. "You go ahead. I need to have a word with Preston."

"How about goodbye?" He flashed a snide smile, then turned and walked toward the office.

"Okay, everybody, show's over," I addressed the onlookers. "Back to work." I stepped over to Preston, and took his hand. "Why don't you wait for me in the kitchen? I won't be long."

Deena draped a sisterly arm around him. "Come on, Preston. I could use a cup of coffee."

With Preston occupied, I joined Bradford in the office. "Long night at the station?" I sat down in the chair next to his.

He scrubbed a hand across his scruffy chin. "No, early morning flower shopping. I called in a couple of favors. They weren't too happy with me dragging them out of bed before dawn."

My tongue felt glued to the top of my mouth. "The case is over."

"Just beginning for Fallon. The D.A. will have his hands full with this one. Halsey clammed up, but the others took plea deals in exchange for turning State's evidence against Halsey."

"How did he convince them to go along with his plan?"

"They were in so deep they had no choice. The only way for them to escape jail time was to trust Halsey. Bad choice."

"And Snellgrove?"

"Unrequited love pushed him over the moral edge." He surprised me by laughing. "Idiot."

"Sophia is a cold fish. They deserve one another."

"Oh, and we found the missing manuscript among Halsey's possession."

"Yeah? I guess that's good news for some folks. Bad for others." I didn't bother concealing my amusement. "What happens now?"

"It's bagged and put away for evidence. After the trial, who knows?"

My gaze caressed every muscle. "So you're free to leave Whiskey Creek." My voice bottomed out.

He reached for my hand. "I'm leaving in the morning." His luminous eyes held mine captive, smoldering.

"So soon? I thought we'd have more time." The words gushed out. "You haven't closed on the ranch."

His finger traced a fiery path up my arm. "I'll be back in a couple of weeks for the closing. I hired a professional moving company to pack and move my furniture, but I need to know how big a place I'm buying."

I inhaled a deep breath. The moment had arrived

sooner than I had anticipated, but I knew what I wanted. Had been wrestling with it all night, and now the time had come to let the others in on my decision. I crossed my fingers for good luck, hoping I wasn't about to make another monumental mistake. "Since I'm only going to say this once, let me fetch Preston." I left the office and made for the kitchen. I'd taken about ten steps when my intuitive knowing picked up an incoming celestial visitor.

"Meet me in the dispensary," Scarlett's voice buzzed in my ear. "This is a family emergency. Life or death!"

The tone of her voice had me dashing for the small room at the back of the salon. Life or death, she'd said. Crap. Death is the food of drama. Scarlett floated over the counter when I bolted into the room and eased the door shut. "What's up?" The words exploded out of my mouth.

"I rushed down here as soon as I saw her name on the list of arriving saints." Scarlett's voice pitched high with excitement. "I had to warn you, although, I could pay heavily for snitching. If the Boss learns I'm down here, I'll be pitching a tent with the earthworms." Scarlett flashed a neon green, then a bright orange, and green again. I ducked down and placed both hands over my head.

"What the hell's wrong with you, Claiborne? I'm trying to warn you about your mother's impending arrival on the long, black train."

I bounced upright. "What? Mama's name is on the list? For Heaven?"

"Don't know her final destination, but she's on the list of arrivals."

"How soon?"

"It hasn't been posted, but soon, she's on the list."

"The list was wrong before."

"Wrong, Claiborne. The list was correct all along. The evil twins are on trial as we speak."

Damn. She's right. Both were on the list. Both are dead. What to do? What to do? I smacked my fist against my palm. "Then I'll stop it. I finally have both my parents together, and Mama's not going anywhere."

"You can't stop the Death Angel, girlfriend."

"I can and I will."

Scarlett cocked her head. "Oh, dear, someone snitched that I'm down here. The Powers that Be are pissed. Listen, Jolene, stay out of it. If you interfere, you'll regret it."

"But Scarlett, you're talking about my mother's life. How can I stand by and do nothing? At least tell me how they plan to take her out so I can stop it."

Scarlett faded in and out. "I only know she's on the list. Don't know the time or means. Could be an accident. Or murder. Or natural. Doesn't matter. She's headed for the judgement seat. Accept it, Jolene. And please, for my sake, stay out of it."

"Forget it. Scarlett. I'll fight Heaven and Hell for my mother."

"You just may have to. The Dark Powers are always on the prowl for another soul to steal. Don't say I didn't warn you." Scarlett faded away, leaving me alone. I hesitated for a moment, my brain scrambling for a plan. Nothing. Not deterred by my lack of brainpower, I bolted out of the room and dashed down the hall for my workstation to retrieve my shoulder bag. A surge of enraged injustice fired up my step, and I pounced on Holly as I rounded the corner. "Holly, cancel my appointments. Tell Deena I had an emergency and will call her later."

Curious faces turned my way as I collected my handbag with my gun tucked inside, and retracted my steps back to the reception desk and to the rear of the salon. Outside, I dashed for the Mustang and slung open the door.

"Stop, Jolene! What about us?"

I pivoted at Bradford's roar. "I have to leave, Bradford. Wait for me." I slid behind the wheel.

He bound for the car. "How long do I wait?"

"As long as it takes." I fired up the engine, and possibly the end of our relationship.

He reached the car and leaned in the open window. "You have an hour. After that, I'm gone"

"Fair enough." I jerked the gearshift into drive. His face mirrored his disappointment, but he stepped back, allowing me passage. Our gazes locked in silent battle. Mama's face transposed over his, and the spell broke. With desperation's call to action, I hit the gas, and the Mustang bucked in pursuit. Destination: the farm. After that? Wherever fate led me on this critical mission to stop Heaven from murdering Mama.

And now for a sneak peek at Jolene's next escapades!

Bein' Dead Ain't No Excuse

by

Penny Burwell Ewing

The Haunted Salon Series

Chapter One
The List

Picking a fight with heaven isn't for the faint of heart, or even for the strongest heart. It's reserved for the stupid, like me. Only a pig-headed Southerner would lift her fist to the sky and issue a challenge to the Master of the Universe to a duel of wills. But that's what I did when Mama's name landed on Heaven's list of arriving saints.

Scarlett Cantrell, that's my gal pal from the Other Side, alerted me of Mama's impending departure on the long, black train. Well, that doesn't fit into my plans at all. I have two beaus fighting over me, Deena's wedding is less than two weeks away, and Billie Jo's expecting a baby in the spring. How can we Tucker gals get along without our mama? Well, we can't. That's why I'm speeding toward the farm—to prevent Heaven from playing target practice with Mama.

I arrived at the farm in a cloud of red dust, and bolted from the car for the back kitchen door in pursuit of my sainted parents. Bursting through the door, I found an empty kitchen much to my disappointment.

"Mama?" I called out. No response. "Daddy?" No answer from the empty house. Retracing my steps, I checked the garage for their cars. Check. They were here somewhere on the farm. Half out of my mind with worry, I sprinted for the barn and heard the murmur of angry voices as I drew near the opened doors.

"Now you listen to me, Annie Mae Tucker," my father's stern voice rose above the clucking chickens and shuffling hooves. "We're selling the farm and moving to Florida."

"And I say different." Mama's voice pitched high. "We've got a new grandbaby on the way. I'm staying put."

"And I'm selling the farm and moving to Florida, old woman."

"Over my dead body, asshole. This is my home and you can't sell it without my signature. What are you doing? Let go! Stop, Harland!"

With those angry words spilling out into the frosty morning, I scrambled through the opened doors to witness my parents tussling on the upper hayloft. I hesitated, my mind not quite processing the scene unfolding before me. Before I could open my mouth to protest, Mama let out a scream and pitched forward off the loft and landed with a soft thump on a hay pile below.

The scream on my lips burst out as I rushed to her side and bent over her still figure to brush the dried grass from her pale face. "Mama?" I patted her face. "Can you hear me?" From the loft above, I could hear Daddy's frantic cries as he scrambled down the wooden ladder.

"Land sakes, Annie Mae!" he bellowed as he sank down beside me, his hands shaking as he lifted her limp hand. "You trying to kill yourself?"

At his words, I shot him an angry look. "You pushed her," I accused. "I saw and heard the whole thing."

Daddy blanched and pulled back in surprise, but before he could respond to my hurtful words, Mama moaned, and then opened her eyes. "I'm fine, just winded." She smiled up at Daddy. "Harland, help me up."

Together, we stood Mama on her feet. "Are you sure you're okay?" I asked her as I plucked strands of hay from her short, graying blonde hair. "I'll believe you should be checked out at the emergency room. That was a nasty fall."

"Nonsense," she huffed. "Just a minor accident." With shaking hands, she brushed hay from her worn jeans. "I slipped and fell, that's all."

"Minor accident? I closed my eyes and blew out a breath. "Pushed is more like it."

Daddy made a noticeable sigh. "Now, Jolene, don't be silly. I didn't push your mama. I grabbed her when she slipped. I tried to *prevent* her fall."

Scarlett's warning rang in my ears, and I ditched the rest of my common sense. "I see it differently." I plunged ahead blindly, "With her dead, you can sell the farm and disappear with all the proceeds. Disappearing *is* your specialty."

Mama pinched me hard on the upper arm. "Leave the past be, Jolene. We paid for our mistakes a hundred times over, and we'll not apologize again." She linked her arm in Daddy's. "Now apologize to your father."

The words stuck to the roof of my mouth as the full impact of my accusation hit me. Heat flooded my face as I continued to stare in mute silence at my father who seemed to wither in height with each passing second. His once proud face wrinkled heavily with the downward turn of his mouth, and his eyes shifted away when I tried to capture them with mine.

Once again, my impetuousness had reaped immense damage. As usual, I hadn't stopped to think about the consequences of my rash actions. Words once spoken are hard to take back. Especially when you've just accused your father of attempted murder.

"We're waiting, Jolene." Mama's snide voice cut into my thoughts. "And why aren't you at work? The salon is short-staffed with Billie Jo out. Deena's nerves are frazzled with wedding preparations, and here you are provoking hard feelings with your sharp tongue."

Daddy put an arm around my shoulders. "Leave her be, Annie Mae." His voice softened. "Tell me what's got you jumping at shadows, honey."

I slipped my arm around his waist. "I'm sorry, Daddy. If I'd taken the time to think things through... I misjudged you..." My words choked on a sob. "But Mama's in trouble."

He steered me out of the barn. "Let's go up to the house. Annie Mae can whip up a quick breakfast, and you can tell us what's going on with you."

Mama kept silent as we climbed the back porch steps and entered the warm, cozy kitchen. She headed straight for the refrigerator and pulled out a slab of thick-cut bacon, her pursed lips never cracking a smile. As she set about frying the bacon, Daddy poured us both a cup of strong, black coffee and joined me at the table.

He squeezed my hand. "Okay, honey, tell us what's on your mind. Whatever's going on, we'll handle it as a family."

Okay, the time had come, but as I sat there staring into Daddy's gentle brown eyes, I choked. How do you

4

tell your mama that her neck is on Heaven's chopping block? The words stuck in my throat, and my head pounded from trying to make sense of an impossible situation. I couldn't find the right words or a gentle way to break the news, so I just opened my mouth and released the bomb. Mama dropped her fork into the sizzling bacon grease, and Daddy got up from the table and walked out the kitchen door without a backward glance. And me—I was left running full speed toward disaster with the brake line cut.

****

"You told them what?" Deena's shrill voice blasted over the rock-n-roll tune streaming over the salon's speakers. Of course, several heads swung in our direction with avid curiosity in their gleaming eyes.

I grabbed my sister's arm and propelled her past the flower garden in the reception area and into her office. "Damn Deena, give me a break, will you? Every vulture in Whiskey Creek is out for new gossip."

Deena snatched her arm out of my grip. "Give you a break? Ha! You're the one who peeled out of here this morning and left me here to deal with *your*"—here she paused for emphasis—"boyfriends." She waved two fingers under my nose. "Not one, mind you, but two. Why can't you settle for one man like the rest of us, Jolene?" Her voice rose. "And those damn flowers are giving me a headache."

The flower garden was a result of clashing testosterone and the almighty male ego. It had started with Preston Neally's autumn bouquet and ended with Bradford's insane attempt to woe me away from the young doctor. And now Deena's office and reception area were filled with floral arrangements of every size, shape, and color. Oh, boy, what a story, and I don't have time to fill you in on the details.

"I'm sorry, but I had an emergency, Deena. A life and death emergency." I tried to touch her, but she moved away with her face pulled into a frown.

"Another cockamamie ghost thingy," she blurted, and spun around to face me, her eyes spitting fire. "We're short staffed with Billie Jo out on maternity leave, Holly gave her two-week notice, my wedding is ten days away, and we're closed up in my office discussing another one of your *situations* instead of my nuptials. It's always about you, Jolene, and I'm sick of it. And your brash actions have injured two great guys. I hope they both dump you."

We stared at one another for several seconds, and seeing all the hurt and anger in Deena's eyes, I knew the time had come for me to lay it all out on the line. On hearing Mama's dilemma, Deena would probably stroke out and blame me, but I needed her help. Billie Jo's too. Mama's life was more important than her wedding, or Preston and Bradford's delicate feelings. To hell with them, and anyone else who got in my way.

Being the big sister, and tired of her silly tirade, I grabbed her upper arm and propelled her to her desk chair. "Sit down and shut up." I applied my superior weight, and she collapsed into the chair. "Maybe you didn't hear me when I said that Mama's number's up."

Deena's upper lip curled in a contemptuous twist. "Get real, Jolene. I'm tired and stressed out this morning, and fed up with the drama. Really, Mama's number's up? What nonsense. And what does that mean, 'her number's up'?" Her eyes sparked rebellious fire at me.

A first for her, I assure you, as normally I'd just whip her ass like I used to do growing up. Now, I just plain felt sorry for her, and didn't have the heart to mess up her face right before her big day. However, my patience can stand so much without breaking down altogether, and I was close to losing it. The earlier scene at the farm had zapped my usual calm demeanor, and I had no way of knowing when the Death Angel would swoop down and murder Mama.

"Deena, honey." I patted her cheek with the tip of my finger. "Mama's on 'The List'."

"What list?"

I rolled my eyes heavenward. "Good Lord, Deena. The list! The list! Haven't you been listening?" I clenched my hands to my side to keep from strangling her.

Confusion clouded her face. "I don't recall you mentioning a list."

I inhaled a deep breath, held it, and then exhaled at the count of ten. "When I met you at the back door. I told you about it then."

"Aren't you going to ask me about Sam and Preston?"

Dingbat! "What about them? They're gone. End of story."

Although my voice didn't betray my doubts, inside, my heart hammered against my chest as adrenaline pumped through my veins like a gasoline pipeline. I had dashed out of here so fast this morning that I had been unable to name the victor—because I had made a choice.

My choice. I could chuckle about it now. Dating two men had come down to this. Chose one, everyone demanded, so I did, but the chance to reward the winner never happened. Because of Scarlett, and that damn list.

My choice?

A word about the author...

Penny Burwell Ewing was born and raised in Fort Pierce, Florida. Growing up in a Southern coastal town gave her the best of small town living where the residents look out for one another.

Her interest in writing began in the 1970s when she consumed every bodice-ripper published and decided to try her hand at entertaining herself. It worked, and she is now working on her fourth novel. Once a professional cosmetologist, Penny draws on her humorous experiences behind the chair to add spice to her Haunted Salon series. She currently resides in Tifton, Georgia.